DREAMING
OF
AUTUMN
SKIES

V.C. Andrews® Books

The Dollanganger Family
Flowers in the Attic
Petals on the Wind
If There Be Thorns
Seeds of Yesterday
Garden of Shadows
Christopher's Diary:
    Secrets of Foxworth
Christopher's Diary:
    Echoes of Dollanganger
Secret Brother
Beneath the Attic
Out of the Attic
Shadows of Foxworth

The Audrina Series
My Sweet Audrina
Whitefern

The Casteel Family
Heaven
Dark Angel
Fallen Hearts
Gates of Paradise
Web of Dreams

The Cutler Family
Dawn
Secrets of the Morning
Twilight's Child
Midnight Whispers
Darkest Hour

The Landry Family
Ruby
Pearl in the Mist
All That Glitters
Hidden Jewel
Tarnished Gold

The Logan Family
Melody
Heart Song
Unfinished Symphony
Music in the Night
Olivia

The Orphans Series
Butterfly
Crystal
Brooke
Raven
Runaways

The Wildflowers Series
Misty
Star
Jade
Cat
Into the Garden

The Hudson Family
Rain
Lightning Strikes
Eye of the Storm
The End of the
    Rainbow

The Shooting Stars
Cinnamon
Ice
Rose
Honey
Falling Stars

The De Beers Family
"Dark Seed"
Willow
Wicked Forest
Twisted Roots
Into the Woods
Hidden Leaves

The Broken Wings Series
Broken Wings
Midnight Flight

The Gemini Series
Celeste
Black Cat
Child of Darkness

The Shadows Series
April Shadows
Girl in the Shadows

The Early Spring Series
Broken Flower
Scattered Leaves

The Secrets Series
Secrets in the Attic
Secrets in the Shadows

The Delia Series
Delia's Crossing
Delia's Heart
Delia's Gift

The Heavenstone Series
The Heavenstone Secrets
Secret Whispers

The March Family
Family Storms
Cloudburst

The Kindred Series
Daughter of Darkness
Daughter of Light

The Forbidden Series
The Forbidden Sister
"The Forbidden Heart"
Roxy's Story

The Mirror Sisters
The Mirror Sisters
Broken Glass
Shattered Memories

The House of Secrets Series
House of Secrets
Echoes in the Walls

The Umbrella Series
The Umbrella Lady
Out of the Rain

The Eden Series
Eden's Children
Little Paula

The Sutherland Series
Losing Spring
Chasing Endless Summer

The Girls of Spindrift
Bittersweet Dreams
"Corliss"
"Donna"
"Mayfair"
"Spindrift"

Stand-alone Novels
Gods of Green
    Mountain
Into the Darkness
Capturing Angels
The Unwelcomed Child
Sage's Eyes
The Silhouette Girl
Whispering Hearts
Becoming My Sister

V.C. ANDREWS®

DREAMING OF AUTUMN SKIES

G

GALLERY BOOKS

New York London Toronto Sydney New Delhi

G

Gallery Books
An Imprint of Simon & Schuster, LLC
1230 Avenue of the Americas
New York, NY 10020

Following the death of Virginia Andrews, the Andrews family worked with a carefully selected writer to organize and complete Virginia Andrews's stories and to create additional novels, of which this is one, inspired by her storytelling genius.

First Gallery Books trade paperback edition October 2024

V.C. ANDREWS® and VIRGINIA ANDREWS® are registered trademarks of A&E Television Networks, LLC

GALLERY BOOKS and colophon are registered trademarks of Simon & Schuster, LLC

Simon & Schuster: Celebrating 100 Years of Publishing in 2024

For information about special discounts for bulk purchases, please contact Simon & Schuster Special Sales at 1-866-506-1949 or business@simonandschuster.com.

Interior design by Erika R. Genova

Manufactured in the United States of America

10 9 8 7 6 5 4 3 2 1

Library of Congress Cataloging-in-Publication Data

Names: Andrews, V. C. (Virginia C.), author.
Title: Dreaming of autumn skies / V.C. Andrews.
Description: First Gallery Books trade paperback edition. | New York : Gallery Books, 2024. | Series: The Sutherland series
Identifiers: LCCN 2024024211 (print) | LCCN 2024024212 (ebook) | ISBN 9781668015834 (hardcover) | ISBN 9781668015827 (paperback) | ISBN 9781668015858 (ebook)
Subjects: LCGFT: Novels.
Classification: LCC PS3551.N454 D74 2024 (print) | LCC PS3551.N454 (ebook) | DDC 813/.54—dc23/eng/20240531
LC record available at https://lccn.loc.gov/2024024211
LC ebook record available at https://lccn.loc.gov/2024024212

ISBN 978-1-6680-1583-4
ISBN 978-1-6680-1582-7 (pbk)
ISBN 978-1-6680-1585-8 (ebook)

Our lives are seasonal.
We die and are reborn like leaves.
It permits us to hope.

—*Caroline Bryer*

PROLOGUE

The very day my mother was killed in an automobile accident and my mother's companion, Nattie Gleason, was seriously injured, Mrs. Lawson, Grandfather Sutherland's head housekeeper, descended on my school like a hawk and practically flew me out and off to Sutherland, my grandfather's mansion. The horrid news was stabbed into me with quick, factual, unemotional statements on the way to the estate. I wanted to leap out of the moving limo, but where would I go?

My father was already living with his new family in Hawaii, where he and his new wife continued working as FAA air traffic controllers. At the time, he wanted nothing to do with me. In his mind, I should have been his spy, told him more so he would have been prepared for the shock of having his wife fall in love with another woman. Somehow, in his mind, his adultery was justified because it was heterosexual.

"Men live by their own rules," Nattie once said. "After all, first there was Adam. And where did Eve come from? Adam's rib. They'll never let you forget it."

As soon as Mrs. Lawson and I arrived at Sutherland that dreadful day, I was taken to a bedroom almost hidden away down a side corridor. After my mother's funeral, I was essentially confined to that one dark and stark room. It was there that I was subjected to months of aversion therapy.

"Therapy" was a very kind way of describing what Grandfather's expert, Dr. Kirkwell, did to me until she considered me "sexually safe," which, in her mind, meant I would not be inclined to develop into a gay woman. She was demanding and frightening, even when she smiled. My hope was that I would never mature into a woman like her despite how intelligent and respected she was. I often wondered if there was anyone who would or even could love her.

What was worse than being someone who couldn't be loved? That was who I felt I was then.

After my therapy, I was released into the rest of the world of the mansion and restricted to homeschooling with my only peer contact being my troubled, brilliant cousin Simon. Simon was two years older chronologically but decades older academically. He was one of those child prodigies who could graduate from college at the age at which most complete the fourth or fifth grade.

But Simon was no one for me to envy, especially after I was able to know him better. I realized he had no meaningful friendships, just some former classmates for whom he might answer a math, science, or history question. For as long as I knew him, no one invited him to his or her house. He never talked about going to a party. His happy smiles were as rare as white peacocks.

Later, however, there was something far worse for Simon. Whether he did so deliberately or not, Simon caused the head housekeeper's fatal fall. Mrs. Lawson went tumbling down the mansion's curved stairway, landing awkwardly and twisted at the bottom. Simon had a mental breakdown because he feared that Grandfather would blame and dislike him for what had happened. For Simon at the time, Mrs. Lawson's death was far less important than how our grandfather would react to it. That was how much he idolized our grandfather.

Maybe Simon and people similar to him, people who had such superior intellects, suffered emotions more deeply.

Mommy once said Simon couldn't pretend. "Your cousin is unable to make things easier for himself by escaping reality. Your aunt Holly cried to me about that often. Sounds funny to complain about a child who can't dream his or her way out of reality, but believe me, I know about that.

"My imagination helped me escape Sutherland every day I lived there. Warm feelings of affection have to be nurtured. One look would tell you that in our Sutherland garden, flowers of love wilted and languished. They were rarely if ever watered with compassion and tenderness."

When she told me about Simon's inability to avoid reality and her desperate use of living more in her imagination, I wondered if that eventually would be my fate as well, especially because of my aversion therapy. I was force-fed statistics and logic condemning homosexuality. Dr. Kirkwell was telling me that I should see everything in the world that way; I should make all my important decisions based on cold, hard evidence and never on the basis of a feeling, no matter how deeply I felt it.

But I didn't want everything to be factual, scientific. I wanted to believe in fairy tales and good ghosts as well as bad. Goodness knows, even though I had hated her, I wished I could pretend that the day Mrs. Lawson died hadn't happened. I was a little more like Simon about it; I couldn't erase it or cover it with something bright and happy. It stuck out in my memory like a sock leaking out of a closed drawer.

Simon was not a violent person. When he was angry, he confined his responses and actions to satirical comments or just dirty looks. Sutherland was a fertile garden for sarcasm and nasty innuendo. Disapproving faces, some ancestral, flashed on the walls of my grandfather's mansion.

Whether I imagined it or not, I felt constantly judged, even by the housekeepers. Often, they would pause to watch me pass by as if they anticipated my shouting out some obscenity or threat. Sometimes I was afraid to touch anything and found myself tiptoeing through rooms and halls. It was as if I wanted to be merely a shadow of myself. Was I reliving my mother's life here? Of course, I wondered if that was what Grandfather wanted at the time. Maybe he thought he was punishing my mother through me.

My mother never got along with her father and continually reminded me how unhappy she had been with her childhood at Sutherland, despite how beautiful it was and how envied she was growing up with tennis courts, a pool, and even a golf course on the property. It was truly an impressive mansion, with its gray-silver stone exterior and grand, oval-shaped mahogany doors. The massive structure overlooked hundreds of acres. My grandfather had the gardeners create a brook close to the house with water running over rocks that was then pumped back up to run over them again.

Once, when my mother and I were looking at the water bubbling over the rocks, she said, "It gives him a godlike feeling because he can change nature, create lakes and rivers as well as mountains if he wants. He even imports different species of birds to see if he can get them to survive here, make it their home."

Despite how other people would find that amazing, she sounded bitter, even sickened by it.

Truthfully, regardless of its majestic beauty and opulence, I couldn't say I ever totally enjoyed going to Sutherland for grand parties and dinners. There was always something shadowy and unhappy about the experience, whether it was created out of my mother's disagreement with my grandfather about her political thoughts or emerged from some family reference that caused an argument about his or her value as a Sutherland. It was as if the mansion forbade unrestrained joy, even on Christmas.

With all this troubled history born in my grandfather's mansion, anyone would think I would flee from the very thought of ever considering Sutherland my home. In a sense, it was almost a betrayal of my mother to do so, perhaps more of a betrayal of myself.

But in the end, that was what I did: I embraced it, all of it, all its history and the pride of being a Sutherland. It was impossible not to think we were special, even though I knew the warning, the ancient advice, that one should be wary of vanity, the devil's favorite sin. Arrogance thinned out the ice beneath your feet. Like Grandfather and all my ancestors, I could very well fall into the cold and dark. But when you're skating with such adoration around you and everyone, especially every servant, is pandering to your needs and wants, after a while, despite how you want to cling to humility, you become deaf and blind to anything other than yourself.

After I had disappointed my father during a trial period of living with him and his new wife and children in Hawaii, I accepted my inheritance of a troubled and harsh family past and a future that wove itself through corridors of unexpected darkness, with skeletons grimacing because of their envy, their arrogance, and their incestuous passions and lust.

I had no one else to blame for my risk of becoming one of them, a Sutherland, except maybe fate, which maliciously brought me back and stood behind, beside, and above me, whispering into my ear while

I slept and smiling gleefully at me in the shadows of every corridor, satisfied that it was having its way. For quite a while, it did.

However, my story is different from the story of some other victim of fate, because I realized that when you are captured by a strong current and unable to swim against it, you can do one other thing. You can swim faster toward where it is taking you and take away some of its control.

And that's just what I did.

CHAPTER ONE

Before Mrs. Lawson's death and my leaving for Hawaii, my cousin Simon enjoyed unraveling family secrets for me. He convinced me to go down to the long and vast basement where many of the Sutherland surprises and mysteries were buried, the most dramatic being the grave of my great-grandfather's illegitimate child, Prissy, the daughter of the African American maid with whom he had actually had a secret love affair. She was the help, a servant. Yet he had risked his name and reputation to continue his love affair.

In a letter Simon said Great-grandfather had written to a friend but never mailed, Great-grandfather said she had the most beautiful sable eyes and a smile that brightened the gloomiest day. I would have thought it to be a wonderful forbidden romance, if it wasn't for what had resulted.

Prissy, who had been born with progeria, or accelerated aging, had been kept in the bedroom where I had been kept during my aversion therapy treatment. Her existence was an embarrassment to the Sutherlands, as Mrs. Lawson had me believe I was. I was given Prissy's clothes to wear. Seeing her grave in the basement was so unexpected, and it was probably the most shocking thing I had seen in Sutherland. Her birth and death had been successfully kept hidden from the rest of the world. I had heard no reference to it, not even from my mother.

There were many more secrets buried in cartons and trunks in what I considered the Cemetery of Memories, a cemetery that included Grandmother Judith's diary. In her diary, which Simon had found in the basement before I went to Hawaii, poor Grandmother Judith revealed that she really hadn't belonged here. For her, marriage to my grandfather had become a form of entrapment. She was caged and looked for ways to avoid the condemnation of the Sutherland spirits, spending her time on charities and doing whatever she could to be away from Sutherland.

I wondered if Grandfather had ever read it before sentencing it to what he thought would be eternal darkness. If he had read it, why wouldn't he have destroyed it along with so many other unpleasant facts? It was truly like everything to do with Sutherland was a holy relic, even things that would ordinarily embarrass other families.

Simon was gleefully right: there was much to learn in the shadows, in the corners, and under the dusty old sheets in the basement, and he was an effective guide, having spent so much time alone there, fascinated by his discoveries. No one enjoyed privately sharing something as much as someone whispering a forbidden truth.

It was the reason Simon had emerged from his self-isolation at Sutherland to greet me at the front door when I arrived from my failed trip to Hawaii and my supposedly new family. He had a new forbidden truth. He was as gleeful as ever and so anxious to share it with me.

Despite my personal disappointment, sadness, and even fear of returning to Sutherland, I was willing, even anxious, to hear about Simon's discoveries. He was driving the shadows out of Sutherland and perhaps in an odd way turning it into a true family home for both of us, because you couldn't live in a house with so many unsolved family mysteries and think of it as a home.

"I've discovered a new and very important secret," he whispered, with his eyes blazing, and then he stepped aside so that I could enter his world. "You must come right up to my room," he added, with that Sutherland tone of command, loud enough for Aunt Holly to hear. He leaned in again to whisper. "We'll wait for the right opportunity." He reached for my hand, which surprised me.

"Let her get settled in first, Simon," Aunt Holly said, obviously not knowing what he was referencing. I could see she thought that whatever it was, it was part of his dark condition. On our way home from the airport, she had stressed how slowly and carefully I should engage with Simon.

"He is still like a time bomb. You can see it ticking in his eyes. It breaks my heart, but I try to look undisturbed and not make matters worse. It's frustrating when that's all you can do as a mother."

Emerson, my grandfather's limousine driver for decades, was carrying my suitcases and waiting behind us. He had started driving for Grandfather in England, and when Grandfather found a loyal employee, he'd import him to serve no matter where in the world he or she was living.

Simon looked surprised at what Aunt Holly had said. It was as if he had never known I had left and been gone that long. It gave me an eerie feeling. Perhaps he had envisioned me in my room all this time, maybe even had gone there and believed he had seen me, even spoken to me. He obviously either ignored the luggage or refused to see it.

"There'll be plenty of time for you to talk once Caroline settles in, Simon. Maybe you can join us for lunch outside today," Aunt Holly said, with a wide smile full of motherly hope.

"Not hungry," he said. "And it's not lunch conversation."

He glared at the luggage now as if it were all some unwanted do-nation, started to turn, and stopped. There was actual pain in his eyes because of my silence while he paused. I could see he had wanted me to defy Aunt Holly and join him. I wanted to assure him I would, but before I could promise anything, he turned away again and hurried into the house, rushing toward the stairway as if he was afraid to be seen out of his bedroom. I looked at Aunt Holly, who sighed deeply.

"I don't know which is a bigger challenge for you, Caroline, Hawaii and your father or Sutherland and Simon," she said. "It's sad to see him so indifferent to reality and worse to see you feel guilty about it."

I was going to just burst out with an explanation, describe the importance of the Cemetery of Memories for him. However, she stepped into the mansion quickly, as if she wanted to clear the way for me and make it safe.

Mrs. Lawson's replacement, Mrs. Fisher, came hurrying down to the foyer to greet us. Her thick-heeled black shoes echoed on the tile, reminding me of Grandfather's mahogany walking stick when he walked through the house. She approached us with her right hand on her right hip bone, as if she was a western gunslinger. She wore a flowery white short-sleeved blouse and an ankle-length black skirt. She didn't look as old as Mrs. Lawson, but she didn't look that much younger. Maybe she was in her late fifties.

"Age is a sneak, especially for women," I overheard Nattie tell Mommy once. "It oozes into your body like water into a napkin. You don't see it spreading; it just does."

I think they were doing their makeup together at the time.

"Well, hello there, lass," Mrs. Fisher said. "You're a pretty little thing, aren't you?"

Thing? I thought. *Why call me a "thing"?* I didn't ask, but I didn't smile either. I stared at her the way Mrs. Lawson would say was impolite. Maybe it was Nattie's fault because she had described herself at my age so well that whenever I looked at an older person, especially someone over fifty, I would wonder what he or she had looked like at my age. I'd dwell on it so intensely that I didn't hear what he or she was saying. Often, I had thought that Mrs. Lawson was never a young girl. She skipped years like you would skip over a pond of dirty water. In a different way, she suffered what Prissy had suffered.

Mrs. Fisher had silvery gray eyes and graying brown hair trimmed at the nape of her neck and at her cheekbones, the hair so straight it could have been ironed. Her nose was a little too long but not really sharp. Her lips looked crooked, but maybe that was just her smile, which she held so long, it seemed to weaken into a disapproving smirk when I didn't smile back or say anything. Little brown age spots were scattered on her forehead and on the crests of her cheeks, as though God had tossed them at her like an afterthought as he was returning to heaven.

"I'm Mrs. Fisher," she quickly said to break my silence. "Your new head housekeeper."

Mine?

I looked at Aunt Holly. Emerson paused and said, "Mum," to her and then walked on ahead with my luggage. We had started to follow when Mrs. Fisher stopped us by putting her hand up like a security guard.

"Mr. Sutherland wants to see her immediately," she said, nodding at me. Then she looked at Aunt Holly and added, "Alone."

As soon as I had set foot in Sutherland, I thought a cold bolt of lightning had been shot through my breast. This just added ice to it. I couldn't even take a deep breath. Mrs. Fisher turned and held her right arm out and down, dividing me from Aunt Holly and urging me to hurry along. When I didn't move, she loudly whispered, "He's waiting. You don't want to keep your grandfather waiting."

I glanced at Aunt Holly. I knew she disapproved of how Mrs. Fisher was speaking to me. Her eyes darkened, and her body stiffened.

"Go on. I'll wait for you," she said, practically speaking through her clenched jaw.

"Oh, I can show her up afterward," Mrs. Fisher said.

"She doesn't need to be shown up. She's lived here," Aunt Holly said sharply.

Mrs. Fisher held her wooden smile for a moment and then relaxed.

"Of course. She'll be fine," she said. "She's been through far more than most young girls, losing a mother so tragically and then upsetting her father by doing something so foolish on a beach that she almost drowned. Poor thing. He sent her back like a defective tool or something."

She clicked her lips while she looked at me.

"I'd hardly call her that, Mrs. Fisher," Aunt Holly said sternly. "And I don't think it is to anyone's benefit to put it into headlines like news bulletins."

"Oh, you're right. I do apologize about how that must have sounded. I'm sure she's a strong one. She'll rebound quickly from all of this," she added, waving her hand across the front of her face as if she was fanning away some bad odor. "We'll all be here for her."

Just how much about me had Grandfather discussed with her? Did she know the details of the aversion therapy, too? Did she know all about Nattie?

"Of course we will," Aunt Holly said, really more to me.

Mrs. Fisher softened her expression again and provided a warmer smile, but I didn't smile back or say a thing. Aunt Holly squeezed my hand gently, and I started toward Grandfather Sutherland's office, imagining the waves of rage he would send at me the moment I entered.

CHAPTER TWO

I knocked and heard his gruff "Come in." He said it twice, as if he had been waiting for hours, even though I knew he would know exactly when I had arrived.

I opened the door slowly and stepped in as soon as I could squeeze through. Then I closed it and leaned back. He looked like he hadn't moved from his seat or changed his clothes since I had left for Hawaii. He had been quite optimistic about it and had given me money and my mobile phone then, along with his warnings and hopes.

"Sit," he said, nodding at the chair in front of his desk. He leaned back in his leather chair and then pressed his fingertips against each other as if he was about to say a prayer. Usually, that meant he was about to criticize someone or quietly issue a stern warning.

I glanced to the right at his secret inner office. Were my mother's ashes still in the urn on a shelf in there? Simon had been the one to tell me about it. An empty coffin had been lowered into my mother's grave. It was one of the deepest-buried secrets at Sutherland. But believing the urn was still there, and that in a real sense my mother was close to me, gave me some comfort.

I sat, my back straight, my hands folded in my lap, and I looked at him as directly as he was looking at me. I didn't know if I was imagining it or wishfully thinking it, but I thought I saw a soft smile leaking into his face. Maybe he couldn't see how I was trembling beneath my facade of courage and that pleased him. I often thought my grandfather expected people would fear him as much as if not more than they respected him. Anyone who showed courage, especially his granddaughter, interested him more.

However, he quickly retreated from whatever pleasure he had felt and sat forward, his hands flat on the desk, looking like he would simply growl. His lean jaw was firmer, smoothing away the shallow wrinkles. I was always intrigued by how his gray hair hadn't conquered all the rust-colored strands. For a moment, I was fixated on the tiny patches of color, as I had often been. It was as if the man who had once had a full head of hair that striking rust color was battling hard and somewhat successfully against age. He had some secret, some power.

I knew he was very handsome in his youth. My mother admitted that, according to Grandmother Judith, when he was a young man he had a smile that could charm a witch. In his place was this elderly but regal-looking man whose power seemed to radiate and subdue anyone who confronted him. In the moment of heavy silence, I struggled to keep any tears from even beginning to form. I wasn't going to plead for his sympathy. Surprising as it was, he didn't look like he wanted that from me anyway.

"Why do you think you got into trouble so quickly over there?" he asked.

I could see in his eyes how important my answer was going to be to him. No excuses, no shifting of blame, nothing that could shield me even dared to come to mind at that moment. That was how powerful Grandfather's stare could be: it could certainly stop any self-serving thoughts, especially anything even hovering around dishonesty.

Simon once told me that Grandfather was the only one who could tell what Mona Lisa was thinking. I didn't understand what he meant until he showed me a picture of the painting.

Besides, I had wondered the same thing about myself. What had led to my quick downfall with my father?

"I trusted too quickly and was too desperate to have friends."

He simply stared for a long moment, as if my words were being translated, and then he sat back again. This time, there was no misinterpretation of his slight nod. There was a glimmer of approval, and for anyone summoned before my grandfather, that was enough to let hope breathe.

"I always forget the great need you young people have to have friends. You would think that would be a need more when you're older."

"Didn't you when you were young?" I asked, feeling even more courageous now.

"You have no better friend than yourself," he said sharply. "I knew that the day I was born."

"Isn't that lonely?" I quickly asked, sounding like a lawyer in a trial.

He didn't smile. "Independence is more valuable. The more friends you have, the more vulnerable you are, as you've already discovered."

I didn't respond, but I was sure he could see I didn't agree.

He sighed. "Speaking of that, I should have realized how susceptible to bad advice and ideas you still were. Drugs, nearly drowning?"

"I didn't mean to . . ."

He put his hand up.

"Don't start making excuses. If you put yourself in a place where someone can take advantage of you, it's all your fault. Recognize the mistake and correct it."

My father had used practically the same exact words.

"Okay," I said in a small, low voice. His eyes widened. "Okay," I said, loudly and firmly.

"Good. I have no intention of prolonging this conversation. As I said, you don't have to dwell on having friends, but I realize you can't continue to be homeschooled here. To get right to the point, there is a private school I will have you attend. It's not very far from here. Emerson will take you and pick you up. If he's busy, my man Sanders will handle the transportation."

"Private school?"

"It's where your uncle Martin went and where your aunt Holly went as well, The Oaks. It's a small school compared to the public ones. And expensive," he added. "Misbehavior can lead to expulsion, and parents, grandparents, whoever paid the tuition, lose it. I don't like losing money. I think of everything I dislike, I dislike that the most."

"So maybe I should just go to public school," I said. I could almost hear my mother coming back at him. "That way you have no risk."

"NO. We don't need that," he said in his usual confident manner. His words were stamped in my ears. "It's better you go to a place where no one has preconceived ideas about us born out of gossip. The faculty at The Oaks does not gossip. They know they would be dismissed immediately. The families sending their children there are well established and respectable. Just as we are."

We? I thought. I couldn't remember him including me like that before when referring to the Sutherlands.

"It sounds snobby," I muttered, loud enough for him to hear.

"It's special, not snobby. 'Snobby' is a word envious people use. Besides, there are tuition grants for those who can't afford it but qualify.

I make considerable contributions to the school that enable them to award those scholarships. Truth is, my money created it."

"If the faculty knows that, maybe I'll be treated like some princess. That might be worse than gossip."

Now he did smile, but it was a smile of sarcasm. "Hardly. You'll be treated tougher because you are a Sutherland. The principal, Mrs. Rich, won't tolerate even a minor infraction of the rules. There is a golden rule that was set down, and she enforces it strictly: no favoritism. Net worth . . . do you know what that means?"

"I think so. Like adding up everything you own and all the money you have."

"Good enough for now. Anyway, Mrs. Rich blocks that out of any student's biography."

Mrs. Rich? I thought. Was that her real name, or had she changed it in order to be a principal in a school for the wealthy?

"Although it's early August, you will be taken to the school to tour it and to meet Mrs. Rich. The school year there begins a week before Labor Day. It's a longer school year. There are fewer holidays, but the faculty is paid twice what public-school teachers make.

"This personal one-on-one visit with Mrs. Rich will be the only advantage you'll enjoy. Of course, Mrs. Rich has been made aware of your social issues. Out of respect for me, she will keep an extra eye on you."

"She has more than two?" I said. Again, it was my mother's voice.

He nodded, sat back, and looked out of his side window toward the golf course. There were three men playing. They were surely business associates, I thought, being rewarded for obedience.

"I know what you've inherited," he said, still staring through the window. "I'm not as intolerant of the disagreements someone might have with me as you've been told. Sutherlands have spirit and courage. When it's proper, I encourage it. They are the building blocks of self-respect. I expect that someday it will be the same for you."

But according to Aunt Holly, it was not an expectation for Uncle Martin. Vaguely, I wondered why not and if I should bring that up, but I dared not challenge Grandfather now. I remembered how angry he would get when Mommy tried to stop him from being so nasty to Uncle Martin. It was practically the only time his face turned crimson in reaction to something she had said.

He turned back to me. "What you have to learn, something your mother didn't learn or care to learn, is how to be more diplomatic. Sometimes you can be more successful going indirectly for something rather than head-on. Political. As you have more involvement with others your age, teachers, and so on, you'll learn and understand what I'm saying. Something tells me you will understand better than your mother did.

"And to show you I have confidence in you, despite the unfortunate Hawaii episode, I'm going to give you a very important assignment while you are here now and when you come home from school and on weekends."

Assignment? Would I have to write another letter to Daddy pretending it was from my mother or something similar? He rid me of that thought quickly.

"I wouldn't have been so quick to pull the trigger as your father and his new wife did, but they have other issues, especially your father, who apparently has taken on more baggage than he had intended. Most men who marry or remarry women with children do. You have to have a lot of faith in the way this woman has brought up her children. It's a crapshoot and I think he lost."

"You mean Dina," I said. Surely he didn't mean Daddy's stepson, Boston. "Do you know about everything that went on in Hawaii? Did my father tell you, give you daily reports or something? Do you know how she treated me and how . . ."

The expression on his face grew more stern.

I took a breath. I had never been this courageous in front of Grandfather. Perhaps I had finally reached the point my mother had reached. Knowing all he had done to her, I thought he would open his mouth and blow me out of his office and that would be that. I'd be sent to some place where I'd be so isolated as to be forgotten. But he surprised me again.

"That's not important right now. Suffice it to say, I don't rely solely on anyone's opinion of anything, including opinions about you."

Had he had someone else keeping track of things in Hawaii? It was the first time I had heard him even suggest that he didn't agree with my father. Dared I think I was truly being given a new start, a new chance to prove myself?

"What's my assignment, then?" I asked.

"Simon," he said, which nearly took my breath away.

"Simon?"

"I had high hopes for him and continue to, but there are many dark places for him yet to pass through. I've had the best medical care for him, psychiatric care, not that I put that much stock in it. The point is, he is lost right now. I want to see him regain his brilliance and his ambition. I'm sure it's all still within him but just under a cloud. I want to know more about that cloud. Something even his psychiatrist can't see is causing this . . . this extreme behavior."

"He just thinks you're angry at him about Mrs. Lawson."

"No, it's gone beyond that. That's a psychiatrist's easy way out. Don't need to hire anyone for that. And I don't want that whole issue discussed.

"I've offered Simon many opportunities to redeem himself, to live up to being the Sutherland he wanted to be. I observed how close he got to you before . . . it all changed. As far as I could see, you were a good influence. I know you have no psychiatric training, whatever that means, of course. In my opinion, he just needs . . ."

"A friend?" I ventured.

"Another portal."

"I don't understand—portal?"

"Another way out. What he tells you, you will tell me, and I will confer with Dr. Sachs, his psychiatrist, if I think there's any value in it. Somehow those people twist simple things into Greek myths.

"I'm just concerned for Simon. Of course, I know he's suffering inside from past actions, but there's something else as well. Trouble with his father, his mother, maybe girlie things."

"Girlie?"

"Whatever you end up calling it," he said sharply. Flushes of anger seemed to rise and then fall in his face. "I'm not denying that you have your own troubles; it's just that you struck me as being more under-standing, maybe because of those problems."

Problems? I thought. Was he thinking Simon might need aversion therapy? To start with, I wanted to tell him I hadn't needed it; it was wrong to assume things about me. But I was afraid to spoil this moment between us.

"Look, don't think of it as some sort of obligation I'm placing on you. What I'm saying is that you'll have an open door to my office when it comes to being a portal."

I said nothing. Portal? Wasn't this being a spy? If Simon found out I had told Grandfather something he had said to me, what would happen then?

Maybe Grandfather could read minds.

"But I know young people," he continued. "Don't let him think you're some sort of undercover agent for me. Understand? Don't men-tion this. It will drive him deeper into the darkness. If you do what I ask, you'll be helping him, not betraying him, and that will help me do what has to be done to restore him and make him potentially produc-tive, Sutherland productive."

Who's going to help me? I wondered. *I want to be productive.* Maybe he read that thought, too.

"Mrs. Fisher is quite aware of our family difficulties. She'll keep an eye out for both of you."

"Someone else with three eyes?"

His face seemed to freeze. "Be careful, Caroline. There's a difference between insolence and courage. Now, as I was saying, I've known Mrs. Fisher a long time. You can trust her. I don't hire people I can't trust or even if there's a question of it. I can have her take you over for the school tour. Emerson is occupied with something else tomorrow."

"Can't Aunt Holly do that?" I quickly asked. "She went there. She'd be more familiar with it."

He thought a moment. "I suppose. I'll tell her."

"I'll ask her," I said.

He finally smiled. "Okay. You ask her. Maybe it would be better for you to take a little more charge of your life, mainly your responsibilities. Go on and get settled in again. Every day is a new start. That's the first thing I think of when I wake up."

I rose. As soon as I turned my back, he said, "I intend to make sure your father is sorry he let you go. His patience is limited because of his past and his present choices, and limited patience leads to mistakes."

It took me so by surprise that I paused with my mouth open, I was sure, when I looked back at him.

He nodded. "Just a moment," he said, and opened his top desk drawer. "I want you to have this now. Consider it a bribe," he said, and smiled.

I stepped back and took the box that I knew held Grandmother Judith's sixteenth-birthday ring, the topaz. I opened the box and looked at it. Then I looked at him. His eyes were so focused on me that I couldn't breathe.

"Thank you," I said.

"Thank your grandmother. Remember, she had that in her will. Take good care of it. I'm sure you will."

Was it possible? Did I smile with affection? It really did sound like he cared about me and I wasn't just another burden or obligation. Did he really like me?

Could he really be my grandfather?

Wait.

Beware of those words, I could almost hear Mommy say from the inner closet.

You don't know what your grandfather means by "I'm sure you will." Don't think automatically that he favors you. I fell for that a number of times when he said something complimentary about me. In the end, my father disliked me even more.

Those imagined words made sense when I remembered what she had said about Grandfather after my father had left us: "Your grandfather often enjoys making others feel sorry. He feeds on someone else's misery."

For the first time, I was confused. Was she right, or was she just like him because she would never permit herself to see any good in him?

Dared I doubt my mother?

Worse yet, did I dare trust my grandfather?

CHAPTER THREE

Aunt Holly was waiting in the entryway, sitting with her legs crossed in the big brown leather chair. Her eyes were closed and her forehead crinkled like that of someone who had a headache. After seeing how Simon was, it wasn't hard to understand why she would have one almost all day. As soon as I shut Grandfather's office door behind me, her eyes snapped open. I could see the concern on her face. Had Grandfather bawled me out? Did he threaten me, take away all my privileges? Would I be locked away again but just in a different room from the last time or maybe even back in the same one?

She stood up as I approached her, her smile too full of worry to be bright.

Should I tell her everything? Should I risk losing her sympathy and concern for me? I wondered. Who had been a better friend to me recently than Aunt Holly? She took me secretly to see Nattie before she died. She took quite the risk to do that for me. Shouldn't I take a risk for her?

However, the moment I did, Grandfather would know, and maybe he would never again confide in me as he just had. But I knew she was expecting me to reveal everything fully, maybe exactly the way Daddy had expected: without delay or caution. Still, I hesitated. Besides, wasn't it Nattie who had advised me not to lie even when you think it's necessary in order not to hurt someone?

"Then what do you do?" I had asked.

"What they do in politics," Nattie had said. She knew; she had worked for the U.S. ambassador to France. "You just tell part of the truth."

Now I told Aunt Holly, "Grandfather wants me to go to a private school, The Oaks, the school you and Uncle Martin attended." I burst out with it as if I might otherwise explode. At least, that was one of the two big headlines, the other being basically that I would spy on Simon.

She didn't look all that surprised, but she did become more thoughtful. "Really? I should have anticipated that and prepared you." She shook her head. "Your grandfather is always one step ahead of the rest of us. His personal private school for the Sutherlands."

"He provides scholarships for worthy young people who can't afford it," I said, trying to maintain my excitement.

The whole idea actually frightened me. What sort of a private school would Grandfather create? Would I be under a magnifying glass everywhere? Talk about spies . . . I could be in a nest of them. Could I ever trust my classmates? He might have lied to me. Everyone might know my secrets.

She nodded. "Yes. He basically created it, even though there are no mentions of Sutherland on any wall or a dedication. Ordinarily, he's not that charitable. Anything he does is anonymous when it comes to charities. It's almost as if he is ashamed to be known as someone who would help those in need," she mused, mostly to herself. "Martin and I began in the seventh grade there. I was enrolled as soon as your uncle Martin was enrolled. My father had great respect for your grandfather. Practically used the same toothpaste. He has that effect on men about his age—always did, always will."

"He didn't send Mommy there, right?"

"No, but no one knows why he does or doesn't do anything until he tells you," she added. "Best guess is that he believed only his son who would be in his business should be well educated."

"But he wants to send me there."

"Yes. He does work in mysterious ways."

She studied me in expectation of more information.

"He wanted Mrs. Fisher to take me to see it, but I asked if you could."

"Of course." She smiled. "I'd like a tour myself and to see what changes have been made. But did he bawl you out for what happened in Hawaii?"

"No. He just told me to correct whatever mistake I had made. The worst he said was that I was too trusting."

"Really? I wish he'd be as kind to Martin. Okay. You might as well get your things unpacked. I'll see about lunch. Maybe Simon will change his mind and join us now that you're back."

That frightened me a little. Everyone was seeing me as some sort of miracle worker, putting all their hopes for Simon on my shoulders.

"Didn't he ever since I left?"

"Shortly after you left, he began skipping lunch or took something in his room. I tried having my lunch with him in his room whenever he did that, but he wouldn't eat if I did. He'd say he wasn't hungry or claim he needed to be alone with his thoughts. I've tried being insistent, but he turns to stone. Believe me, I've cried myself to sleep over him many times. He sulks so much at dinner that Grandfather probably would want him to eat in his room then, too. There is still a lot of work to do on him. For all of us," she added with a hopeful smile. "He has a good doctor, not that your grandfather would let anyone less in the door."

"Grandfather doesn't believe in psychiatry when it comes to Simon. He believed in it when it came to Dr. Kirkwell and me," I said, barely hiding my bitterness.

"I'm sorry I couldn't do more about that."

"Oh, I'd never blame you."

She smiled and then shook her head. "I know your grandfather is losing his patience. He has told Martin that a number of times since you left. Twice he almost put him back in the clinic. Simon won't come home to us.

"I wanted Martin and me to move in here, but Dr. Sachs says that might reinforce Simon's belief that there is no other world but Sutherland. He'll never think of our home as his home.

"If your grandfather gives up on him, he'll surely give up on himself. Whatever Simon's processing now, he wants done here. Personally, I don't think he ever could believe in anything more than he does in Sutherland. That is definitely one thing about him your grandfather enjoys."

"But surely Simon wants you to be happy, too."

"He doesn't even talk to me that much, let alone his father. His psychiatrist thinks that is not unusual, considering his situation. It's not easy for us to know what to do or expect. Despite his faults as a father, Martin is suffering over him, too," she added, smiling. "That's one good thing."

What a funny way to put it, I thought. *She's happy Uncle Martin is suffering.* "Misery needs company," Daddy used to say. Now I was tempted to tell Aunt Holly what Grandfather had asked me to do, simply to help her feel better. Was I the only one he had told of his deep concern for Simon? For everyone else, he put on his usual demanding face. Sutherland rules, Sutherland behavior, was what he was demanding from them, not love or compassion.

Again, I thought it was curious how honest and concerned Grandfather had just been. Was he being honest? I wondered. Or was his concern for me tied to his concern for Simon? The failure of one of the Sutherland grandchildren was trouble enough. Two might seriously damage the family name. Who was the future of this family? Was that his real reason for thinking about us and not genuine sympathy and worry, a grandfather's sympathy and worry?

Young people my age were easier to read and understand. They needed more time to hone their skills of deception. Would I ever reach Grandfather's clever way of hiding his true emotions and feelings? Did I want to be like him? Once again, I would ask myself if I wanted to be a Sutherland, especially since I knew that my mother hadn't.

Aunt Holly mistook my deep thinking for fear. "Don't worry," she said, taking my hand. "It'll all be fine. We all have to have hope."

I nodded. If she only knew how often I hadn't even tried to hope, I thought.

She and I walked up the stairway together. I hadn't been on it for a while, but the moment I took the first step, the images of Mrs. Lawson lying awkwardly and broken near the place where I now stood came rushing back and so vividly that they almost took my breath away. Aunt Holly saw the look on my face and glanced at the area that locked my attention. She said nothing for a few more steps and then paused, turning to me.

"Maybe you should rest for a while. Traveling all night, even if you slept some on the plane, can be very tiring, as well as all the emotional ups and downs you've experienced in the past day or so. Don't worry about unpacking everything right away. It'll keep. Just rest and freshen up for lunch."

"Okay," I said. My voice sounded so thin and insecure, the voice of someone who had become a little girl again.

We paused at the top, and I took a breath. Within the surrounding six or so square feet, everything about my life and Simon's at Sutherland had undergone a dramatic change. Would I think about these things every time I went up and down these stairs? Would the images return in more vivid nightmares because I was back here? I shuddered as if a cold blast of wind had come swirling around the corner. Aunt Holly took my hand. Perhaps she thought about all this, too. Perhaps she had her own nightmares.

"Seriously, are you all right, Caroline?"

"I'm okay," I said with trembling lips.

We walked to my room.

When Aunt Holly opened my bedroom door, I knew I wasn't okay. It was as if all the bad memories had been waiting there for me. Images and words, especially Mrs. Lawson's scream, came rushing back at me. The fears I had smothered under the bedcovers and the horrid moments during Dr. Kirkwell's administration of aversion therapy, fears that I had locked away in the closet, as well as the uncertainties I had about Grandfather and the longing I had for my mother, came at me like a tidal wave.

I hadn't realized until this moment how successful I had been at leaving it all behind me when I had arrived in Hawaii. It had been blown off by the trade winds, but now, for a moment, it felt like I hadn't really been there—that it had been some wild, wishful dream. Whether she could see it all in my face or not, Aunt Holly put her arm around my shoulders and hugged me.

"I know that you wanted to leave this behind and start a new life with your father. I'm afraid you'll have to do what I have done for so many years: take what you have and mold it to your needs and desires as best you can, hoping things will be different someday soon."

"Changes don't come easily to Sutherland," I said. "If they come at all."

She smiled, hugged me tighter, and laughed. "No one knows how smart you really are, but they'll see. My money is on you, Caroline."

She kissed my cheek and let go. "Do you want any help with anything?"

"No, I'm fine. You're right. I'll take a short rest before doing much more."

"Okay. It's turning out to be a beautiful day. I'll go see about setting up lunch on the patio," she said.

"Where's Uncle Martin?"

"At the city office, his second home. Maybe his first," she added with a grimace.

"What did he say when he learned I was coming back so soon?"

"Whatever your grandfather told him to say," she said, then squeezed my shoulder and left.

I closed the door, and for a long moment I simply stood there looking at what had been my mother's room before it had been mine. My mother had shown it to me only once before Grandfather had put me here. We had never stayed overnight at Sutherland. Even if there was a heavy snowfall during and after dinner or Christmas, anytime, Mommy would insist on our going home. I wanted to stay. It was an adventure back then, and Daddy was willing to stay, too, but Mommy was adamant.

"I wouldn't sleep anyway," I recalled her saying once. "Too many ghosts."

I knew she wasn't fond of her room the way girls I had known from school were fond, even proud, of theirs. When she showed me what had been her room, she said it was deliberately kept from being too personal.

"As you can see, or will someday," she said, not intending to be prophetic, "it's like . . . as impersonal as so much of Sutherland, with its long hallways and large rooms where even echoes feel out of place."

How could echoes feel out of place? I really didn't understand what she had meant then. I was too young and too far from what my life here was to become. But it was clear to me now. Being gone from it and living in a bright, warm world even for a short time seemed to make everything my mother had said about it louder.

The hardwood floor still looked newly stained, and the walls were that neutral light brown. Obviously, despite my having left, Grandfather had made sure it was kept up as if he had anticipated my return any day. Maybe he always knew what would happen. Truthfully, he didn't seem that surprised. I even imagined him looking in periodically to be sure it was made ready without delay. The shine on the floor hadn't lost its glitter. I remember when I first stepped off my bed here, I was afraid of smudging the gleam that made you think you could ice-skate on it. It looked the same right now.

The only picture still on the walls was one of a racehorse my grandfather once owned, Cutter, a cinnamon-brown horse that nearly made it to the Kentucky Derby. How many times had I heard that story and been expected to be grateful the picture was there? It was a beautiful horse, but I, and I'm sure my mother, would have liked some colorful landscapes, anything that would give the room some feminine warmth. I don't know why I would have expected otherwise, but the black mechanized window curtains hadn't been replaced with something more attractive, something softer. The coffee-and-cream area rugs on both sides of the king-size oak bed, and the bed itself, with its nondescript starched white comforter and pillows, looked as clean as they had the day I left for Hawaii.

I sighed with disappointment, probably like a convict who had violated her parole and been returned to the same cell. Despite how my stepsister, Dina, turned out to be, I did prefer sharing that room with her in Hawaii. There was the patio and all that brightness flowing through the windows. It was a girl's room. Mommy called this room a "late-nineteenth-century motel." It had its matching dark brown bedside tables and a matching bureau with an oval mirror above it in an oak frame. None of the furnishings had anything embossed on them, no birds or flowers, not even some squiggly design. They were as plain and simple as could be.

I hoped I would make new friends at school this coming year, even at a private one with a smaller population. Would I ever want to bring a new girlfriend here? She'd be excited about seeing Sutherland but then let down when it came to seeing my room. In the back of her mind, she would wonder, *Are you a guest here or a granddaughter?*

Mommy had told me this room, her room at Sutherland, was deliberately made dark and neutral. There was purposely nothing especially feminine about it. She had said, "It was a subtle way for my father to say that what I wanted didn't matter. The image of Sutherland mattered. I guess that was equally true for my brother, Martin. We could have easily exchanged rooms. We had the exact same furniture! There was probably some sort of sale if you bought two of the same thing. My mother wasn't permitted to add anything, especially to the room I was now using."

Mommy claimed that, back then, Grandmother Judith was even afraid to spray her cologne in her room. It had to reek of the scent of the mansion, a manly scent.

"The mantra was that Sutherland had to remain inviolate and remain as it was. If he added anything, it was just to make it more majestic. Truthfully, however, I always suspected that my father wanted a second son." She thought a moment and added, "A second boy would have been like an insurance policy for him. In some ways, that explains most everything."

What did Grandfather want now? Was Simon supposed to be that second son? Was that why he was showing this concern and enlisting me to help? Recalling my mother's words made it seem like I was looking at the Sutherland world through her eyes. Could I really change anything?

Was it possible that I could someday get Grandfather to redo this room so I'd feel it was my room? If he was making new demands of me, shouldn't I dare to make one of him? And then I thought that after what he had told me about what friends meant to him, how little, in fact, and how they were more of a liability, how could I complain about being embarrassed to bring any of mine to this room? He'd simply say I was better off. What argument would work?

Exhausted from all this thinking, I opened one of my suitcases, looked at my luggage, and then flopped onto my bed. I closed my eyes. Aunt Holly was right to suggest some rest, but what I really wanted was to close my eyes and envision palm trees, hear the sound of the ocean, and feel those comforting warm trade winds. Clouds looked dabbed onto the blue and gradually shifted so that I could stare at them and begin to see shapes, even faces. The sky met the horizon, and when the sun set, the colors were dazzling. I imagined the sun was the tip of God's forefinger. It was as if he was putting out the candle. I told no one, especially not Dina. Most everyone else took it all for granted.

Her stupid expression, "Just another day in paradise," made paradise sound ordinary.

Suddenly, my stepbrother, Boston, came into my mind the way something was lying in wait just below the surface of all your thoughts to be remembered. When I had first met him, I had thought he resembled Daddy in his build. From the way he held himself, always conscious of his posture, I suspected he wanted to be like my father. He did have what I called proud shoulders. Looking at him from behind, someone might easily mistake him for Daddy. He had his mother Parker's lighter brown hair, but it was cut in the same style Daddy kept his in, a military look. He had beautiful hazel eyes and a firm chin, with straight, full lips. Everything about him seemed highlighted, maybe because of his Hawaiian tan, especially those eyes.

Of everyone in my father's new family, Boston was the saddest about my leaving. Those last minutes we spent together before I was taken to the airport would probably be embedded in my mind forever. I could sense his feelings for me and for the first time had thought of myself as someone's potential love interest. He had made clear his intention to visit me here in Sutherland. Had he said that just to be nice?

Perhaps even more important, in that short time, I could see his great desire to leave and become someone independent, out from under my father's shadow even though he respected him in so many ways. He loved his mother, and despite all that he criticized about his sister, he would do what he could to protect her. He simply had doubts she would survive herself. She was, unknowingly, her own worst enemy.

Right now, conjuring his image and especially his smile, I felt like a schoolgirl infatuated with some rock star or movie star. I had never really felt that way toward either. Often, my mother had warned me about the love interests she predicted I would experience. "I used to feel guilty that I didn't have the same passion my girlfriends had for this or that boy and have as intense a crush on that young teacher or this handsome fatherly one. You have to rely on your own feelings and not someone else's, but perhaps they'll be nothing more confusing for you. They were for me.

"Beware of first loves," she had said. "Sometimes doubt or caution is a good thing even though it's so inviting to leap into a relationship. Oh, why am I telling you all of this now? You're so young," she had exclaimed, her hands flying up like sparrows.

I had the feeling she was desperate to tell anyone about herself. Sometimes it was so important to voice your thoughts, no matter who was listening. I always thought it was strange to want to talk to your-self, but maybe it wasn't.

"When are you old enough to fall in love?" I had asked. Was there a certain age?

She had laughed and then turned terribly serious.

"When you know who you really are," she had said. "Only then, because you'll really understand what makes you happy, as opposed to what someone else thinks should make you happy."

I thought I did know myself back then, but now I had no idea who I really was and what I should think. Should I drive away all my thoughts about my stepbrother, Boston? Whom could I confide in when it came to these feelings and thoughts now? I was afraid that I would be embarrassed telling all this to Aunt Holly. She was nice and had loved my mother, but she wasn't my mother, even though I could sense that was who she was trying to be for me.

In my world, there were gaps between myself and everyone I knew. Sutherland was not a place for lonely people, or maybe it was the ideal place for them. I had accused Grandfather of being lonely without friends when he was younger. Maybe he had been lonely all his life, even when he had a wife and children, and was lonely now. Maybe I was more like him than I had imagined. When he was growing up, did his father treat him like a disappointment? Neither of us could escape the dark cloud that had put over us. Was he the first to know we shared this feeling? Was that why he sounded like he thought he could trust me?

Should I be happy about the similarity or sad?

Or maybe I should be more afraid.

CHAPTER FOUR

There was a loud knock on my door. Before I could say "Come in," it opened, and Mrs. Fisher appeared. I sat up. So much for my privacy, I thought. She entered, perusing the room as if I wasn't even there and she was checking up on the maids.

"Oh, you haven't even started on your luggage. You poor dear. Let me help you," she said, moving toward my suitcases.

I put my hand up the way she had when I had first entered Sutherland today.

"No, it's all right. I'll get to it."

She tilted her head.

"Really. Independent, are you? The ship that won't sail with the fleet." She stared at me for a few moments. I felt uncomfortable, almost angry, until she added, "Just like my daughter was."

"Was?"

She folded her arms across her breasts and stood straighter, posturing like someone who had been accused of something terrible.

"She married a man from India and died there of hepatitis. My husband had refused to acknowledge the marriage, so she did a runner."

"What's that?"

"She ran off with her new husband. We had to find that out from strangers. She had left no forwarding address. My husband forbade me to try to find her. In a way, my family story is not terribly different from yours. We unexpectedly lost people we loved the most, and that makes the pain deeper. We should be good friends, mates. People who share similar family tragedies usually are."

"Why didn't your husband want your daughter to marry a man from India?" I asked suspiciously. I didn't want to share any family tragedy, and I didn't think it was similar, even though it was surely as terrible.

"Oh," she said, moving to sit at the foot of my bed. "My husband was a man who lived at the wrong time. He thought it was still the time when the sun never set on the British flag."

"Why didn't it set?"

She spoke quickly, as if she had memorized it all to recite it. "We ruled so many places in the world, even India once. We were in every time zone. He was all pomp and circumstance. He had been a butler to a knighted architect. When I met him, I thought of him as a life raft. My own father had died, and my mother wasn't doing well. I made meager pounds working in a department store, even though I was an associate manager. Women are discriminated against everywhere. Except in Sutherland, of course. Your grandfather respects people who work hard and fulfill their duties.

"And so here I am, speaking to you. See, we have a lot to share."

"It's not the same thing."

"What's not?"

"What happened to your daughter and what happened to my mother and then me."

"Well, as I said, we both lost somebody we loved so deeply."

"If you loved her so deeply, why did you let your husband do that to her?"

I knew I could ask the same question about my grandmother Judith after Grandfather just about disowned my mother, but, like my mother, I always thought she cowered in his shadow. Was Mrs. Fisher the same sort of wife? Was that why she got along so well with my grandfather? Despite what she was telling me, did she accept that women weren't as important?

She winced but kept her wooden smile. No matter how she responded, it wouldn't diminish my reference to love, especially when it came to her daughter. So she had a better life with this arrogant Englishman. Did that really matter?

Certainly, I had a better life here when it came to wealth, but look at how much different life was when you had a mother to love you. No one here would ever hold me like my mother had or kiss and cherish me in that special way, not even Aunt Holly, who was trying. The word "love" itself would be weaker, emptier, if someone could just step in to fill that gap and put your mother on a shelf of memories.

How come Mrs. Fisher didn't seem to feel that loss so much that she would always cry talking about it? It was almost impossible for me to talk about my mother without its bringing tears to my eyes. I was so much younger than Mrs. Fisher, but I could sense how altered the world was without that deep love that a mother and a daughter shared. Everything, even the most ordinary thing, seemed different without it. It was as if a color was forever gone, an incomplete rainbow.

Mrs. Fisher quickly reacted to the disapproval in my question, a question I never dared to ask Grandmother Judith. She curled her lips into a sharp sneer. "All women don't have the same sense of independence your mother had and, I might add, the finances to permit her to be that way. Some people have an easier time being heroes and heroines."

Heroine? I thought. *By just loving your daughter?* I bit down on the words before they rode a wave of anger through my lips.

She quickly changed her sneer into a smile so false it could be like slipping on a mask. "But let's talk about good things, about the future. Your grandfather has asked me to keep a special eye out for you and—"

The door was thrust open again.

This time, it was Simon.

He was wearing a brighter shirt, red with a white collar. I knew he had a number of colorful shirts—I saw them hanging in his closet— but he seemed always to choose something darker. I remembered when he wore the white tennis sneakers he was wearing now. He said his father had bought them for him with the prospect of them playing tennis. As far as I knew, they never did while I was here. Sometimes he wore them as a subtle reminder, and then he put them away "with all the other dead promises."

"Excuse me," he said, looking at Mrs. Fisher. "But I was coming to escort my cousin to lunch."

He was polite, even sweet.

"Oh," she said, rising quickly. "That's very nice."

I was just as surprised as she was. He had been so adamant when Aunt Holly asked him to be at lunch with us. I thought he had sounded downright angry about it.

"I haven't had time to change," I said.

"No wonder," he said, looking at Mrs. Fisher. His eyes flashed a little anger. "You haven't had much time to yourself."

"Oh, of course." She rose. "Did you want any help, Caroline?"

"I'm fine. Thank you, Mrs. Fisher. Simon, I'll be with you in five minutes."

I tried to sound as firm and determined as my grandfather could sound. Earning respect and being treated the way someone mature and independent should be treated were probably more difficult at Sutherland than anywhere else, but the moment I left Grandfather's office this morning, I felt I should strive for that. After Hawaii, I was a hair's width from becoming an orphan.

"Five minutes? I hope so," Simon said, smiling, without his usual ironic humor. "I'm hungry." He opened the door wider, indicating that Mrs. Fisher should leave. She glanced at me suspiciously and walked out. Did she think I knew he would come to fetch me for lunch?

"I thought you weren't hungry," I said.

He smirked as though I had said the dumbest thing. This was more like the Simon I knew. "Of course I'm hungry. When did I say I wasn't?"

"What? We . . ."

"Besides, Grandfather is going to attend."

"I just assumed he would."

"You can never assume anything about Grandfather. I like that he's attending because everyone makes it more important. He'll expect me since you've returned. I don't like disappointing him, and why would I skip lunch anyway?"

"But I thought . . . I mean, Aunt Holly said you often don't eat lunch with everyone."

"My mother exaggerates. It's part of being a mother, especially when she talks about her own child or children."

"My mother wasn't like that."

He laughed.

"She wasn't," I insisted.

"Whatever," he said with a Simon shrug, lifting and dropping his shoulders with that familiar arrogant confidence I thought he had lost.

The joy in his face certainly contrasted with the dour expression he had when I first arrived. I was afraid to say or ask anything more about it. I pressed my lips shut. *Don't do anything to ruin this*, I thought. Was this the effect my being here had on him already? It boosted my ego, which desperately needed a boost.

"Oh, I see Grandfather gave you Grandmother Judith's ring."

Instinctively, I put my hand over it. Would he quickly conclude, as Grandfather had joked, that I had been bribed to spy on him? It wouldn't surprise me. Simon could reach a conclusion with lightning speed.

"Yes. She had left it to me in her will."

"I remember that. Something about after your sixteenth birthday. Nothing goes on in Sutherland without Grandfather's approval or knowledge."

He looked like he was going to get angry again but then smiled.

"*L'État, c'est moi.* It was true for Louis XIV of France, and it's true for Grandfather. Lucky we're on his good side."

"We are?"

"Why not?"

Grandfather would love to see him like this, I thought. Maybe he knew something magical would happen to Simon when I returned. I almost felt guilty getting credit for it. All I did was appear.

"I guess I am hungry, too. Let me get out of these travel clothes. I'll be right out," I said. The less I talked about the change in him, the better.

"I'll wait at the top of the stairs," he said, as though that place no longer had special meaning. I'm sure I looked surprised, but he didn't see it. He turned and left, closing the door.

I rushed to wash my face, brush my hair, and change into a blouse and skirt. When I opened one of my suitcases, my Hawaiian clothes stared up at me, but I didn't dare wear any of them now. I didn't want to talk about Hawaii and especially relive the last days.

After I stepped out of my room, I saw Simon standing at the banister at the top of the stairs and looking down. Was he seeing the horror that I saw, reliving those moments? Would everything quickly return to the way it had been? Was he realizing what I had felt? As I drew closer, I saw that if he was, he was determined not to show me. He turned, smiling widely.

"You look like you grew up overnight," he said.

"I do?"

"That can happen. It's not time but events that mature and also age us when we're older," he said, returning to his teacher tone of voice. People who didn't know Simon would think he was simply arrogant. That was probably why he never had friends, whether close to his age or even older.

"Brilliance can be either a blessing or a curse," my mother had told me when I expressed how amazed about him I was.

He paused, hearing himself speak that way, and quickly smiled. "Madam," he said, imitating a Southern gentleman, and held our his arm. I couldn't recall him ever behaving like this. If I showed too much surprise, he might feel silly and return to being the Simon I knew.

"Thank you, sir," I said.

He laughed. I took his arm, and we started down the stairs.

"Did you finally play tennis with your father while I was away? I see those tennis shoes look more worn."

"What? Oh. No. They're comfortable. I feel spry and alert walking these stairs and these long hallways when I wear them. Once in a while, I go for a run around the property. Tennis? Dad and me? Grandfather has been keeping my father busy seven days a week. Lucky for him, there aren't eight."

"You run around the property?"

"Sure. Fresh air and exercise. Can't have my nose in a book all day and night."

This didn't sound at all like the Simon I knew before I left and the description of him that I was given afterward. Why hadn't Aunt Holly mentioned the good things? Why hadn't Grandfather Sutherland? Could he have done all this in secret?

He held his smile and really did look quite alert. I almost felt grateful for all that had occurred to bring me back. Fate's plan had backfired. Maybe it was important to help someone else before helping yourself. Or maybe it was really the same thing in the end. I supposed someone might say, "We're all selfish when you get down to it. Good deeds make you bigger, stronger, and brighter in the eyes of others." In this case, I was aiming straight for Grandfather's eyes.

Simon was still holding that brighter smile and walking as if he had just stepped out of a plane and onto a cloud. Now that we were about to see Grandfather, it made me a little nervous. Would he think I had revealed his secret assignment for me and Simon was behaving this way to cover up his anger? Could something explosive happen at lunch and cause my return to be as traumatic as my leaving Hawaii?

I had to keep talking. "Do you like Mrs. Fisher?" I asked.

"I don't know as I've developed a definitive opinion about her. Some people think first impressions are the most meaningful, but I've always liked learning as much as I can about someone or something before reaching a conclusion. Of course, if Grandfather likes her, I do. It's just that she . . ."

"Tries too hard to be liked?"

"Yes, that's it. Very astute. You pick up the right vibrations when you meet someone new. Maybe you've inherited your father's air traffic controller instincts."

"Really?"

"On the other hand, good intuition is a Sutherland trait. You can't help but have the vision. Sometimes I think Grandfather can see through walls. He can certainly see through insincerity or ulterior motives. People like Grandfather, of which there aren't many, don't need lights in the dark. I've made sort of a study of famous men and women who fit that description."

"Have you?"

"As a footnote, not as a major subject. Carl Jung's theory of the collective unconscious helped me understand a bit. We'll have to talk about it one day."

He just leaped years ahead of me, as usual, I thought. Simon was really brilliant, and that sort of intelligence surely couldn't be stifled forever. He'd get back to being who he could be. But why was he talking about all this when we were alone? What about his new secret? Couldn't he suggest it before we saw anyone or stepped out onto the patio? In the entrance when I had arrived, he looked like he would explode if he didn't get the information to me.

At the moment, he just looked ahead with that gleeful smile frozen on his face. He was walking briskly and still holding my hand. I was about to bring up his urgency to tell me what he had discovered, but Aunt Holly appeared before I could say anything.

"Oh, how nice you look, Simon. I'm so happy you decided to join us."

"Do I really look nice?" He glanced at me. "Or is this just a mother's natural exaggeration?"

"No. You do look nice," I said.

He smiled at me and turned to Aunt Holly. "In that case, thank you, Mom."

"Your father has decided to join us," Aunt Holly said, her face brightening even more.

"It'll be nice to have the family together for Caroline's return," Simon said.

Did I hear right?

The Simon I remembered would have said something sarcastic,

and that wasn't a wry or sardonic smile on his face now, either. He looked honestly happy about it. I glanced at Aunt Holly. She was smiling warmly at me. *She thinks he's being this way only because of me,* I thought.

I wanted to whisper, "I haven't done anything," but I dared not do anything to spoil the moment.

Actually, having such a possible effect frightened me. Now that I gave it more thought, I didn't want to be responsible for anyone else. Right now, I was struggling to be responsible for myself.

The table on the patio had been set. Mrs. Fisher was standing over it as if she was going to leap at a fork that was just a quarter of an inch too far to the left. Clara Jean was bringing out the salad bowl. Perfectly on cue, Grandfather; his CEO, Franklin Butler; and Uncle Martin were approaching. Simon would usually make a comment like "They're walking in step with Grandfather. They won't breathe unless he does."

Instead of making a comment, Simon rushed to pull out the chair for Aunt Holly and then for me, as if he wanted to show Grandfather he was a gentleman. Grandfather paused at the end of the table to watch and then sat. Maybe no one but me could see the glint of approval in his eyes when he glanced at me.

Uncle Martin slipped into his seat the way someone who didn't want to be counted late for class might. Franklin sat to his right, close to Grandfather. Whenever he attended a dinner or lunch, he always seemed to be between Grandfather and Uncle Martin. People in Sutherland were set in their places like pieces on a chessboard at the start of the game.

I don't know why, but it suddenly occurred to me that I had rarely ever seen my grandfather without his usual gray or tweed jacket, but today, an August day with a cool breeze that signaled the oncoming autumn, he wore a very light, well-fitted blue-gray jacket with a dark blue tie. He wasn't wearing this when I saw him in his office. He appeared more festive now. Uncle Martin was in his usual charcoal jacket and matching gray tie. I hadn't been gone that long, but he looked older, more stressed. He always squinted at the dinner table as if Grandfather had cast a spotlight over him, but today the lines around his eyes looked deeper.

Clara Jean began to serve everyone salad.

"What's for lunch?" Simon blurted. "I'm starving."

Grandfather looked at him as if he wanted to be sure Simon had really spoken. He glanced at me before answering him.

"I believe Mrs. Wilson has prepared fresh turkey sandwiches," Grandfather said. Then he sat back.

Uncle Martin hadn't said hello or even really looked at me.

"Have you discussed my proposal for your schooling with your aunt Holly?" Grandfather asked me.

"She has," Aunt Holly quickly replied. "I look forward to going and seeing the school myself."

"Good. Franklin?"

"All the arrangements have been made for Caroline to be there tomorrow at ten a.m."

"Be where, exactly?" Simon asked.

"Caroline is getting an introduction to and a tour of The Oaks, the school she will attend," Grandfather said, and started to eat his salad, which was the signal for everyone to begin.

"Oh. Well, I've never been there," Simon said, "even though you and Mom attended, Dad."

Grandfather paused to look at Simon as if to be sure he had heard right. Uncle Martin paused, too, but checked Grandfather's face first to see if Grandfather was displeased. I wondered how often Grandfather had placed the blame for Simon's condition on him. Mommy always said that Grandfather was too hard on Uncle Martin. "Of course, Great-grandfather wasn't what anyone would call an ideal husband

and father, either," she had said. *What's more complicated than a family?*
I wondered.

"Do you want to go?" Uncle Martin asked.

"On the tour?" Simon said. "Sure. Always wondered why you
never sent me there."

"What?" Uncle Martin looked at Grandfather. "We provided
special private teachers for you, Simon. The moment you entered ele-
mentary school, we all knew that was going to be your future," Uncle
Martin said, again looking at Grandfather, I was sure to be confident
it was the correct response. "You were asking questions before the
teachers asked. Sometimes, they said, you took up so much class time
that there was little left for the others. We did what we thought was
best for you."

"And thanks for that, Grandfather, and you, too, Dad."

Uncle Martin recognized that I was sitting there, that I was back.
He smiled at me with a slight nod. Could that mean, I wondered, that
Grandfather had confided in him, describing my new assignment? I
hadn't told him anything, nor had I done anything but arrive with my
tail between my legs, I thought, and everyone was acting as if I had just
moved a mountain because Simon was in a happy mood.

"Very good. I look forward to your reactions to The Oaks," Grandfather said to both of us. "Dress properly, and be ready to leave in time
for the ten a.m. meeting. Any questions?"

I looked at Simon.

He shrugged. "I'll certainly fit it into my schedule," he said. He
held his expression for a moment and then smiled.

His father laughed nervously, and Aunt Holly squeezed my hand.
Out of the corner of my eye, I saw Mrs. Fisher smiling. It was truly
like some magician had waved a wand, washing away my depression
and trepidation. Funnily enough, I wondered if this would all make
Daddy upset.

I wasn't suffering enough.

I was grateful but also afraid that if they credited me with something good about Simon, they might blame me if something bad about him now occurred.

Mrs. Fisher continued to stand to the side, directing Clara Jean and her assistant in clearing things off the table and bringing out food. Mrs. Lawson used to hover like this, I thought, but she rarely spoke. She simply watched and spoke with her eyes.

Maybe it was the tension or maybe it was the trip and the emotional impact of my return, but suddenly I was feeling sleepy. Aunt Holly was the first to notice. I had no interest in dessert, and by now, Grandfather, Franklin, and Uncle Martin were talking about other investments and business decisions. Simon listened, but I was anticipating him leaning over to whisper about his new secret. Instead, he ate his dessert and continued to listen to the business talk, but differently from how I recalled him listening to these sorts of details in the past. Right now, he almost looked amused, as if he knew something none of them did.

They were so eager for Simon not to be depressed that they didn't see the differences in him, I thought.

"I think Caroline needs to take a nap now," Aunt Holly announced when there was a bit of a pause.

Everyone stopped talking and looked at me as if I had just sat down at the table.

"Of course," Grandfather said. "Reacclimating is always a little exhausting. Whenever we went on a trip, especially a long one, your grandmother," he said, turning to Simon and me, "always liked to arrive a day ahead of me so she could be fresh when I arrived."

"Like a tomato, fresh," Simon quipped.

Grandfather stopped smiling. "No. Rested, not irritable."

I thought Simon was going to react to Grandfather's displeasure.

"Didn't you need to rest, too?" I asked quickly.

"Better equipped for travel," he said.

"You kept yourself busy, so time flew by," Simon said.

"Exactly."

"Time is the stream I go fishing in," Simon said.

No one spoke.

"That's Thoreau, Grandfather," Simon added. "You have an original copy of *Walden* in the Sutherland library. Third shelf to the right of the door."

"Thank you for the information," Grandfather said. It was hard to tell from the light in his eyes whether he was annoyed or pleased.

There was a note of that familiar arrogance Simon could have in his voice. How much of the old Simon did Grandfather really want back?

Aunt Holly rose, sensing a need to end any tension. "I'll see to Caroline getting some rest."

Grandfather nodded.

"Welcome back," Uncle Martin said unexpectedly.

Welcome back? I didn't know what to say. Didn't he understand that I was here because I was rejected by my father and his new wife? Why *welcome*? If he wasn't blaming me, why didn't he at least sound sympathetic? Was there no other place but Sutherland in the world, no other place to live and prosper?

I looked at Simon, but he avoided looking at me. *Does he finally feel sorry for me?* I wondered.

"Maybe now I should help with the unpacking," Mrs. Fisher said.

"No, it's fine," I said quickly and firmly. My voice sounded almost exactly like Grandfather's. "Aunt Holly and I can do it."

She nodded and took a step back. I had a surge of regret. Perhaps I was being unfairly harsh. I glanced at Grandfather. His eyes narrowed, but he looked more thoughtful than upset with my behavior and tone.

I kept my eyes looking down at the table when I rose. The sun had slipped behind an oval cloud, as if nature wanted to get the spotlight off me.

I looked toward the garden that had been my mother's favorite part of Sutherland. Was that just a shadow smoothly appearing between two bushes, or my mother's spirit reminding me that she would always be here, always supporting me? Maybe Aunt Holly felt it, too. She put her arm around my shoulders, and we walked back into the house.

"If this is any indication," Aunt Holly said, "then Simon is returning to us. I know it's sad for you to be back here, but as my mother used to say, there's always some unexpected good hovering behind or under some sadness."

"I didn't do anything or say anything that would cause him to change so quickly. I'm just as surprised as you are."

"I know. It's always funny how we're quick to recognize our faults but often need someone else to help us see the best in us."

What's the best in me? I wondered. *Not crying and moaning about my own problems, hiding my real feelings so it looks like I've accepted my fate? Is obedience all that is expected of me: do what I can for Simon, go to a new school, and sew up my thoughts in a sock and drop it into a corner of my closet? How can I oppose it? Aren't I being given a second, even a third, chance?*

Aunt Holly had me lie down while she unpacked my things. I must have been quite tired. I didn't resist. When I opened my eyes again, she was gone, and everything had been hung up and put away. I glanced at my watch and saw that hours had passed. But before I could sit up, Simon opened the door and peered in without knocking.

My first thought was that the Simon who had just spent lunch with me wouldn't be that impolite. Maybe he had just been pretending at lunch. The hardest thing to believe about his emotional and psychological suffering after the death of Mrs. Lawson was that he would not be a step or two ahead of everyone else, even Grandfather. He was weighed down by his own darkness.

He was wearing a different shirt, one of his dull gray ones, and was no longer wearing those white sneakers. There were other things about him that looked different. Maybe it was just the light in his eyes. He seemed more in a daze, the brightness gone from his face. He even looked a little angry. Had something happened after I had left the patio?

"What?" I asked, scrubbing the sleepiness out of my eyes.

"If you've finally rested enough from your trip home, we can go down to the basement, and I can show you the new secret," he said.

CHAPTER FIVE

For a long moment, I simply stared at him. He wore the same expression he had when he had left Aunt Holly and me on my arrival at the front entrance. The anger he had displayed then had returned, brighter and deeper in his eyes. I wasn't afraid as much as I was confused. It was as if we hadn't had lunch, as if I had fallen asleep and dreamed it all as soon as I had been left alone in my room. My mother once told me that sometimes you could wish for things so hard in your dreams that you believed they had come true when you awoke.

With impatience clearly written across his face, Simon leaned back against the doorframe and tapped his fingers on the wall as if he was playing piano keys. It wasn't only the expression on his face that startled me. His whole demeanor had changed. He stood stiffly, his shoulders poised as if he was expecting a blow to the back of his neck.

I had the suspicion that he had been acting at lunch just to please Grandfather. He was so smart. Had he suspected Grandfather wanted to use me to get to him? Was that why he was showing off, acting so pleasant and suddenly interested in everything? Did he want Grandfather to be happy with me, or was he toying with both of us? What would I say if he came right out and asked me, "Are you our grandfather's new spy, a young Mrs. Lawson?"

Often, before I went to Hawaii, I thought it would be more difficult to lie to him than to Grandfather. Even Aunt Holly had said that Simon could x-ray whatever reasons or excuses she used for anything and see the truth: "In ways that were disturbing, I thought my son was older than me sometimes."

"Well," he said now, fixing his darker eyes on me. "It's the best time of day to go down there." He looked up at the ceiling, making it obvious he was doing so to quiet his impatience. "This is the lull before the Fisher storm."

"What's that mean?"

"Sutherland weather report," he said, still looking at the ceiling. He was looking at it so intensely that I looked at it as well. Did he see something I didn't see, like a hidden microphone or camera?

"Fisher storm?"

He snapped his attention back to me. His face was ghastly, haunted, his cheeks whiter, and his lips pulled backward so hard that I could see the molars in his mouth. He clenched his teeth, too. Such a display of rage now was terrifying.

I'm not equipped to handle Simon when he loses control of his emotions, I thought. *I'm barely equipped to handle myself.* Maybe Grandfather was subtly punishing me rather than depending on me. Maybe that was why I thought I heard my mother whispering warnings.

Simon continued to stare coldly. I hated these short silences between us. When he did that, I couldn't help but hold my breath. Would they lead to the calm and clever thoughts for which he was so well known once or the spiral of some emotional hurricane?

"I'm just trying to understand, Simon. Everything isn't as clear to me as it is to you. Fisher storm? You mean Mrs. Fisher?" I asked as calmly as I could manage.

"She pokes her nose into everything, every nook and cranny of this place. I can feel her eyes on me almost all day and night. Don't tell me you don't feel that, too, even in the short time you've known her."

"I thought you and I agreed about her. She tries too hard. You didn't make it sound so terrible only hours ago."

"Of course, she's not as bad as Mrs. Lawson was," he said, ignoring my point. "At least Fisher attempts to disguise her impatience and condemnation with those nauseating smiles. Unless she was talking to Grandfather, Mrs. Lawson never smiled. Mrs. Lawson could burn a hole through you with her glare. The servants didn't simply rush off to correct something; they fled. Her dark shadows are still fading from our walls. I'm looking forward to when they're completely gone. I'm sure you know exactly what I mean.

"Nevertheless, let's avoid Fisher. She's idolizes Grandfather just as much as Mrs. Lawson did. Not unexpected. Who works here and doesn't? He has this special Sutherland power over his servants. It's as if he can see everything they see, see through their eyes."

"You make 'Sutherland' sound like profanity." *Which is totally unusual for you*, I wanted to add, but hesitated.

He grinned impishly. "It is what it is. You can't be happy being in this family, not after all you've been through under Grandfather's watchful eyes."

"Maybe we're both making Grandfather seem greater than he is, Simon."

"Ha. He is what he is. Mrs. Lawson proved that."

"What does that mean?"

"She was like Satan's Beelzebub, his assistant in hell."

"You are saying Grandfather is Satan?"

This was my cousin who really did think the sun rose and went down when Grandfather opened his eyes and closed them to sleep. All he had ever shown me he wanted was to be another Grandfather Sutherland.

"Mrs. Lawson," he said between his clenched teeth, as if just saying her name explained everything. He continued to glare expectantly at me.

I knew my mouth was open, and I was staring at him in disbelief. I hardly thought he'd ever mention Mrs. Lawson, much less practically justify her death and his causing of it.

Continuing to smile weirdly, he added, "But you shouldn't look so surprised about her replacement, Caroline. You know Grandfather," he said, looking up at the ceiling again. "He only hires people who would die for him, and you'll soon learn why that was especially true for Mrs. Lawson. Lawson. We should have called her Lawless."

He laughed, a thin, evil-sounding giggle of delight.

"Simon," I said in a voice just above a whisper.

I knew he heard me, but he continued to look up as if to ignore me.

I stood up slowly. "Simon," I snapped as sharply as I dared. "We shouldn't talk about her or say things like that especially. What if someone else hears you, especially Mrs. Fisher?"

He turned back to me, looking surprised. "So? You think she might rise from the dead or come out of the walls?" he replied, far more nonchalantly than I had anticipated.

"What?"

"Maybe she's possessed Mrs. Fisher. That's possible, isn't it?" he asked, his eyes wide open. "Spirits do that. They go into personalities that at first seem different from theirs so you won't know they are there. You know that, don't you?"

He looked like he was seriously considering it and wanted me to agree. He wasn't making any sense. Simon was never one to talk about spirits. He believed only in what he could see and touch. This was frightening. Rushing out and down to get Grandfather or calling Aunt Holly flashed through my mind, even though I knew he'd probably never talk to me again.

But this was what Grandfather wanted from me, wasn't it? I felt trapped, spinning with confusion. One moment everything looked wonderful and hopeful for both of us, and then this.

He didn't wait for an answer while I pondered. He walked out and stood there looking back in at me.

"Well?" he said. "Are you coming or not? Once you learn what I know, you won't be tiptoeing through this mansion. You won't be so timid."

"I'm not timid. I'm trying to remain calm after what's happened to me."

My eyes froze with tears. He grunted,

"Calm? You're far from calm. The eye sees not itself but by reflection."

"What's that supposed to mean? Can't you just say what you mean, Simon?"

"You don't see yourself the way you really are," he replied. "No one does."

"Even you? What do you see when you look in the mirror now? A very short time ago, you were smiling, trying to make jokes. What should I believe?"

That question seemed to go deep. For a moment, he looked like he was going to cry and admit he had serious problems. But the look was gone almost as quickly as it had come. He seemed to parade through a myriad of emotions, as unsure as a blind man walking between burning buildings. His face flushed.

I was afraid to say anything else. For sure now, one of my words could cause him to explode. Everyone would blame me just as quickly as they applauded my positive effect on Simon.

"Are you coming or not?" he said again. I had no doubt he would leave and maybe avoid speaking to me again. Grandfather would be upset. I had driven him deeper into the darkness, not drawn him out of it.

I pulled out a light blue sweater hanging in my closet, slipped into it, and followed him.

"Women change clothes like chameleons change colors," he muttered to his right, as if someone else was walking with us.

"Why did you change your clothes?" I asked. We approached the stairway. Would it always feel like I was stepping onto a ledge? "You looked so nice. Your mother was so pleased."

"Was she? I don't choose my clothes; they choose me."

"What's that supposed to mean? You keep talking in riddles."

He turned abruptly onto the steps and then paused.

Here it comes, I thought, *telling me he didn't choose his father, either, or something just as terrible to say.*

"Forget about all that. Just walk softly. Everyone is taking a short rest before the late-afternoon and evening chores. This place is like a battleship. I'm surprised we don't get any 'Now hear this' over a loudspeaker. Grandfather is taking a nap or something. Tiptoeing is required. Lord have mercy if you disturb Zeus."

There it was again: his anger toward our grandfather, and so vehement, too. He turned and began walking down the stairs quickly. I had to hurry to catch up to him. Was he descending with his eyes closed? How could I get out of this? All I was doing by going along was encouraging his instability.

"I should be resting, too," I said. "I've had a traumatic past few days."

He turned before we had gone too far, his normal gleeful Simon smile spreading over his face like a broken egg yolk. "Traumatic? Your vocabulary is improving. Maybe you should get into trouble more often. You'll be like me, graduating way before you were expected to. Mistakes can make you stronger in the end. Look at it this way: you'll be more careful about stepping into the ocean." He started walking quickly again.

"That's not funny, Simon. If you were really interested, you'd let me tell you all about it. Maybe then you'd be more considerate. No one really warned . . ."

Before I could say anything else, he put his hand up and froze. I waited. Maybe I was still readjusting to my return, but I didn't hear anything at first, not a whisper of movement in the huge house, not a telephone ringing, not anything being switched on or off.

And then, down the hall near the doorway that opened to the room where I had been kept prisoner, Mrs. Fisher emerged. She looked angry about something and didn't so much as glance our way as she crossed to follow the hallway toward the kitchen. She did walk softly, almost gliding an inch or so off the floor. How did he hear her? He knew every creak in this house. He wore this mansion like another layer of skin. It had always been a living thing to him. Did he even know there was a world outside?

"Did you see her face? Someone's going to get it," Simon whispered. "Someone left something exposed, something that shouldn't be out of a dark closet."

He smiled. Why did these dark mysteries make him so happy? As with everything at Sutherland, there was always one more layer of reason, one more hidden thing. It was as if we all lived in a world beneath another world. Peel away a surface, peel away a smile, and you discovered a different reality. Perhaps that had always been true and always would be for those who lived at Sutherland.

"In there? What could they be doing with that room? Is it being changed? Will it be made into my room now? Maybe Grandfather doesn't want me living in what had been my mother's room. Maybe he wants me to forget her. What do you know about it? What have you seen?"

He didn't reply. He started to walk, but I reached out to touch his shoulder and made him pause again.

"What about that room?"

He stared again as if he had no idea what I was asking about.

"Didn't you hear me? Have you been in there since . . . since I was?"

He looked at me guiltily, on the verge of apologizing, maybe, but then continued walking toward the basement door.

"Simon? Have you?"

He paused.

"Tell me, or I won't go a step farther."

He sighed as if he was putting up with a child. "I looked at it from time to time to remind myself."

"Of what?"

"What they did to you, Dr. Kirkwell and Mrs. Lawson. They both enjoyed it too much, especially Mrs. Lawson. But you know all of that."

"Grandfather hired them," I said angrily.

He was causing me to relive it. Maybe he was right to avoid talking about it. Would I ever forgive Grandfather, no matter how nice he was to me now?

Simon laughed unexpectedly.

"Why is that funny?"

"It's not funny. One day, we'll remind him." His smile lifted off his face like a frightened sparrow. "He shouldn't be above reprobation."

"What? What are you saying?"

"Above criticism. I guess your vocabulary has a ways to go."

"That's arrogant, Simon. Just because you're a walking dictionary . . ."

"Oh, please. Let's go. As I said, we have only a small window of time. And then—"

"And then what?"

"You'll understand everything."

"Everything?"

He approached the basement door, opened it softly, and looked at me.

"Well?"

The indecision and minor panic I felt weren't something new, despite the pins and needles I was to navigate since Hawaii. Every time I turned a corner in this house, from the day I had returned to it after the aversion therapy months ago, I was in some sort of crisis. Now it seemed even more true.

Maybe I should have begged my father to give me another chance, even though in my heart I knew that was a fruitless hope, despite how passionately I expressed my regret. It was always part of who he was and what he did in his profession never to reverse a decision. Perhaps, in the end, I really had to be more like him and my grandfather and stifle compassion until it shrank to a speck of my personality.

I knew how Daddy felt about it, and I surely understood where Grandfather stood when mercy was an option. They believed people recognized when you didn't have self-confidence, especially when you made a decision. But how did you know when you had too much ego, when you thought you were so right and everyone else was so wrong? In the end, wasn't that really a weakness? Eventually, wouldn't that destroy you? My mother certainly thought that was true of her father and mine.

Simon was showing his impatience again, opening and closing his fists and clicking his lips. He could have a breakdown right here and draw the whole house to us. I really had never told Grandfather or Aunt Holly about our previous trips to the Cemetery of Memories. They'd be surprised at how often I'd been there with Simon. I was just as guilty of keeping secrets. Both would be so disappointed in me. Maybe they'd blame me for Simon's behavior then and now. I imagined Grandfather reneging on anything hopeful he had said. I could hear him mutter, in fact, "I guess your father was right about you. You're too much like your mother when it comes to respect for this house and its heritage."

Tears threatened to emerge from my eyes. What choice did I have? Turning back and hiding in my room was not an option. For better or for worse, I had signed up for this when I accepted Grandfather's request. "Accepted" was a dream word. As my mother said about my father after he had left, "When he says 'Jump,' I'm supposed to ask 'How high?'"

I hurried to Simon. We slipped in, and he flipped the switch to illuminate the stairs and turn on the scattered lights of the cavernous basement below.

Darkness fled to every corner and dimly lit area. Boxes, crates, and old furniture with dusty covers seemed to perk up and rise to the floor as if they had been sleeping just below the surface of the old, cracked concrete. Spiders raced to a safer place on their webs. Rats and mice fled to their havens between boxes, in deeper corners, and under the dusty covers. It was a cemetery, I thought. What secret lay in wait?

And would I wish that it was never unburied?

CHAPTER SIX

It hadn't been that long since I had last been down here with Simon, but the basement looked different to me. Now I noticed how the air that leaked in stirred the dust that swirled under the dimly lit bulbs. The stale odor of old things with their mix of scents was sharper and more unpleasant. Surely nothing, not the old trunks, old furniture, lamps, or cardboard boxes, had its original tint. It was the land of the faded. Perhaps it was because the brightness and sharp colors of Hawaii still lingered so firmly in my mind that the sight of the Cemetery of Memories was so unattractive this time. At the moment, I didn't want to spend another minute in it.

When we heard footsteps above, Simon put his hand up so we wouldn't move or talk. They disappeared to our right, and all was almost completely silent again, but before we moved, we heard the sound of water running through pipes on our left and farther in.

Simon smiled at me. "The house is swallowing something," he said. "Hope it doesn't swallow us."

It really sounded like he thought the mansion was a giant whale or something. Why did he want to live here so much if he had such dark thoughts about it? Did he always have dark thoughts about himself? Was that why he felt he belonged? Maybe what I believed was his arrogance was really more a cry for help. I'd never dared suggest it to him. But after all, everyone, from his grade school days until now, had told him he was different.

I hated it when my stepsister, Dina, implied that I was. She practically had me believing it. That would have been a better answer for Grandfather. I got into trouble because I didn't want to believe it.

When that noise from upstairs stopped, Simon beckoned, and we walked forward. He turned about where I knew Prissy's grave was located. Was he just going to bring up all that? Maybe he had forgotten all that he had shown me.

But then he turned to his right and stopped to pick up a carton and quietly place it on the floor between us. There was a smaller, flatter carton beneath it.

He looked up at me with a smile of accomplishment, his eyes blazing like the eyes of someone who had lost a gold ring and finally found it through painstakingly clever detective work. I could see that he was anticipating my being as excited as he was.

When I had first come down here and seen the things he had discovered, I did share some of that interest and enthusiasm. Of course, I was emotional. It wasn't long after I had been locked up in what I learned had been Prissy's room, so naturally I was shocked by the sight of her grave. That gave me the idea of calling this basement a Cemetery of Memories.

But it felt different now. There was nothing magical. This was just buried old things, smelly and crusted with time and darkness. Attics and basements weren't meant to be visited frequently. They were homes for the forgotten. Maybe I was still tired and suffering from my Hawaii experience. Simon could see how I felt about being here. I knew I was cringing. The light in his face darkened into a grimace.

"What's wrong? You don't seem interested."

"I forgot how *ugh* it was down here," I offered as what I hoped was an acceptable excuse.

"Ugh? How could you even think it? Everything in this basement spells us," he said. "I expected you would understand and realize how important it is, especially after what you've been through."

"Nothing feels like me." I embraced myself. "It's cold and dank here, Simon. There must be mold everywhere. What is it you want to show me? Can't we do this quickly?"

"Quickly? Yes, quickly. The faster you go, the more you miss, Caroline. I walked by this many times and never realized it was here," he said, gently kicking the small carton.

"What is it? Is the new secret in there?"

"Yes. And it's an even bigger secret than Prissy."

Even bigger than Prissy? A secret child buried in secret? Was it even legal for her to be buried in a basement? Not that I could envision the Sutherlands being held accountable for anything they had done.

I stepped closer, feeling my heartbeat quicken.

Were all families like this, floating above a graveyard of revelations that potentially would change who they were and fill them with new disappointments and fears? It was like being reborn every other day or week. Your birth certificate could fade. No wonder I used to be jealous of my classmates who had much simpler family lives, almost downright boring ones, with normal birthday and holiday celebrations. Their fathers weren't perfect, their mothers weren't startlingly beautiful, and their grandparents weren't kings with business empires.

Our neighbors used to call us the Robot Family because we were so picture-perfect and moved seamlessly from morning to night, never changing when chores would be done or when my father would get the mail. But the truth I knew deep inside me was that no one was as envious of us as I was of them, especially now.

Simon's smile changed again. He looked as jubilant as a surgeon who had made an incision and discovered the hateful tumor. The changes he had gone through from the moment he had come to my bedroom after lunch were frightening me cold to the bone. I looked back at the stairway. Maybe I should just flee and tell my aunt and my grandfather that it was too hard to help Simon. I'd confess about all my visits to the basement with him, combing through papers and pictures buried for one reason or another. I'd even admit to reading Grandmother Judith's diary and learning how much she hated being here. Would that be enough?

Can't I just live my own life, go to school, and make real friends? I'd promise to avoid the Dinas, get good grades, and make my grandfather and aunt and uncle proud. But maybe it was impossible. Kings and Sutherlands couldn't have ordinary lives. They had to love a different way. Heck, they even had to eat a different way.

Simon knelt and carefully opened the flat carton.

"Never in a million years would anyone else have believed that Grandfather would keep these. But I know that's how intense he is about documentation, even if it's not to his obvious benefit. He taught me that there's always the possibility your lawyer could find something helpful later. Never throw away a receipt or a note. He's so strong and confident to keep this. It's the warrior ethic. Grandfather always says life is a war with yourself as well as others. He claims he was born with his hands fisted. Maybe I was, too."

"Hands fisted? I don't understand. What war? What is this? Why are you speaking so nastily when you refer to Grandfather? You used to chastise me for saying critical things about him. You just went to lunch because he was going."

He acted as if he couldn't hear me. For a moment, I wondered if I had even spoken. Maybe it had been only thoughts I hadn't voiced.

He held up a packet of envelopes bound with a piece of leather string and smiled as if my merely seeing it was the answer.

"What is that?"

"Letters from a Miss Lorna Stanford."

"Who's that? Letters to who?"

"To whom," he said loudly. It was as if something took over him to be correct and be perfect grammatically and factually. He took a deep breath like someone about to go underwater.

There was a trembling in his lips that sent a nervous sting to my heart. He looked like he could cry or scream. For a moment, I thought he was going to put the packet back into the carton. Despite my curiosity, I wished he would and we would go back upstairs.

"All right. To whom? What is this, Simon? Why do we care about someone named Lorna Stanford? To whom did she write those letters?"

"Letters to Grandfather at the time of her engagement to be married."

"Engagement to Grandfather?"

"No. Grandfather was married, and not for long, either. Some might even say he was still in his honeymoon days."

I shook my head. He still had the trembling in his lips and was stumbling on words, like saying "ether" instead of "either." I felt myself growing paralyzed with fear. This was not Simon.

"What does that mean, Simon? Please, I want to go back to my room."

The basement grew darker, danker, closing in on us as if every old thing, every carton, even Prissy's spirit, wanted to hear this conversation.

"Why are those letters so important? What are they about? What do you want to tell me?"

"First they start rather desperate and then they become more demanding."

"Of who—whom?"

"Grandfather."

"But you just said Grandfather was already married."

"Grandfather *was* already married; Grandfather was already married," he repeated in a calmer tone, and he slapped the packet of letters so hard on the carton that I winced and even stepped back. He pressed the packet to his forehead and just stood there staring through me.

"Simon? Please explain. I'm getting cold. I'm still tired and . . ."

"It's Grandfather's fault, not mine!" he burst out, wide-eyed.

I just stared, waiting for more explanation, afraid to move a muscle or utter a sound. He looked like every other moment he had to remind himself I was there. His eyes would grow distant and then focus sharply on me.

Finally, he pulled a letter out of the packet. "She claimed Grandfather took advantage of her. She doesn't use the word 'rape,' but she might just as well have used it. She goes into amazing detail for someone who was too drunk to protect herself. How could she remember, huh? Any one of Grandfather's attorneys could have cut her to pieces in a courtroom."

He held the letter out. "This is quite racy. You know what that means? It's almost pornographic, and that—"

"I know what that means, Simon. I don't need to read it. I believe you. Dr. Kirkwell showed me a lot of racy things, some making me sick to my stomach."

He nodded and dropped the letter into the open carton. Then he held the remaining letters like a hand in a card game. I was thinking he would say, "Pick one."

"Grandfather paid for the cover-up. He wasn't going to let this go public, but I doubt her future husband believed the story. She supposedly went traveling with a friend, something of a last fling as a single woman, and got sick overseas so she could stay away for months. From what I'm reading between the lines, her future husband just went along with it.

"In this letter," he said, holding another one up, "she basically demands that Grandfather hire her husband to be a high-paying executive in one of the Sutherland companies."

He laughed gleefully.

"He bought him off. You know Grandfather. He says nothing is right or wrong. It's just a matter of price when it comes to being right. He said that at dinner more than once. You were there."

"I don't remember the things he said and says as well as you do, Simon. You've been with him longer than me."

"It doesn't matter. Her husband got sick a few years later and died of colon cancer."

He laughed again.

"Sutherland luck, huh? No one to worry about. And no child to worry about."

"No child? What are you saying, Simon? This Lorna got an abortion or gave the baby up for adoption?"

"No."

"No?"

He wasn't looking at me. He was looking past me to my right. A chill went through me. He was gazing so hard that I turned to look. Had Mrs. Fisher snuck down here to watch us? There was no one there, unless his mental turmoil permitted him to see spirits. It sent a cold chill through my shoulders and up the back of my neck. I had to get out of here.

"Simon?"

"She wouldn't get an abortion. She wanted the baby. Makes sense, makes sense?"

"What makes sense?"

He was still looking past me. Again, I glanced to my right. It was as if he was talking to someone else now.

He laughed again; he laughed so hard that his eyes teared. He scrubbed at them and then tilted his head when he looked at me this time. "Don't you see? There would be no Simon," he said. "Where would Simon be?"

"What?"

I glanced at the stairway. Surely, he was on the verge of another serious breakdown. Maybe it was seconds away. I should just run and get help, I thought. Wasn't this what Grandfather really wanted when he said I would be a portal, someone to watch for Simon having another nearly suicidal episode? He looked at the stairway, too, and then at me. I was sure he could read my thoughts. He took a step to the right, as if he wanted to prevent my fleeing.

"You don't understand yet. You'll see. It's not my fault; it's Grandfather's fault. Read."

He shoved the letters at me. Too frightened to do otherwise, I took them, but I didn't open any.

"I don't want to read them. I want to go upstairs, Simon."

"She was here; she gave birth here," he said. "That was the deal."

"Here? The basement?"

Maybe that made sense. This was the Cemetery of Memories.

"No, upstairs. In Sutherland. I know the room, too. I'll show it to you, one of the guest ones never used since. I'm probably the only one who notices those things. Something always told me there was a reason it was kept so special."

He paused, smiling as if that was a great accomplishment.

"I'm getting so confused, Simon."

"No confusion. Grandfather lost that negotiation. The great Sutherland negotiator lost." He started to laugh but stopped and looked angry again. "Grandfather lost. Don't you understand what that meant? Grandmother Judith lost, too."

"Grandmother Judith? How did she lose?"

"She had to give birth to the baby who wasn't hers."

It was so illogical. That actually made me feel better. He was hallucinating. Surely.

"How can you give birth to a baby that's not yours, Simon?"

"You're so innocent that you can't imagine sexual deception."

"Don't tell me that, Simon. I've heard it enough. Just explain what you're saying."

"I'll spell it out for you. You isolate yourself when you would show, and everyone is told you're pregnant. Then, when the baby is born, you pretend you gave birth. Grandmother Judith had to do it; it was the only way she could have any self-respect. How do you marry someone and accept that some other woman had his baby, made a baby with him during your honeymoon?"

His clear logic was like a bee sting. I held my breath and shook my head. What baby? Whom did he mean?

"That wasn't in her diary," I said. "You're making things up. You found her diary. You let me read it. You read it."

His smile widened. It was more of a Simon smile. It actually made me feel less anxious.

"We were both fooled there, Caroline, sweet Caroline. Grandmother Judith didn't write that diary. I didn't see it at first. She had such good penmanship, but something about the way the *t*'s were crossed and the *s*'s. Check the handwriting in the diary yourself against these letters. You don't have to be expert at it. She took over her life, you see. She always wanted to be Grandfather's wife. This was a way for her to be it. She made him say 'I do,' and then she was Mrs. Sutherland for all practical purposes. She went to sleep believing it. Maybe even Grandfather believed it."

I looked at the letters.

"Notice the envelopes," he said.

"What about them?"

"There are no stamps. They were hand-delivered, like a summons. You know what a summons is." He laughed. "Grandfather knows. He's sued many people, and many have sued him."

He was right; there were no stamps, but there was no name, no address, either.

"I still don't understand. This Lorna took over Grandmother Judith's life? She even wrote her diary?"

"That's what I'm trying to explain. Gradually, in more and more ways, she slipped under his bedsheets. She crawled into Grandmother Judith. You'll see. It was Grandfather's fault. They can't blame me."

"Why do you keep saying that? Blame you for what? A baby?"

He looked like he had frozen, and then his lips trembled again. My mind began to spin with answers. I glanced at the letters in my hand and then at him.

"Who was Lorna Stanford? Simon? Who was she? Did my mother know her?"

"Oh, yes, but she didn't know the truth. But I know it, and now you know it."

"My mother knew her?"

"Of course. It's why she had so much power over everyone here. Don't you see?"

I started to cry. "I don't, Simon. I'm so scared that I can hardly breathe."

"Are you?"

I nodded.

"Of me?"

"Yes," I said.

"You should be. I wouldn't hurt you, but you should be."

"Why?"

"Lorna Stanford was Mrs. Lawson, and her son . . ." He brought his right hand to his throat as though the next words were choking him. "Her son is my father."

Did my heart stop and start?

"I killed my own grandmother, and it wasn't an accident. I deliberately pushed her," he said, and laughed. His laugh just stopped, but he held his mouth open as if he was screaming.

I dropped the letters, turned, and ran toward the stairway.

CHAPTER SEVEN

Mrs. Fisher saw me come out of the basement and hurry to the stairway. She stood near the entryway and watched me with her hands clasped on her stomach. I hurried up the stairs faster without looking back. My whole body was still shaking. Trembles came in ripples from my legs up, so as soon as I was in my bedroom, I lay down and stared up at the ceiling.

My mind was flooding with questions. *What do I do? How do I tell Grandfather what Simon discovered and what it has done to him?* Every time Grandfather looked at me, would he see the face of someone who knew a terrible thing about him, about this whole family? Would he want to get rid of me, simply get me out of his sight? He could do anything. He could ship me off to a foster home anywhere, even in another country, to be sure I wouldn't tell anyone or that whomever I told wouldn't care.

What about Uncle Martin? Could it be possible that he never knew the truth about himself? During the time I was out of what had been Prissy's bedroom before I went to Hawaii, I never noticed Uncle Martin treating or looking at Mrs. Lawson as anyone other than the head housekeeper. I saw no affection between them. Did she tell him he was her son? Would Grandfather have forbidden that?

Maybe Grandfather wasn't out-negotiated. He wanted everything to be as it was. Mrs. Lawson didn't have to threaten him to become his shadow wife. It was difficult to believe that anyone could force Grandfather Sutherland to do anything, but if it was his own fault, he might not have had much choice.

All these questions wanted to lounge around in my head and punish me for tinkering with the Sutherland past. I never understood what my father meant when he told my mother, "You don't disturb the dead. It's an unfair one-way conversation." She had complained about her ancestors, accusing them of terrible things. I understood now, but could I take my father's advice and ignore what had just happened?

And what if I didn't get up right now and go down to tell Grandfather any of this? Would my silence matter?

You're not good at hiding your thoughts, Caroline, I told myself, especially from a man as clever and insightful as my grandfather, who made his fortune outwitting competitors. Daddy once told Mommy, "You can criticize your father if you want, but don't get into a poker game with him."

I wondered if I could confide in Aunt Holly and leave it up to her to decide what to do. She was really trying to be a mother to me now. On the other hand, would my revelations shock her to the point where she didn't want to have anything to do with the Sutherlands? She seemed always on the verge of leaving.

What real hope did I have that things would change between my grandfather and me? It was very difficult to like someone who knew a terrible secret about you, about your life. Dina had taught me that in Hawaii. All my choices, comments, and even my thoughts were so much more important now. I had needed my mother so much for her advice these past months, but never as much as I did at this moment.

As I looked around this bedroom, I felt even lonelier and more lost. There wasn't anything to cling to, anything to bring to my cheek and feel warmth and comfort, nothing to trigger a warm memory of my mother or the sound of her voice. Grandfather had made sure that anything of my mother's was removed. There wasn't a stitch of her clothing, not a handkerchief, nothing from her school life, not even an old hairbrush that would have some strands of her hair in it. It was as if Grandfather had created a special vacuum cleaner to suck up anything even vaguely reminiscent of her, and yet . . . he kept her ashes in his secret closet.

I wondered why even more. Did he really think that gave him satisfaction, revenge? Did he go into that closet to gloat? As bizarre as it sounded, did he want to control everyone, even after they had died?

Secrets in the basement, secrets in my grandfather's office . . . the madness of Sutherland pounded in my head like slow but heavy drumbeats in a funeral march. What was more, I thought, if there was insanity in the Sutherlands' blood, it was possibly in mine.

When I was younger, I thought it would be something great to be like my grandfather, but now I feared that all my relationships, a marriage, even how I treated my own children, would be as flawed and unsuccessful. You could move a thousand miles away, meeting totally different people, even change your name, but you couldn't escape your family secrets.

Should I be afraid of becoming an adult?

I always thought happiness would come in waves when I was an adult, that I would be able to make my own decisions and be my own person. Children could be happy, for sure, but their happiness was fragile, dependent on the adults in their lives and how happy they were. How could that truth be taught to me any more clearly than it was now?

I pressed my knees to my chest and embraced myself, folding over so tightly that no one could ever get me loose enough to stand, much less live here. I made it hard to breathe. Maybe I could crush myself to death and be with Mommy.

I didn't want to envision Simon frozen in a scream below, but that image kept flashing before me. Desperately, I pushed my thoughts back and back, searching for something happy, something that would warm my heart and make the world colorful and welcoming again.

But the darkness was too strong. All the shadows in Sutherland had banded together and were right outside my door. They blocked even a twinkle of hope.

It might have been five minutes before I sensed the hand on my shoulder squeezing tenderly.

"You poor child," I heard her say. It was as if the sound of her voice came through a long, dark tunnel of tin, more like an echo.

I felt my body soften, my legs relax.

"You don't have to tell me anything. I can see from the way you are that the experience was devastating to you. All I can tell you is, in time it won't be. Nothing kills sadness faster than burying it in new minutes, new hours and days."

Slowly, as if I was just learning how to do it the way a baby might, I turned and fluttered my eyes open to look at Mrs. Fisher. I wondered just how long she had been there. Had she heard me say something to myself, heard my calls for Mommy? Was that why she had said "the experience was devastating"?

Maybe she had gone first to Grandfather to report that she had seen me flying up out of the basement, and he had told her to go up to my room and be that third eye. Had he sent someone to the basement to fetch Simon? What had they done to him? Would he think I had sent them?

"Have you seen Simon? Where is he?" I asked.

"I'm more concerned about you," she said, stroking my hair and smiling. "My darling little girl."

My darling little girl? I stared at her; she was looking at me so strangely.

"We need to worry about Simon," I said, and sat up sharply.

She kept her smile, a smile wrapped in a memory so thick that she couldn't hear me. It frightened me, overcoming my spark of courage, so I sat back so she couldn't stroke my hair. She took a deep breath and straightened her back into an ironing board. Before she spoke, she pressed her lips together so hard they turned pale.

"Ever since I began working here," she said in a more familiar tone of voice, her English correct voice, "I have noted that he's been going down to the basement. I told his psychiatrist. I wanted to change the lock on the door, but he claimed that would be too harmful at the moment. He said we shouldn't restrict him from any part of the mansion or grounds. Imagine that. People with special knowledge can be quite arrogant at times.

"Admittedly, I know about this much about psychiatric care," she said, holding up her right thumb close to her right forefinger. "But you don't have to have a doctorate to know that you, Caroline, need tender loving care. I'm not going to let you go running off to India."

"What? Why would I do that?"

Although I had no tears, I scrubbed my eyes. Maybe I wanted to be sure I was seeing her and not imagining all this. She was speaking like someone in a dream. My surprise woke her out of it.

"Oh, that's just an expression I use these days. If I could have stopped her . . ."

Tears formed in her eyes instead of mine. Could I be more

confused about how I should react to all this? I was supposed to feel sorry for her? Was that what she wanted? How selfish. I thought she was supposed to look out for everyone.

"Simon is more disturbed than he ever was," I said, pronouncing each word with a deliberate crispness. "He is so disturbed that I got terrified and ran away from him. He has to be helped right now."

She took a deep breath, looking firmer. "He has a session with his psychiatrist tomorrow afternoon. I'm sure it will be fine. While you were away, he had frequent outbursts."

"No, you don't understand. He might still be down there right now and—"

"No. He's in his room. He went there shortly after you went up the stairs."

"Then you saw how he was?"

She shrugged. "As I said, he's been like that since I arrived. I don't think this psychiatrist has made an iota of progress with him. Maintaining the status quo. That's what I call it. If his parents asked my opinion, I'd tell them."

"You saw him at lunch. Do you think he looked the same just now as he did then?" I asked in a louder voice.

"No, but he goes in and out of his moods. I was told to expect it because that's a symptom of his illness. Besides, dear, you shouldn't worry yourself about it. You can't take on everyone else's problems when you have enough of your own. Your heart is too big for your hands."

"What?"

"If anyone should know, I should. My daughter was like you, only worse sometimes." She leaned forward to whisper, even though we were alone in my room with the door closed. She even glanced at it, which made it seem even weirder.

"I think she married that man just out of spite. Goodness knows she was stubborn and spoiled. I spoiled her, but that was my husband's fault, you see. He was so mean to her sometimes. I had to compensate, try to make her happy. I'm sure you understand. Your mother probably did the same thing when you think clearly about it. Right?"

I didn't answer. This was not a good time to bring back those memories. And how would she know any of that anyway? She was the last person I'd confide in. Her sincerity was an eggshell with nothing in it. I wanted to tell her that I didn't have to have a doctorate to know.

She went on as if I was fascinated with every word she said. I had the feeling I didn't really have to be here. She'd sit on my bed and recite it all anyway.

"And then that would lead my husband to become angrier, just as I'm sure it made your father. It was what your grandfather calls a no-win situation, a double bind. We must avoid that, mustn't we? That's what we would be in if we went and told your grandfather about all this right now. His patience is being tried as it is. No, the thing to do is put this in a closet for the time being. It's just another episode."

She held her smile and stood with a look of contentment on her face. She was probably about to say, "End of story."

"No, it's not just another episode," I said. "And I can't just forget about how he just was and put it in a closet. There's no closet big enough. Simon's very disturbed about Grandfather and . . ."

"Oh, in his state, everything is disturbing in one way or another." She waved it off casually, as casually as she would an annoying fly.

"This is more," I practically screamed.

"Oh, dear, dear. This is why you should spend less time with him. Besides, what are you going to do, run to your grandfather for every little thing Simon says he's discovered about him? You'd wear a path into the floor. Your grandfather is a rich and powerful man. All powerful men have things in the past they'd rather not be discussed. Just forget whatever Simon is telling you now."

"I told you. I can't do that."

"You have to. It's better for Simon if you do, and probably better for yourself. Don't you know the expression 'Don't kill the messenger'? It means blaming the person who brings bad news about you or your loved ones even though it's not his or her fault. You don't want to go to your grandfather with something Simon told you today. He'll tell you more tomorrow."

A new thought bloomed. "How do you know what I've learned is bad news for my grandfather, news that would make him angry to learn I knew?" I asked suspiciously.

She held her wooden smile and didn't reply. She was more difficult to read than my father. His focused eyes could turn to glass, and all you could see was your own reflection. My mind raced with the possibilities behind Mrs. Fisher's words and stone-cold smile. How much did she really know?

"Trust me, I know enough to decide these things. My daughter discovered things about my husband that enraged him when she threw them in his face."

"I don't think any of that was like this," I said. I was tired of her comparing her life with mine.

"Oh, you'd be surprised. As surprised as I was. I resented her myself for digging those things up. People bury the darkness in their past. They pretend none of it happened or refuse to believe their own eyes. People lie to themselves to survive themselves. We've all hurt someone, deliberately or not. Guilt preys upon us like termites, eating us until we are afraid to be alone with our own thoughts."

She laughed, almost a witch's cackle.

"Imagine the granddaughter of Cain. Why would she want to hear about what he had done to Abel?"

It came, sizzling through me like a flash of lightning. She knew about Mrs. Lawson's letters. She had read them, and she had put them back. She knew Simon would bring me down to them. She wanted all this to happen. She could have stopped it simply by appearing in the basement before Simon opened the box.

But she didn't. Why didn't she?

She wasn't just trying hard to get us all to like her.

She wanted us to need her.

Maybe that was all her daughter wanted, to be needed. If anyone was lying to herself, it was she. Maybe none of it was her husband's fault; maybe she drove her daughter to run off.

And Grandfather trusted her so much, trusted her with Simon's and my life.

What did she really want?

CHAPTER EIGHT

The look on her face told me she saw me realizing all of it. It brought a different smile to her face. She wasn't angry or afraid. It was crazier. It was as if she was proud of me for figuring her out.

"You've followed him to the basement, haven't you?" I asked. "You didn't simply report it to his doctor. You did more. You watched him going through everything. You spied on him."

"Well, not all the time, obviously. I had more important things to do, but I wouldn't call it spying. As I have said, I was brought here to do more than simply supervise servants."

"And when he left the basement, did you look at what he had looked at?" I demanded.

Her eyes widened. "You are a bright little girl. I thought so when I first laid eyes on you."

"Then . . . you knew it all before I did. And you wanted me to know, too."

"Wanted you to know what?" She shrugged. "I have no idea what you're talking about. Would anyone doubt me, even your grandfather? Why would I lie?"

She looked at herself in the mirror.

"There's no deception in my face. See? You can make it all disappear. You're in control of your own thoughts. Take charge of yourself. There is nothing to know. Don't look at the world through Simon's eyes. Those eyes are distorted right now. That should be your attitude, and mine.

"Again, Simon's behavior just now is not different from any behavior I've seen since I've been here and especially since you've been away. He'd scream at something he thought he had found and go running up to his room. All I did was make sure he didn't harm himself. I reported everything to his 'brilliant' doctor. It's his problem, not ours. He's the one making the big money on it."

"But that's not true. Simon is worse than he was before I left. Who knows what he might do to himself because of what he found?" I said.

"Only if you tell. He'll feel betrayed. He'll get over it. I'm sure, in his mind, it's no different from whatever else he found. All that about Prissy. There are terrible things buried down there. Just tuck this particular experience away. Keep it our secret until it fades like so many other things he's discovered and reburied."

"I don't believe that. Anyway, why is it our secret?"

"What I told you was true: you and I share the loss of someone so dear. We understand each other, the loneliness and fear we can endure. Secrets about our families and our futures are born of all that. I want you to know that I'm here for you. And in a deep way, I'm here for Simon as well."

"No. You're here for my grandfather, not me or Simon. You just said it a moment ago. He brought you here to do more than supervise servants or run Sutherland."

"That's the same thing in the end: protecting your grandfather and you and, yes, poor Simon. Don't worry. In time, you will understand. You will love yourself and your grandfather more," she said. "You and I have so much reason to care for each other. What ties two people closer than important family secrets? We'll protect each other, you and I, and of course, Sutherland. Surely, you want that, even more than ever now. Just do what I say.

"Otherwise, I might tell your grandfather that it was you who found the letters, and you showed them to Simon and told him those things, which has only made him worse."

"I would never have done that."

She shrugged. "Who knows for sure what you'll do and not do? You're trying to get your grandfather to like you, aren't you? Imagine what he'd think of you if he found out you made up things and told them to Simon, which only made him worse than he was. And then you went and told them to your grandfather as if Simon had told them first to you."

"Why would you do that, tell my grandfather such a lie about me?"

She shrugged as if the answer was obvious. "When a daughter or a granddaughter disobeys, you have to be stern."

"But I'm not your daughter or your granddaughter."

My head was spinning. I was being locked up again.

"That doesn't make sense," I said.

"It will," she insisted, in a sterner tone of confidence and with impatience in her voice. "I'm not going to waste any more time arguing with you about it. Now, take a shower and get yourself ready for dinner. I'll come back up here if you're not downstairs in twenty minutes," she threatened. "You have to listen to what I say if you really want to protect Simon and yourself."

She smiled coolly.

"You will learn it's best to trust me."

"You can't force someone to trust you," I said.

She laughed. "In the end, you will force yourself. We all do. Now, we're going to have a family dinner and please your grandfather," she insisted, pounding out each word like nails into a board. "Don't just change your clothes; change your face. Blank pages. They're safer. Empty your eyes when you get ready."

"I can't do that."

She gave me a smile so cold this time that it sent a chill up my spine. "Of course you can," she said in a sweetened tone. "Your grandfather is looking forward to having a nice dinner with his family. Simon, at lunch, pleased him. Finally, there's a little relief in this house. Don't go spoiling it."

"Simon won't go to dinner now. He may never go to a family dinner again. Grandfather will be even more angry."

She sighed deeply. "You don't know your grandfather as well as I do. He won't be surprised if Simon doesn't appear tonight. Or he'll seem disappointed, but the man pretends to be disappointed. He's what my husband used to call unflappable. He's prepared for everything."

Why was she so confident? My heart pounded with the possibilities.

"Does my grandfather already know? Did you already tell him what Simon discovered in that box and then told me?"

"And spill more of that vomit into the halls of Sutherland?" she asked with an ugly, twisted grimace. "No, no. Didn't you just hear what I said about the messenger? It would apply to me as well as to you, silly girl. Once you make an accusation, you're forever tied to it, true or not. Just do as I say, and all will be well."

"But . . . when he looks at me at dinner wondering why Simon isn't there this time, especially after thinking I was making progress with him . . ."

"Don't worry. I'll be there to protect you."

"Protect me from Grandfather? How are you going to do that? Stand between us?"

"Why, no, darling, sweet girl. I mean, protect you from yourself, of course. I didn't succeed at that when it came to my own daughter, but I know how to correct it. I won't let you down."

She opened the door and then turned to me.

"If you don't listen to me, you'll be out there in this big Sutherland home all alone."

"My aunt Holly—"

"Will be devastated if you tell her what Simon brought you down in the basement to learn. That family, your uncle and aunt's, is held together by weak glue as it is. What would you accomplish? You'll just be the hated messenger again. Tell her what Simon revealed to you today, and she won't take you to see that school tomorrow. She will hate to be a part of any of this. She seems strong, but she lost a child. Who did she have to cling to here, especially after your mother became persona non grata? Her mother-in-law? We know what a limp plant she was.

"And now you want to tell your aunt that Simon believes he didn't have her as a grandmother? She wasn't her mother-in-law? I don't have to tell you how she feels about her husband. There isn't a servant here who doesn't talk about it. All you will do is cause her to feel lonelier and more lost, especially if she becomes suspicious of you.

"No, Caroline. I'm the only one giving you good advice right now. You'll see. You'll be thanking me."

"But . . ."

"So many people go in and out of shadows, even in a fully lit room. I understand that, and you are beginning to understand. It's a heavy load for any young girl to carry, but especially you. And although I'm so much older, it is for me, too. Age doesn't make the truth less powerful. If anything, it makes it stronger. I was honest with you, so you know what I'm advising is wise. I have the unfortunate experience of dealing with loss and deception. You can profit from it."

She held that same smile. Yes, it was a smile of self-confidence, a Grandfather Sutherland smile, but I could see how it was frayed at the edges.

"If you made a big mistake with your daughter, why can't you make one with me?" I shot back at her.

She stopped smiling. "That's more reason why we need each other now more than ever. We'll make sure neither of us makes a big mistake. Won't we, darling girl?"

I didn't speak. Her words sounded more like a threat. I just watched her leave and close the door. It brought the same deep chill Mrs. Lawson had brought when she shut the door behind her and left me in Prissy's room that first day, the day of my mother's death.

I'd never really escaped, I thought, even when I had some good days with Daddy and his new family in Hawaii. Doors could be shut in your mind. They could trap your good memories to the point where you had to struggle to rescue them.

What choice did I really have? I could make matters so much worse for Simon, and she was right, I would hurt Aunt Holly. A deep sigh of defeat told me I would do what she had ordered me to do. I would take a shower and dress as nicely as I could for dinner. I would put everything Simon had said in the same darkness where I kept all the Sutherland secrets.

However, Simon wouldn't appear, and then Grandfather would look at me with questions in his eyes, and maybe his look would force me to tell him, despite what Mrs. Fisher had said. Yes, that could happen. She didn't understand what was now between my grandfather and me. She wasn't in the room with me when I first arrived. Surely, she didn't know the assignment he had given me. *She can't help me*, I thought. *She's the one deceiving herself.*

But right now, I had to do what she had asked me to do. I had no doubt that she would return and stay until I did what she wanted. Like someone preparing herself for rejection and abandonment, I rose and decided what I would wear.

Afterward, when I stepped out of my room, I debated going to Simon's. I was afraid of how I would find him and terrified of what he would do when he saw me in my brightest blue dress, my hair brushed. Why, he would wonder, wasn't I as devastated as he was?

Maybe that was good; maybe it was better to bring this all to a climax. Ironically, we'd both escape from Mrs. Fisher. The very roof of Sutherland could come down from the vibrations of all the anger expressed.

Didn't I want that?

I paused at the top of the stairs and looked toward Simon's corridor. Downstairs was a world of lies and make-believe. It was an unreal world. My mother knew that. She had confronted it, and she thought she had won when she married my father and began what she believed was a different life. In the end, her actions didn't lead her to the freedom she dreamed of having. Sutherland had an ally in fate, and not only did she lose her dream as a result, but she lost me and the future she had hoped I'd have. I was sent back here. We both were. Even her ashes were imprisoned.

Go to Simon, I thought, *and bring the house down, defy everyone: Mrs. Fisher, Daddy, and especially Grandfather.* I was about to do it.

"Hey," I heard, and turned to look at the stairway. Simon was standing at the bottom. "I'm hungry," he said, and beckoned. "C'mon."

He was standing right where Mrs. Lawson's body had lain broken and dead. Dressed in another bright shirt, a turquoise blue, he widened his smile. His hair was neatly brushed, and he wore a pair of black pants instead of jeans. He had those tennis shoes on, too. For a moment, I couldn't speak or move. Then I thought, *He's doing this for me so I won't be caught in a crisis.* He had snapped out of his own panic and guilt after Mrs. Fisher had seen him go to his room. He was still smarter than anyone, smarter and more clever.

I started down. The moment I stood before him, I knew that what I hoped wasn't true. The look in his eyes was too bright. He wasn't pretending for my sake. He was really different. This was a lot more frightening than even the basement.

"It's Mrs. Wilson's meat loaf. I can smell it a mile away," he said. "And she always has an apple pie for dessert when she makes meat loaf. I memorized her menus long ago."

He paused as though he was hearing a voice only he could hear. The pause was deep, his eyes foggy.

"Simon?"

"Oh, sorry. Lost track of my thoughts for a moment."

He nodded and smiled.

"You look very nice, Caroline," he said.

"Thank you," I whispered. I was still holding myself as if I anticipated a real electric shock.

"So, I was thinking about tomorrow," he said, turning and then reaching back for my hand. "The Oaks has only two hundred students, grades seven to twelve. Your current class has twenty students in it. You'll almost get the same one-on-one instruction I've had. That's good and bad."

"How's it bad?"

"You can't claim the cat peed on your homework," he said, and laughed.

Ordinarily, hearing him laugh would have made me feel good, but right now, it sent what felt like drops of an icicle streaking down my spine. Everything about these moments didn't feel real. There was a happy bounce in his walk, and he wore a smile that looked frozen around his lips.

This can't last, I thought. I held my breath the entire way.

When we entered the dining room, I was surprised to see Grandfather already seated at the table.

Mrs. Fisher was standing just behind him, her gray eyes more like flint stones flickering. She didn't take them off me, intimidating. Grandfather was turned to his left and reading some papers, something that had always annoyed Grandmother Judith. Mommy would say something like, "Why don't you bring your guns, too?"

He'd snap the papers or just hand them to Franklin, who would then quickly put them into a briefcase. Often, he would ignore her and, after everyone was seated, sign something before handing it to Franklin.

Now he folded his papers and looked at us.

"Here we are," Simon announced. "The future of Sutherland."

Grandfather didn't smile. His eyes flitted to mine, but I swallowed my thoughts, terrified that I could unleash the Simon who had been in the basement a short time ago.

Uncle Martin and Aunt Holly came rushing in and broke the heavy moment. Something had delayed them. Grandfather gave Uncle Martin a look of reprimand as they sat.

Simon pulled out a chair for me, and then, after I sat, Grandfather said, "It's good to know there is a future."

Simon laughed, and Grandfather turned to me with warm approval. I felt like a liar, the liar Mrs. Fisher had predicted I might become.

But I didn't look away.

And just like that, the things Simon had told me and Mrs. Fisher's threats fell back into my darkest thoughts like some smothered nightmare.

But I was certain.

It was all waiting for a better opportunity to come roaring back.

And I didn't see how I could survive at Sutherland when it did.

CHAPTER NINE

Grandfather began our dinner by making some announcements about successes in various Sutherland enterprises. His boasting wasn't a surprise. He had made these sorts of proud revelations almost every time Daddy, Mommy, and I had dinner at Sutherland. One time, when he went on and on about it, I remembered Mommy getting him very angry by asking, "Is this a family dinner or a business meeting?"

"I'd think you'd be happy to share in Sutherland success," Grandfather had snapped back. "Anyone would think so, but why am I not surprised you aren't?"

That started another family argument, until Daddy seized Mommy's arm. She looked at him and stopped talking. Her arm was red where he had seized it. I could see the imprint of his fingertips. As usual, Grandfather glared at Uncle Martin, defying him to offer any opinion or even try to say something that would calm everyone down. He would never dare agree with my mother against my grandfather. Even if he merely looked like he did, Grandfather would scowl so hard at him that he practically shrank in his chair.

However, this time, Grandfather was kinder to Uncle Martin than I had seen him be at most dinners, complimenting him on one of the company's achievements he had announced. Simon kept saying, "Great, Dad, great," whenever Grandfather paused in his description of Uncle Martin's success. Finally, Grandfather stopped talking altogether and looked at Simon with annoyance rimming his eyes.

Ordinarily, Simon would blanch, sit up straight, and look as apologetic as he could. This time, Simon giggled and muttered, "Great, Dad," one more time, almost defiantly. No one uttered another sound in the smoke of Grandfather's anger. We began eating, not like hungry people as much as like people seeking a way to escape the possibility of the next words uttered setting off a bomb.

Throughout, I tried to keep my eyes focused on the dinner and ate slowly, occasionally looking at Aunt Holly, who seemed to possess my mother's ability to read silences. I could see the questions in her eyes. She looked from Simon to me, but I didn't move or say a word. She surely wondered why I was avoiding her eyes. My father used to say, "When you look guilty, you probably are, and the good part of you won't let you disguise it." Close to the end of their marriage, he would glare at Mommy when he would say this. Now I believed she looked away or down many times more out of fear for me than for herself. Despite how curt he could be to both of us, I never thought his rage at my mother would be directed at me with the same intensity.

Toward the end of dinner, Grandfather reconfirmed that Aunt Holly was taking me to The Oaks in the morning. He looked from me to Simon, who still wore that plastic smile. Couldn't anyone else see that it was more like a mask?

"Then there'll be three of you for certain?" Grandfather asked, looking at him.

Instead of replying, Simon rose. "Please excuse me," he said. "I have some important things to address since I'm going to lose the morning tomorrow. Good night, Mother, Father, and, of course, Grandfather."

Everyone looked speechless. He was speaking now as if he was addressing total strangers, people he had just met.

"Oh, yes," he said, turning at the doorway. "And sweet Caroline." He hummed the Neil Diamond song as he left.

I turned to Grandfather, who I expected would shout something after him. He often criticized Mommy for naming me after a song instead of an ancestor. But he simply looked at Mrs. Fisher, who nodded slightly and followed Simon out. His eyes shifted quickly to me. The silence at the table was so deep that I thought I heard everyone's heartbeats. I fumbled for thoughts, a way to explain Simon without any real revelations about today in the basement. I knew that Grandfather was expecting something from me, something informative about Simon's behavior. What could be more informative than what had happened in the basement?

How do I begin? My mind fumbled for thoughts as I struggled to compose a less devastating way of saying, "He discovered that his grandmother was not Grandmother Judith, and Simon admitted to deliberately pushing her down the stairs."

"I just realized," Aunt Holly said, "that Simon's doctor is coming in the morning. Those sessions are more important than ever."

She took Grandfather's attention off me.

I breathed out.

"Of course I'm aware of that, Holly." He glanced at me. "Anticipating it, I discussed it with his doctor, and he thought it might be good for Simon to get out and take interest in something other than

Sutherland. He'll see him in the afternoon," Grandfather said, and then he turned to me again. "Unless you have something to add, some reason for him not to go."

Terror jumped into my heart, flooded up into my eyes. Surely he could see. I looked desperately at Aunt Holly. Uncle Martin was staring at me oddly. It was as if he had just woken and realized all that was happening, especially that his son was under psychiatric care. Grandfather surely had never disguised his embarrassment and disappointment over it. I could just imagine how many times he had lectured Uncle Martin about failing as a father. I doubted my uncle would counter with the same accusation, citing Mommy.

Grandfather didn't turn away. How could he want me to speak up, blurt it all? I realized he would not put this pressure on me in front of Aunt Holly and Uncle Martin if he knew the truth, knew what Simon had discovered. As far as I could tell, Mrs. Fisher wasn't lying. She hadn't told him. She really was keeping a secret from Grandfather, a big secret. I wondered now if everything she had told me was the truth and, in a deep sense of the words, we were to look out for each other. On the other hand, Grandfather would be greatly disappointed in me, and he would surely fire her when he discovered it.

"Simon needs his doctor," I said. "More than a trip to see a school he won't be attending."

Grandfather raised his eyebrows. I held my breath. I was bouncing from one conclusion about Mrs. Fisher to the other. Now, from the look on his face, I concluded she had lied. She had told him what Simon had explained to me in the basement hours ago. Grandfather was so arrogant and confident that he would reveal it all in front of Uncle Martin and Aunt Holly and then reveal how I had greatly disappointed him. I braced for it.

And then he smiled. There was no arrogance or anger just below the surface, either. Something amused him. "Everyone is an amateur psychiatrist," he said. "It's why I don't trust the science. Sometimes you can't tell who's gone to college and who hasn't."

He directed the last part at me.

I felt the heat in my face when I blushed. If I had felt any smaller, I would have had to sit on someone's lap to reach the silverware. Contrary to fear and embarrassment, I felt irritation surge into my blood. It had surely brought red roses to the crests of my cheeks, blossoming out of the anger. It was unfair to use a secret between us to mock me. Maybe my wrath would be nourished mostly by Mrs. Fisher's look of satisfaction. Now I felt sorry that I hadn't told Aunt Holly everything when I came out of Grandfather's office.

"You asked me to be a portal, Grandfather." I gave him my best version of Mommy's defiance.

"Portal?" Uncle Martin asked, looking from Aunt Holly to Grandfather.

"What does she mean, Willard?" Aunt Holly asked.

Whenever she was formal and very serious with Grandfather, she called him by his middle name. He signed everything J. Willard Sutherland. When I'd asked Mommy what the J meant, she first said, "Not Jesus." Daddy had snapped at her simply by saying her name: "Linsey!" Mommy had looked at him angrily and then turned to me and said, "Just James. It was too pedestrian."

"What's that?" I'd asked.

"Common," she'd said. "There are too many named James and only one named J. Willard Sutherland."

That answer hadn't made Daddy any happier. He glared at her for a few more seconds, shook his head, and continued to read a booklet from the FAA. Mommy said when he read one of those, the house could burn down around him. I remembered moving so quietly around him, I even held my breath until I got to where I was going.

Now Grandfather looked like he wasn't going to speak to Aunt

Holly. I was shivering inside, imagining what would come next and trying not to look scared. Later, she would surely want to know why I hadn't told her what Grandfather had asked me to do. She'd naturally wonder what else I'd kept from her. And when she ever found out what Simon, I, and Mrs. Fisher now knew and how long I had known it without telling her, everything warm around us would drift off like smoke in a strong breeze.

"Willard, a portal? What does that mean? Why don't Martin and I know about this if it has anything to do with Simon, especially now?"

"That's between Caroline and me," he said firmly. "A grandfather and his granddaughter can have private talks."

He didn't often call me his granddaughter. Aunt Holly obviously liked that, but she looked at Uncle Martin, obviously encouraging him to speak up.

"Well, what do you mean, then, when you say it's more important for Simon to see his doctor than visit The Oaks, Caroline?" Uncle Martin asked softly. I didn't think he ever asked anything as firmly or sharply as Grandfather.

"Doesn't everyone see how different Simon is?" I asked, looking from my grandfather to my uncle and aunt. "I mean . . . in so short a time?"

"Well, we thought that was because you were here and he didn't feel so alone," Uncle Martin offered meekly, making it sound like a feeble excuse. "Right, Holly?"

She looked at him and then turned sharply to me. "Do you want to tell us something else?" Aunt Holly asked, now with a firm demand in her voice. She was upset about my keeping the portal thing secret. Tears burned my eyes. No matter how this ended up, I'd be the one who did the wrong thing. Why was I somehow always blamed for things others did in this house?

All three of them were looking at me expectantly. I felt the same way I had felt in the fifth grade when I was onstage and the moment came for me to read my favorite poem to the audience. Mommy was sitting there with some of the other parents. Daddy was at work. Most of the other students had their fathers there to watch. I remembered thinking how lucky they were.

My throat choked up. I began to speak, deciding I would start with saying that Simon had discovered a big family secret. Maybe Grandfather would stop me then and say something like, "We'll discuss this later." But before I could start, Mrs. Fisher entered.

"He's fine," she said. It truly was as if she had been standing just outside the door, waiting for her chance to save me.

Grandfather held his gaze on me a few moments longer, realized I wasn't going to speak, not now, and then looked up and thanked her.

"We'll talk about all this some other time. Despite a little hiccup here and there, it was an enjoyable dinner," he said, putting his hands flat on the table and pushing himself up. "Martin, before you leave, let's go over a few points in your Ekland proposal. It's overall very good," he added, more for Aunt Holly, I thought, than Uncle Martin.

Uncle Martin looked at Aunt Holly like a child waiting for his mother or father to say it was okay.

"Go on, Martin," she said. "I'll spend some time with Caroline." She turned to me. "We'll go to the grand living room."

That made my heart race. The grand living room, with its large fieldstone fireplace and its thick gray area rug over the slate floor, was used only for very important family discussions. The last time I was there was for a discussion about Grandmother Judith's funeral. Grandfather always sat in his regal chair, looking like he was speaking down to his subjects. Mommy hated that room. She said there was something about it that made everyone in the family more like the servants.

I understood why she said that. There were more portraits of my great-grandfather and his wife, as well as a painting of a castle near

Edinburgh. Supposedly, one portrait featured an ancestor who could have become the king of Scotland. There was a scroll in a glass case with the family history written in an old language, Gaelic. Above it was the family crest, featuring three stars. How could you defy a Sutherland edict or demand in that room? The weight of decades, a century, intimidated you.

Aunt Holly nodded at me and started around the table. I glanced at Mrs. Fisher. I wondered if Aunt Holly somehow already knew the secret, maybe always did. Mrs. Fisher saw the question in my eyes. It wouldn't surprise me if my aunt knew and had never revealed knowing because of how it might hurt Uncle Martin, even more than Simon, perhaps. Sutherland was a garden in which to grow family mysteries and riddles. Mrs. Fisher shook her head. She knew my question. I had spoken with my eyes. But how could she be so sure? She hadn't been here that long. Her confidence in knowing everything she had to about this family was growing annoying.

I rose and followed Aunt Holly like someone carefully walking around a dark pit.

"I know you're constantly worrying about Simon now," Aunt Holly said, her voice still testy. "That's okay, but just know there is just so much you can do, or I can do, for that matter. The events leading up to all this would have shaken the bones of a grown man, and we both realize how seriously Simon takes everything.

"If this has something to do with something he said, don't take the things he says or believes to heart, especially now. I couldn't even begin to tell you some of the odd things he has said to me in just the past week or so about Grandfather, about Grandmother Judith, even about himself."

"Like what?" Could it be something more horrible? Nothing would surprise me, really. Simon had so many thoughts and ideas twisted and curled like snakes in his troubled mind.

"Oh, it wouldn't help to repeat any of it. Later he won't remember what he said," Aunt Holly replied.

Could she ignore what I had recently learned if I told her? Would she simply believe he had made it all up? How would I know unless I told her what he had said and what had happened to him? Again, I thought that once I fully confessed, she would distrust me even more. The messenger was blamed for the message.

Ironically, the only ally I would have in this house would be Mrs. Fisher.

We turned the corner into the hallway leading to the grand living room.

"Oh, your grandfather is so irritating sometimes. I'll have to describe to you one day how your mother and I imitated him. After we had snuck a few glasses of wine."

She laughed.

No, she didn't know the great secret, I concluded. She wouldn't be this casual. She didn't understand how much more serious all this was. *I have to tell her the truth. I have to be the one. I have to do something*, I thought. Who knew what Simon would do to himself tonight? They must realize that they saw a stranger at dinner. Surely, everyone realized how serious it was.

And if he did do something to himself, how could I say I knew such a terrible thing was eating away at him and kept it secret because Mrs. Fisher thought I should? Aunt Holly would rightfully say, "But you hardly knew the woman, and I know you weren't fond of her from the start."

What then? How many members of my family could I disappoint and drive away? Grandfather was probably already angry at me for saying "portal." He might change his mind about everything.

We entered the room. I felt like I was standing on a cliff.

"Simon frightens me because of how different he can be in so short a time," I said. "He's like two Simons now."

"Oh, I know, sweetheart. He's searching for himself. That's what his doctor thinks. We have to be a little more patient."

She sat on the sofa and patted the place beside her.

"No," I said. "There's more. I can't be patient, not now."

Aunt Holly looked at me expectantly. I couldn't keep the tears from glistening in my eyes. Everything would get even worse in a few moments.

"Oh, Caroline, of course. This is just too much to bear after all you have been through. But that's my point. Best to leave it to his doctor and not do anything that would intensify the situation."

"No," I insisted. "I can bear it, but it's too much for Simon to bear."

She nodded. "So your grandfather wanted you to be a portal. Were you supposed to spy on all of us?"

"Oh, no, just help with Simon."

She saw the tears in my eyes and took my hand. "Yes, you probably can, but it was very wrong for your grandfather to put so much responsibility on your shoulders, especially now. Your mother would be even more furious at him."

"But I want to help."

"Of course you do. You're someone with a generous heart, your mother's daughter, thinking more about him than yourself."

That was what Mrs. Fisher was saying.

"But . . ."

"Of course, you're trying to find yourself, too. We understand."

"No." I paused, took a deep breath, and began. "Simon goes down to the basement and looks at old things, family things."

"He is fascinated with his father's family history, has been since he was five. When he found out there were family heirlooms down there, he was eager to go. Of course, when he was much younger, I wouldn't let him go by himself, even though he was very mature for his age."

She leaned forward, smiling.

"I knew that when he asked to stay here from time to time, that was the real reason. He's like a research scientist looking for the cure of some disease. He can be that intense when he sets his mind to something. When he was ten years old, he would rattle off ancestral details like the family historian."

"I've been down there with him more times than you know. I was down there today, and . . ."

Mrs. Fisher came rushing in, her hands held high, shaking her head. She looked as frightened as I felt.

"What is it?" Aunt Holly asked.

"It's Simon. He was screaming in his room and pounding on the wall. I didn't want to just burst in on him and maybe drive him to do more, so . . ."

"Oh, no," Aunt Holly said, then rose and hurried past her.

Mrs. Fisher remained standing there and then turned to look at me, a calmer expression washing over her face and into a satisfied smile. Then her eyes narrowed threateningly.

"You don't know what you're doing," she said. "You'll destroy him and yourself for sure."

"He wasn't screaming just now?"

She shrugged. "Inside, I'm sure he is."

"You were eavesdropping on me and Aunt Holly just like you were eavesdropping on all of us in the dining room."

She shrugged again. "You can thank me later," she said, and walked out.

I waited a few moments, shifting between anger and fear, and then walked out quickly. Just as I reached the stairs, Aunt Holly began descending.

"He's all right," she said. "Sleeping. I don't think we should wake him. Maybe he screamed out in a dream."

She paused a few steps above me.

"What were you about to tell me?"

I glanced to my left. I could see Mrs. Fisher just at the corner. Would she be watching me and listening to me constantly?

Aunt Holly's face was radiant with curiosity. "Caroline? You said you were in the basement with Simon today. And?"

"I saw Prissy's grave," I said. Nattie's advice had returned. *Tell part of the truth rather than lie.*

"Oh. The biggest stain on the Sutherland name. Your uncle Martin is so worried that after your grandfather goes, those who know will broadcast it. The irony is, the more power and prestige you have, the more fears, too. Was Simon telling you how disturbed he was about that? Was that what frightened you about him?"

"No . . . he wasn't upset about it. It was one of the things he wanted me to know about the family. There were other things, and . . ."

She smiled. "I'm sure there were. To him, it's a museum. Concentrate on the future, not the past. We can't do anything about any of that now."

She continued down the stairs to hug me.

"I'm looking forward to tomorrow," she said.

We heard Grandfather's office door close and saw Uncle Martin in the hallway.

"I'll be here right after breakfast tomorrow," Aunt Holly said.

"But Simon . . ."

"I see Mrs. Fisher is standing guard," she said.

I turned to see her approaching us.

"Get a good night's rest, and don't worry about Simon. He'll be fine. Eventually," Aunt Holly added, with a worried little laugh, her eyes looking upward so that it seemed more like a prayer.

Could God hear prayers in Sutherland? My mother told me that Grandfather Sutherland believed religion was an inconvenience. He would say, "Everything has a limited warranty. Why not earth and all its inhabitants?"

I watched her walk away. Mrs. Fisher joined her to talk with her and Uncle Martin. Whatever she said appeared to ease their fears. I wanted to shout out, "Don't listen to her!" But I was afraid of bringing Grandfather into it, and then everything would be told in one horrible session, the terrible history gushed like an opened deadly wound. Uncle Martin and Aunt Holly started out. Mrs. Fisher watched them and then turned to look at me before she headed back to the dining room.

The impact of all that had happened on this day felt like one of those waves in Hawaii, washing over me and pulling me out farther into the sea. All the lights in Sutherland seemed to dim with that feeling. The early-evening summer sun was retreating from the windows and the draperies. To me, it felt like all that was bright and beautiful was withdrawing from Sutherland, petals closing. The birds were settling in the shadows. Even bats were seeking to circle madly at some other place.

When I looked at the stairway, it seemed to have doubled in length and height, this stairway that I feared would forever loom above me no matter where I lived or went. More than other places in Sutherland, it had its own dark identity. The footsteps of all the ancestors never left it. Ghosts descended, turned, and floated back up it. It curled like the half-closed fist and forearm of the mansion, just the way my father would sometimes curl his when he was angry at someone or something. I could never trust those stairs.

What I realized made me afraid was the possibility that Simon would hear the steps creak and come out. The stairs would do that deliberately. He'd be the first Simon, the one who had shadows in his eyes, the one who had confessed to the evil in his heart. The house was so quiet that a footfall on a stiff step would sound like a gunshot.

Maybe I just wanted to postpone the possibility, but I walked down the hallway to the turn that became the corridor leading to the room that had been my prison. As I approached the metal double doors, I remembered they were so thick that I couldn't hear anyone out here in the hallway. How empty the room behind these doors was. There was nothing on the walls when I had first been brought to it. The floor was different from the hallways. It was a cold gray tile with swirls of darker gray.

It wasn't until after I was released that I learned it had been Prissy's room. It made it even darker to know. Aunt Holly was right to think of it as the darkest, deepest family secret at the time. But now, for me, Prissy's accelerated aging disease suddenly seemed more understandable.

In a strange way, Simon and I were having our youth stolen, our childhoods smothered. The room had brought us three together. As ugly as it was in my memory, I couldn't help but visualize it. I truly hated it but couldn't help being drawn back to it like a moth drawn to the fire that would consume it in less than a second.

"Go on," I heard a voice say in a raspy whisper. "Open the doors."

I turned around slowly. Mrs. Fisher was standing only six feet or so behind me. The light behind her cast her face in shadows, but the glow made the illumination shimmer around her neck and shoulders. She looked taller, larger, and seemed like she was floating. For a moment, I wondered, *Is she really here, or is she part of my out-of-control imagination?*

"Go on," she said. "The only way to overcome your fears is to confront them. Be brave. Open the doors."

She took a step forward. I shook my head.

The shadows seemed drawn to her, streaking her face with a bluish-gray tint. Her eyes deepened. It was as if I could peer through them and see deeply into her.

"Open the doors. They aren't locked. You want to. Go on. Do it," she urged.

I looked at the doors and shook my head.

"You have to open the doors. You know you do. You were drawn here. We both know why. Go on."

I shook my head again and stepped back, but she was there, standing like a wall behind me.

"It's there," she whispered. "Just turn the knob and look inside. How many times have you seen it in your dreams, has it been in your thoughts? You can't get rid of it by ignoring it. Open the door."

Her voice undulated and rolled, rippling in my ears. I felt hypnotized.

"Look directly at what you fear. That's what I do. That's what sustained me. It will help you, too. Go on, Caroline. Do as I tell you. Open the door. Don't defy yourself. Turn the knob. Open the door."

My right hand seemed to have a mind of its own. It rose and touched the cold knob.

"Yes," she said. "Yes. What you think is in there might be. You'll want to know. Turn the knob."

As if I could see through the metal, I saw that four-poster king-size bed back against the far wall. The posts were tall, with what looked like a crown on top of each. To the right was that old school desk, Prissy's desk. The electric shock went through me again, Dr. Kirkwell's special treatment. I couldn't breathe. Those pictures of men and women were flashing, a slideshow of horrid memories.

"Go on."

She was even closer now. I could feel her breath on my neck.

"Turn the handle."

I did. The hinges cried, a metallic scream that grew louder with every inch the door opened, until I was looking in. The faded yellow lampshades on the night tables beside the bed were on.

And there, on the bed, as I had seen it in my grandfather's inner office, was the urn that Simon had revealed, the urn that held my mother's ashes.

CHAPTER TEN

Mrs. Fisher stepped in front of me and slammed the door closed.

"Go to bed now," she said. "You did what you had to do. You confronted your fears. Now you need your rest. You've had a very difficult day, and tomorrow you have to visit your new school and look bright and enthusiastic."

"Why is that in there?" I asked. "And why is it on the bed?"

"I wasn't completely sure you would know what it is, but I'm not surprised. Simon told you about it, didn't he?"

"Why is it on that bed?"

"You wouldn't want to see it on the floor. She has to breathe."

"What? How do you mean, she?"

"Why do people keep their loved ones close, even in urns? There is always something of them there. If you noticed, the curtains are open. I made sure of that. There's light every day, and at night, there's moonlight and stars. Better than a closet, don't you think? A closet is just another sort of grave. I didn't have to do all that, by the way. You should be very grateful."

"Did my grandfather tell you to put it there?"

"Yes."

"Why?"

"He was having a hard time concentrating on his work. Spooky," she said with a crooked smile. "Your mother must have been quite a young woman. Some people can't die even if they want to because the memory of them is so strong. Their voices, their expressions, everything about them is so strong. Once someone gets inside you, he or she lives as long as you do. Graveyards are just . . . commas, not periods. That's how it is with my daughter. That's how it is with his."

"I'm sure that's how it will be with you."

"What does that mean? I'll have a daughter who will hate me and die but not go away?"

"My daughter didn't hate me. And yes, you inherit features from your parents; why can't you inherit some of their fate? Anyway, that's what I believe. You can believe what you want."

"I don't believe that."

"Whatever. Time is a big blabbermouth. It will tell."

She sighed.

"Enough chatter. Let's go to sleep," she said, and reached out to embrace me.

I stepped back quickly. "I don't believe you about my mother's urn. I'm going to ask my grandfather about this."

She shook her head and held her smile. "Always threatening to do things that will end up destroying you. You think it would be wise to confront him with his own fears, make him tell you, a man like that?"

I stared, realizing what she was saying. "But he told you his fear, didn't he?"

"We're closer in age, and I'm here to do his bidding. Older people don't like to admit their fears to younger people, especially when they are trying to guide them. A man like your grandfather—and my late husband, for that matter—wants you to think he's perfect.

"The last thing he'd like you to know is that he is afraid of your mother in any way, even after her death. You're smart enough to know that. Your grandfather is probably the strongest of any man I've met, including my husband, but he has serious conflicts of conscience, well hidden but serious. It all seems too complicated for you right now.

"That's what people are, complex. You don't have a grandmother; you don't have a mother. Your father's disowned you again. You're left with an aunt who is afraid of her own son and doesn't respect her husband. Despite her smiles and oozing love talk, she won't be reliable in a pinch.

"A girl your age needs to have confidence in someone older, dependable, and consistent. I am sure your grandfather brought me here more for you than for him. That's why I told you to trust me," she said. "We have to trust each other. Now, go to sleep. Go on." She beckoned, flipping her hand. "Pleasant dreams."

I didn't move. Her words and what I had seen buzzed like bees in my mind.

"Well? Do you want me to make a scene and alert your grandfather? Because I will," she threatened, and lifted her chin as if she was about to shout.

Panic filled me. I turned around and started back to the stairway, walking faster, more like someone fleeing, fleeing from admitting to myself that she was right. I'd have to guard another secret she and I shared. Maybe she was the only ally I had here now. I couldn't confront my grandfather about this. I wasn't sure what Aunt Holly would do. Look at how much I had been keeping from her. Worst of all, Simon would be in even more trouble, and I'd be the cause of an even bigger setback.

The people I wanted to care for me and share happiness and sadness were being kept too far away because of their own issues and problems. I hated to think Mrs. Fisher and I shared anything, but maybe it was true: she was just as alone. Should I depend on her, trust her?

Practically drowning in mixed emotions, I fell asleep embracing myself and pretending my mother was holding me. Maybe she was. As Mrs. Fisher said, she was there, trapped in the urn but still trying hard to watch over me. I believed spirits lived in Sutherland. Why not my mother's? Would I end up as disturbed as Simon?

Simon didn't appear at breakfast. I ate alone, with Mrs. Fisher looking in occasionally with that smug smile on her face. Aunt Holly arrived at nine thirty. I was waiting for her in the entryway. Mrs. Fisher had laid out the dress I should wear and the shoes. I didn't reject them. Truthfully, I was moving in a daze, hoping Simon would appear and hoping he wouldn't, because once Grandfather looked at him in his darker self, he would turn to me for answers, drilling into my soul with questions until he saw that I knew the great Cemetery of Memories secret.

When Aunt Holly saw me, she didn't seem surprised about Simon not appearing. Worse, I thought, she didn't seem disappointed, either. Was Mrs. Fisher right about her, that she ran from conflicts and, when it came right down to it, wouldn't be strong enough to help me?

"Should we see about him?" I asked immediately after she said good morning. "Simon?"

"No. Your grandfather informed us last night that he told the doctor to keep to his appointment this morning."

"But how did he know Simon wouldn't come down? The brighter Simon, I mean."

It was weird talking about two different Simons, but Aunt Holly didn't even wince. He must have been like this the whole time I was in Hawaii. Like most people, she reduced a painful truth to an annoying, short-lived thing. I could almost hear her whispering to herself constantly: "He'll get over it." But even if he did, who would he become? He was always so aloof from her and Uncle Martin. What sort of family could they ever be?

I so wanted to be as carefree and frivolous as any other girl my age. I wanted boyfriends and parties. Truly, deep in my world of fantasies, I wanted to be like Dina and her friends, who kept themselves in their own world of instant pleasure and excitement. They toyed with forbidden things and ignored worrying about climate change or their futures. My father was right about them. For them, caring as they did only about themselves, concern about finding a means of self-sustaining income, health insurance, the welfare of their future children, a life of purpose, was farther away than Pluto.

But I would have liked even one day without a serious thought.

What was the secret to that? Certainly, Mrs. Fisher, Aunt Holly, Uncle Martin, and especially Simon didn't know it. Grandfather practically forbade it, and my father lived as if such a thing never existed. My mother and Nattie had it, and for a short while, I shared it. But fate had swept in with that thundering eraser and turned those moments of my life into a dream.

"I know what I said about his doctor's appointment being more important, but he seemed so excited about going. I expected him to be down here ready to go, didn't you?"

Aunt Holly shook her head. "I don't know, Caroline. Your grandfather might have ordered him not to go with us. We'll have to deal with that later."

"We could go up to him to see."

"It'll only ruin this whole day for you. For now, let's get you enrolled in The Oaks and give you something brighter to look forward to. Think of it as the beginning of your escape from the problems at Sutherland."

"Yes, but I didn't do so well the last time I escaped."

She put her arm around me. "You will this time." She squeezed my shoulder. "Come on."

I paused at the front door to look back. Mrs. Fisher was on the stairway, watching us leave. I thought she was smiling as if she was proud of me. *She, too, thinks she's my grandmother*, I thought. *Maybe in Sutherland, no one is who they're supposed to be.* I hurried out with Aunt Holly.

"Your grandfather insisted Emerson take us," she said as we walked through the atrium. She giggled like a little girl. "Sutherland-style."

Twenty minutes later, when The Oaks came into view, Emerson said, "I remember the first day I brought your uncle out here."

He looked at Aunt Holly through the rearview mirror.

"Wasn't a cloud in the sky, as I recall. You attended for the first time that same day, didn't you, Mrs. Sutherland?"

"I did. I don't know who was shier, Martin or me."

"Oh, young Mr. Sutherland, for sure," Emerson said. "I think a little afraid, too. I remember I was when I was enrolled at St. Stephen's School for Boys. We really couldn't afford it; it was posh, a factory producing little princes. Those clothes never really fit. I used to call my classmates Tweeds."

He laughed. I knew he was trying to lighten it all for me. I couldn't hide my nervousness.

"Your mum brought you, I'd guess," Aunt Holly said. "And kept you prim and proper."

"Aye, that she did. My dad was at work. He had no patience for childish nonsense anyway. He'd be tickin' off the school cost like a meter in a taxicab. He might as well be riding along with us. I felt his eyes, I did. My mum did, too," he added, laughing.

"You brought Martin to The Oaks, and my mother brought me, probably with similar thoughts."

"And here we are, bringing Miss Caroline," he said.

Only Aunt Holly is not my mother, I thought. *And she's not worried about Grandfather's taxicab meter of school costs.*

The Oaks appeared on the right. It seemed to just rise out of the ground, a reddish-brown two-story building with oak trees on the right and left. The grounds looked more like green carpet, with trimmed low shrubs along both sides of the wide driveway that wound around to the front and to the parking lot on the right.

"Healthy-looking creeping junipers," Emerson said when we turned in from the road.

"The plants are afraid to be otherwise," Aunt Holly said.

Emerson laughed.

"How often does my father-in-law inspect it?"

"Oh, every now and then," Emerson said, as if Grandfather's perusal of the property was top secret. He turned a bit to add, "When they least expect it."

"Sounds right," Aunt Holly mumbled bitterly. "He likes to catch people at their worst."

Emerson didn't reply.

It was an odd time for me to think of it, with all I had ahead of me, but it suddenly occurred to me that Aunt Holly really despised my grandfather. It made sense to dislike those you feared. Had I always disliked my father? Was it only fear of him in my heart?

That certainly felt true for Aunt Holly and her relationship to Grandfather. It was surely why she sympathized with my mother so much and why she disapproved of her husband, was even ashamed of him. Simon was born out of all that. It had to have made her furious. She had lost her daughter to a freaky crib death, and she was losing her son because of the darkness of Sutherland and the power of Grandfather. Yet all that was something she had to keep stifled. Fear was stronger.

But what would she do with the secret Mrs. Fisher and I had smothered, I out of trepidation and she out of obedience? Did she have the strength to threaten him, demand something, finally lord it over him, or would she just flee with Simon as Mrs. Fisher implied?

How did I fit in with all this? Could I do what she had suggested and Mrs. Fisher wanted, concentrate only on myself? Find new friends, dive headlong into a normal young life, put on earphones, swim through frivolous texts, and giggle in the halls of Sutherland? I was a near orphan living in the palace of darkness. Could I step into a new life and be more responsible for myself than I'd ever been? Soon I would know.

Because school hadn't officially begun for students, it was very quiet when we pulled up to the entrance, two wide glass doors with THE written on one and OAKS written on the other. As I gazed at the building, I thought it looked cold, more like an office building with the windows framed in some shiny metal.

Emerson opened the limousine door for us, and we stepped out. The sunshine brought a glitter to the marble steps and entry. Everything sparkled, railings, door handles. It was probably the cleanest school in America, I thought, recalling how often a principal and teachers would be after me and my fellow students to pick up after ourselves. "You show respect for your second home," I recalled my principal saying. Was this going to be my second home when I didn't really have a first anymore?

Emerson went forward to open the school door for us.

"I'll be right out here," he said. "Have a good introduction. And remember, first impressions are usually the most truthful. That's what my mum taught me."

"Good advice," Aunt Holly said.

She and I entered. The dark-tiled lobby looked immaculate and new.

"This was upgraded. The wood floor was replaced and the tile extended. Looks like your grandfather gives it his full attention."

I saw the neatly organized plaques on the right and the glass case containing some trophies on the left.

"None of those are for sporting events," Aunt Holly said. "They're for intellectual achievements. When he was in the ninth grade, your uncle Martin won the school a spelling bee championship."

"He did? I never knew."

"Your grandfather didn't make much of it. Martin told me his father said, 'It's what you do with the words, not how you spell them.'"

A boy who was easily my father's height stepped out from the corridor on the right. He appeared so suddenly and quietly it was as if he had emerged from the wall. His neatly cut bronze hair emphasized his startling blue eyes, eyes that looked almost electric. He had my father's perfect posture with a swimmer's full shoulders. He wore dark blue pants, a light blue shirt, and a grayish blue tie.

My eyes went to his shined black shoes. They made me think of Daddy, who took so much time with his. When I looked up again, the boy was smiling as if he had stumbled on old friends. Did he know Aunt Holly? When he glanced at me, his smile warmed. I felt a tingle of excitement, something my stepsister, Dina, would call "ringing her bell." She'd follow that by singing, "Ding dong, resistance is dead." Sometimes she'd look at a boy like this, sixteen or seventeen years old, and say, "I'd kiss him with my dying breath. Why waste it on myself?"

It didn't make sense to me until just this moment.

"Hello, Mrs. Sutherland," he said. "Welcome to The Oaks. I'm Hudson David. As the senior class president for the upcoming school year, I'm assigned to greeting new students and providing whatever information they need on a tour. I'll bring you to Mrs. Rich."

"Thank you. This is my niece, Caroline."

"Hi," he said. "You're starting the eleventh grade?"

"Yes."

"Great." He put his hand to the side of his mouth, pretending he was giving secret information. "I'll fill you in on some of your class-mates, especially the predators."

"The what?"

He laughed and looked quickly at Aunt Holly. "Just kidding," he said quickly. "The boys in her class don't bring their shadows to school."

"Why not?" I asked.

"They're afraid of them." He smiled, but when I didn't, he stopped instantly. "Right this way."

He stepped back.

"Principal's office still last door on the right?" Aunt Holly asked him.

"Yes, ma'am," he said. "I forgot. You attended The Oaks?"

"Before you were born. I haven't been back for some time. I'm sure there are many changes."

Aunt Holly nodded to me, and we walked into the corridor.

"Where'd you go to school before?" Hudson asked me.

"Colonie," I said.

"Oh. Not that far away."

Decades, I thought. Practically the other side of the world.

He leaned toward me to whisper, but loud enough for anyone to hear. "Beat them in chess last year. Not me. Stuart Martin. Resident genius. The only one he can't beat is himself."

He laughed and moved ahead to open the principal's office door. Her secretary, a woman who appeared to be at the end of her fifties, with layered sandy-blond hair, looked up quickly. Her nameplate read MRS. LOUIS. Her smile was quick, almost like a flashing light.

"Good morning, Mrs. Sutherland," she said, rising. "Mrs. Rich is looking forward to seeing you and Caroline." She opened the inner office door and stepped back.

"I'll be waiting right here," Hudson said. He leaned closer to me to whisper, "Eagerly."

I looked back at him as he sat. His eyes were electric again, stirring me in places where I was afraid to touch myself. If he could do this to me with a smile, what could he do with a kiss? I knew there were all sorts of minefields at a new school, but I didn't think of this one.

I was sure I had just stepped on one.

And I hadn't been here more than ten minutes.

Maybe Aunt Holly was right that I would have a more successful escape from Sutherland.

But I hoped the first thing Mrs. Rich saw when I met her wasn't a blushing, romantically excited teenage girl who couldn't be a serious student.

Emerson's advice still lingered: "First impressions are usually the most truthful."

CHAPTER ELEVEN

Aunt Holly and I entered. Mrs. Louis closed the door behind us so quickly that it gave me the feeling we had just fallen into a trap.

It wasn't dark or gloomy, however. In fact, the office had lighter tile and creamy white walls. There was a silvery wall clock on the right and a painting of The Oaks with mountains in the background on the left. The rear wall was spotted with framed certificates of graduation and awards. Mrs. Rich's desk was long, with an oak front and a darker white top. Everything was so perfectly organized on it, it was as if each item had been designed to be a certain number of inches from another. The neatness and precision reminded me of my father's desk. I didn't see any framed family pictures, nothing warm and comfortable. At least he had some of that.

I had glanced at the wall to the right just behind us after Mrs. Louis closed the door. There were at least ten television monitors, each capturing a different place in the building. She could see most anyone doing most anything.

Mrs. Rich looked up, put her pen down, and then sat back. Her gray hair was cut short. Two circular silver earrings dangled from lobes that looked pasted to her head. She wore rose-colored wide-lens glasses and bright red lipstick. She wore no other makeup. Her face was angular, with prominent cheekbones that for a moment looked more like smudges. She was in a black dress speckled with gold dots. The collar was opened about six or so inches from her heavy bosom, revealing a necklace of multicolored stones. A deep wrinkle ran across the bottom of her neck, which was the only area where her skin wasn't smooth.

"Please," she said, turning her long fingers toward the two chairs at the front of the desk. Her fingernails were as red as her lipstick. I recalled the fake ones my mother had used to match her outfits, something Daddy called "almost heathen."

"Thank you," Aunt Holly said. We sat.

Mrs. Rich stared at me a moment and then moved to her left and revealed she was in a wheelchair. I hoped my mouth didn't fall open; it was that much of a surprise. Aunt Holly hadn't even mentioned it, but then again, she attended before Mrs. Rich had been hired.

Mrs. Rich smiled as if she had anticipated my reaction. She looked friendly, almost amused and understanding, but her immediate question changed that atmosphere quickly. In fact, my whole body tightened to the point where I could imagine it cracking and shattering.

"How do you explain your mother to others your age when they ask?"

"She hasn't—" Aunt Holly began, but Mrs. Rich put her hand up.

"It's very important I hear the answers to my questions from your niece directly, so I get to know her. In fact," she said, tilting her head as though a bright thought had just appeared, "you might want to wait in the outer office."

She said it with a smile, but it had the sound of a stern command. Her smile turned into more of a leer when Aunt Holly didn't speak. She was definitely as surprised by Mrs. Rich's bluntness as I was. The silence lingered like a troubling afterthought.

Mrs. Rich grinned again, but if there was any warmth in it, it was well buried.

"I'm not about to gobble her up, and she has to be able to develop her independence." She looked at me. "Most times in life, there will be no one beside you to hold your hand. Self-confidence is probably the most important subject we teach at The Oaks. You'd like to do that, wouldn't you, develop independence, self-confidence?" she asked me.

I glanced at Aunt Holly, who looked frozen for a moment. She then looked more annoyed, nodding as she spoke.

"Did my father-in-law hire you?" she asked Mrs. Rich. "I know there's a formal board of trustees, but . . ."

"Yes, he did. Almost twenty years ago," Mrs. Rich said. Her eyes shifted quickly back to me, as if spending even a nanosecond on Aunt Holly was too much time wasted. "Caroline? Do you want to be more independent, self-assured?" she demanded.

It had the ring of a threat. Say no or be indecisive, and I'd be denied entry to the school, Grandfather Sutherland or not.

"Yes," I said. Considering my family, or what remained of it, why wouldn't I want to be more independent?

Mrs. Rich nodded, looking pleased, and then looked at Aunt Holly, expectant. There was another long, uncomfortable silence.

"Well, maybe I'll look at the school. There have been many changes since I attended," Aunt Holly finally said.

"I'm sure there have. Hopefully all pleasing to you."

Aunt Holly rose. Before she could say anything else, Mrs. Rich said, "I'll see you when we're finished here. You can give me your review of the renovations," she added, sounding like it really mattered to her.

Aunt Holly nodded, smiled encouragement to me, and left.

I wanted to be in charge of myself, but I couldn't help feeling completely unprotected, dangling on a thread, the way I had often felt before my grandfather and often, especially recently, my father.

Mrs. Rich had gray eyes that darkened when she squinted, focusing on me. Her look wasn't really icy or unfriendly, but her eyes were so unmoving they looked like they had just turned to stone. Even Grandfather didn't have a stare like this.

"So, how do you explain your mother to other young people? You were asked about her in Hawaii, I'm sure."

Mrs. Rich was just like someone my father would say went right to the jugular, adding, "Time wasted is never regained."

I sat up straighter. I could feel Daddy whispering behind my ear: "Act like sheep, and they'll act like wolves." If I could do it with Grandfather, I certainly could do it with her.

"I tell the truth," I said, holding my eyes on hers. "She fell in love with her newest and best friend, someone I loved, too. And they were both in a terrible car accident. I miss them both and always will."

Mrs. Rich nodded. I could see she liked my answer and the firmness with which I spoke.

"None of your teachers will ask you that question or refer to your answer. In fact, no one who works for me will get that personal with you. However, there will be some students, classmates, who will want you to be more detailed, both boys and girls. What did you witness? What did they do to show each other affection? That sort of thing, although they won't put it that politely. My advice is to say you don't know any more than what you just stated. If someone berates you, tries to pressure you or make fun of you, you are to come here to tell me.

"You will quickly see that everyone attending The Oaks is afraid that someone else will have reason to come here. This student body knows my door is wide open and my responses quick and conclusive.

This is not a version of democracy as are most public schools. There are rules here, not opinions. It's a major reason people pay so much to have their children attend The Oaks. They are confident of their safety and their education.

"Obviously, the same warning applies to you. Decorum, respect, and humility. Those are the building blocks of a perfect Oaks graduate. I know what you've been exposed to and what you've experienced. None of that makes a difference here. You are starting this school as if it's the first school you have ever attended."

She sat back.

"Think of it as being your first pair of shoes. You don't want to scuff them. You will get your orientation packet. It will contain the rules, the behavioral expectations. Just read it all carefully. We mean every word that's in it.

"Now, then," she said, grasping a pen and sliding a piece of paper in front of her. "Your grandfather thinks you should take Introduction to Business as your elective."

"He does?"

"You live in Sutherland. The foundation is built from P and L statements."

"What?"

She nodded. "He's right. Introduction to Business is your elective. That's Mr. Kaplan. Like most of my staff, he is no-nonsense. The only excuse accepted for not doing your homework is proof you were in the hospital emergency room."

She tipped the pen toward me.

"Please note the dress code in the orientation pamphlet. We don't have uniforms. Our families like fashionable clothes, but that does not mean the latest teen fad. I doubt you'll ever be dressed improperly, but I know most of the tricks. I had a girl change her clothes after she arrived. Before she could change back to go home, she was gone."

She paused and wheeled herself around her desk to get closer to me. She looked like she was a tall woman, with slimmer hips than I had envisioned. Her shoes were black, with thick heels. I glanced to the right and left to see if there were crutches she used. Perhaps in the closet on the left, I thought.

Although, I imagined she envisioned her wheelchair to be more of a throne.

"Now, I know there is an undercurrent of pejorative commentary about me." She paused, folding her hands together. "Do you know what that means?"

"Yes." *Thanks to Simon*, I thought.

"You don't have to come running to me to tell me what this one or that one said about me. How you react is more important. If you laugh, you're trusted to hear more; if you don't, they'll suspect you are one of the Rich-lings."

"What are they?"

"Students who try to win my favor by revealing what others do. The truth is, most suspect each other. They'll try to get you to say negative things about me and the school. That's how they'll test you. How do you think you will react?"

"I won't do that. I know what happens when people spread stories about you. It's happened to me enough times."

She stared so hard at me that I had to hold my breath.

"That's admirable, but the pressure to find friends is very strong on young people," she warned.

I immediately thought she was piping through Grandfather's thoughts. That was why Aunt Holly asked if he had hired her. They were of like mind. I wasn't surprised. Grandfather was comfortable with echoes.

"I don't care if they dislike me. Real friends wouldn't. My cousin Simon once quoted someone when I was unhappy. He said, 'What doesn't destroy you makes you stronger.' Whoever said it was right. I know I'm stronger and I will be more careful about friends."

She actually smiled, impressed. I relaxed a little. And then I realized that I had already referred to Simon at least twice in my thinking. Sadly, I also thought, *He might be getting destroyed, but he is, in his way, making me stronger.*

"Ah, yes, your cousin Simon. Don't be surprised if some of your fellow students talk about him as if he is a ghost at Sutherland. I've had to deal with that rubbish, too," she added sternly. "I'm sure you know enough not to help spread any ridiculous stories about your family."

"Of course," I said. "Why would I want to hurt myself?"

She nodded again, this time with a truly warm smile.

"There is a young man who is an exemplary student and was not unexpectedly elected by his peers to be senior class president."

"My tour guide," I said. "Hudson David."

"Yes. I find him trustworthy, but I never stop questioning my conclusions about anyone. My advice is you do the same. A little cynicism often saves you from a great deal of pain.

"Now, I will share this with you once and never speak of it again. Like your mother, I was in a terrible car accident when I was just a little older than you are. It put me in this wheelchair. It was quite a disadvantage, but your cousin Simon has the right quote.

"I graduated summa cum laude and went on to marry. We couldn't have children, and that was when I decided to work with children and get into school administration. I met my husband in college, and he went on to be a very successful corporate attorney. He's managed many necessary legal matters for your grandfather.

"Good things can come from bad luck, even bad choices sometimes. You have Sutherland as a result, perhaps, and now you have The Oaks. What you make of it is entirely up to you. If I sat here and felt sorry for myself, I'd be withered and worthless.

"That's the extent of my advice. The rest is up to you. Remember the building blocks for an Oaks graduate."

She wheeled herself back behind her desk.

"I don't say good luck. I say, wise decisions. Go on and enjoy your tour."

I rose.

"Oh, and tell your aunt she can give me her opinion of the renovations now. I see she has seen a number of things," she added, nodding at the monitors.

I looked back and saw Aunt Holly walking slowly through the lobby.

Mrs. Rich's lips softened. She had sounded so official and even a little threatening at the end, but I felt good about having everything set down so clearly. So much, especially at Sutherland, was mysterious and contradictory. Maybe I would enjoy going to school here.

And what was more, I wondered if I could actually like Mrs. Rich. Obviously, Grandfather did. Most grandchildren would feel confident liking the people their grandparents did, but I couldn't help it, now and maybe forever—I first felt suspicious. What had she just said? A little cynicism often saved you from a great deal of pain?

Maybe that was the best advice I had been given this year. I closed her office door softly behind me.

Hudson practically leaped to his feet when I stepped out. Mrs. Louis rose to hand me my orientation packet.

"Welcome to The Oaks," she said.

"Thank you," I said.

Hudson looked like he was waiting for me to breathe. Were the remnants of fear still lingering in my eyes? I didn't think so. On the contrary, I thought Mrs. Rich was right: I did feel more independent, more confident.

"What?" I asked.

"You survived."

I glanced at Mrs. Louis, who also seemed to be astonished by my poise. What had they expected Mrs. Rich would do to me, threaten and frighten me until I was shivering?

"Show me the school," I said with my grandfather's commanding voice, and started out.

"Yes, ma'am," I heard.

Aunt Holly was just coming down the hallway.

Before she could ask me if everything was all right, I said, "Mrs. Rich is looking forward to hearing your opinion of the renovations now."

"Is she?" She looked at Hudson, who had stepped up beside me. "Take good care of her."

"Absolutely," he said. "I'd be afraid not to."

She walked into the office, and I followed alongside him as he began to describe The Oaks.

"Here on the right," he began, opening a two-door entrance, "is our auditorium. It holds about seven hundred fifty people and has a state-of-the art sound and lighting system. Community theaters are always trying to get to use it, but Mrs. Rich is very particular about who comes and goes at The Oaks. Only a few charities have been admitted.

"Mr. Stanley does two plays a year, the second usually a musical. He's your English lit teacher. You should try out for the fall production, *Harvey*, about the invisible giant rabbit. Did you ever read it?"

"No."

"I'll get you a copy. I'll be the male lead, Elwood Dowd."

"How do you know that? School hasn't begun."

"Mr. Stanley gave me the play last year. He didn't have to actually say it. A lot of things are said here without words. Anyway, you should try out for Ruth. Rehearsals are after school and often on weekends and finally evenings. I bet you'd do well."

"Why?"

He shrugged. "I can tell. You have the look of someone who could easily step into being someone else."

"Really? So you can do that, then, if you already know you'll be the male lead. How do I know whether you're yourself or someone you're pretending to be now?"

He laughed. "I was right about you."

"What?"

"You're older than you look."

He thought a moment, looked back at the door, and turned back to me. "I have a great idea. I'm having a small pizza party tonight. My parents are going out. I don't have any brothers or sisters to look after and no one older than I am. There's just going to be four of us, me and my three best friends: Mark Cantor, Paula Reid, and Russel Collins. Getting to know them will be a great head start. That way, there'll be four of us looking out for you."

"Looking out for me? You make The Oaks sound dangerous."

He laughed. "There's all kinds of danger. I'd like you to come. I'll give you the play then, too."

"A party? I doubt my grandfather would let me go. For lots of reasons," I added cryptically.

He shrugged as if nothing was so important that it could prevent me from going to a party. "Let's text about it after you go home and ask. Let me see your mobile. I'll set it up so we're connected."

He held out his hand. *It's a waste of time*, I thought. *With my recent history of going to parties, Grandfather is going to be more than just skeptical.* But I handed him my phone.

After he handed it back, he showed me the gym and what would be my classrooms. His voice changed and became so formal. He was like a different person. I noticed how he looked up at corners and saw the cameras.

"Can she hear what we say, too?" I asked when we started back to Mrs. Rich's office.

"There are rumors that some desks are bugged and those bugs are changed continually so no one can spot them."

"Is that true?"

"Maybe. I've never seen one, but with the Rich-lings out there, she wouldn't need to bug anything anyway."

"She mentioned them and told me what they were."

He smiled. "Nothing gets past her."

"Do you know who's a Rich-ling and who isn't?"

"Everyone," he said. "No one."

"I don't understand."

"Keeping us all guessing about each other is what gives Mrs. Rich her power," he said. He didn't say it with resentment or anger. In fact, to me, it was more like he thought she was clever.

Did that mean he was a Rich-ling? Did I have to watch every word I said now?

Maybe Mrs. Fisher was right.

She was the only one I could trust.

Anywhere.

CHAPTER TWELVE

Aunt Holly looked flushed when we returned to Mrs. Rich's office. She practically leaped out of her chair, looking as if she couldn't wait to leave. I saw that her lips were trembling. Her eyes flickered like candles caught in a breeze. Had I survived Mrs. Rich better than she had?

Her thoughts were circling in the sort of turmoil that follows a nasty confrontation. In some ways, I thought, because of her troubled history and unhappiness, Aunt Holly was weaker than I was. Once, when my mother couldn't hide her anger at her father, she told me that young people like me had hopes of gaining mental and emotional muscle, but older people had to contend with who they had become.

"Your choices diminish," she said. "It is as if the life you were living narrows as you age and you are trapped in a tunnel." From what Aunt

Holly had told me about herself and her marriage to Uncle Martin, I thought that was certainly true for her.

Another troubling thought was born in the corner of my mind: somehow, without her feeling even sadder, I had to stop depending on her. As much as I hated to admit it, Mrs. Fisher was most likely right. Aunt Holly wouldn't ever be the one who helped me at Sutherland. She couldn't even help her own son and had long ago given up on her husband. I almost felt sorrier for her than I did for myself.

"Everything all right?" I asked her.

I expected her to tell me in a whisper that she'd had an unpleasant time with Mrs. Rich and she wasn't surprised Grandfather had hired her.

Instead, she said, "We need to return to Sutherland immediately. Thank you for showing the school to my niece," she told Hudson.

"Oh, I'll escort you out."

Aunt Holly took my hand as if I was a little girl. It was embarrassing. She practically tugged me out of the office. Hudson almost had to jog to keep up with us. I glanced at him so he could see my confusion and fear. Somehow, he seemed unfazed. It was as if people rushing from Mrs. Rich's office was something he had often witnessed.

"I thought it might be nice if Caroline could come to my small pizza party tonight and meet some of my friends," he said as we hurried toward the entrance. "Give her a head start getting to know some of the other students. I suggested she go out for the fall theater production. I'll give her a copy of the play, *Harvey*. I'm sure you probably know it, Mrs. Sutherland.

"Maybe you can speak to her grandfather. He knows my parents well. We'll start about six. I'll personally bring her back by nine if he wants."

Aunt Holly didn't respond. I didn't think she had heard a word he said. She was clearly focused on getting us to the limousine. I glanced again at Hudson, who moved quickly ahead of us to open the school doors.

"Thank you," she told him.

Emerson was standing by the rear door. His look frightened me, too. The lines in his face had deepened. When people got upset or angry, I thought, whatever youthful look they had clung to disappeared. I knew my mother had liked him so much, and now I depended on whatever humor and joy he could flash at us. Unlike so many at Sutherland, he was never afraid to be happy. I couldn't recall seeing him depressed, sad, or angry.

But right now, he was all three.

"We had better get to Sutherland quickly. No more sightseeing," Aunt Holly told him.

"I know," he said, and closed the door after we sat, avoiding looking at me.

I glanced back at the entrance. Hudson was staring at us, glaring angrily, I thought. I was sure he was not used to being totally ignored.

"What's wrong?" I asked Aunt Holly as Emerson drove us away from the school. "Why did we practically flee?"

"Simon tried to commit suicide," she said.

My gasp was so deep that I couldn't speak.

She covered her face with her hands. "After all the time at the clinic, the treatments, a personal therapist . . . I just let this go on and on. And your uncle . . ."

"What?"

"Sutherland means more to him than his own son and definitely me."

She turned away so I couldn't see her tears.

"What did Simon do? How is he?"

I didn't think she was going to answer, but she wiped her eyes and turned back.

"He deliberately tumbled down the stairway."

"What . . . Maybe he tripped."

"No. Mrs. Fisher saw him do it. The way she described it, it was practically a dive. I don't know any more than that," she said, and sat back in silence.

I wanted to keep denying it, but in my heart, I knew the reason it could be true. Was this my fault? Should I have told the secret? Grandfather would be very angry. He had trusted me to somehow prevent this sort of thing. He'd want to know why I hadn't gone to him. I shouldn't have listened to Mrs. Fisher. How would I do it now? Everyone was going to hate me.

I looked back toward The Oaks.

It disappeared when we made a turn and, along with it, maybe any hope I had of starting a new life. I sat back, enveloped in my own silence and guilt. How many times had I been rushed away from something horrible or unpleasant? Leaving our home after Daddy had exploded with rage, Mrs. Lawson dragging me out of school to Sutherland, and leaving Hawaii to be sped back to Sutherland . . . all of it merged into one scream echoing inside me.

When we arrived at Sutherland, Aunt Holly opened the door before Emerson could and got out. She glanced back at me as if she had just remembered I was with her and hesitated.

"I've got her," Emerson said, and reached for my hand.

"I'm okay," I said.

If there had ever been a time for me to be in charge of myself, seize that self-assurance Mrs. Rich had predicted I'd gain at The Oaks, it was now; otherwise, how would I help myself, let alone anyone else? I rushed in behind Aunt Holly.

Uncle Martin was standing beside Mrs. Fisher and talking to Dr. Sachs, a tall, lean, dark-haired man in a brown sports jacket. I vaguely recalled him moving through the mansion like an undertaker guiding people to their seats or their places at a cemetery. Uncle Martin turned quickly to us.

Before Aunt Holly could speak, he said, "Miraculously, no broken bones. Dr. Sachs has him resting under sedation. Father has relieved Mrs. Fisher of any other duty but watching over him for the time being."

Aunt Holly turned to the doctor. "What happened?" she demanded. "Were you able to talk to him, get him to say anything?"

"Yes."

"And? So?"

"Well, it won't make any sense to you right now, Mrs. Sutherland."

"Just tell me!"

The doctor looked at Uncle Martin, who nodded. Aunt Holly glanced at me and rocked impatiently on and off her toes until she looked like a ballerina. Her rage had lifted her. I could see it in her eyes when she glanced at me. She had to have her husband okay the doctor talking to her?

"He claims he was pushed."

"Pushed? Down the stairs? By whom?"

He shook his head.

"Who did he say pushed him?" She held her fisted hands up in frustration when the doctor didn't immediately respond. "One of the servants?"

"No."

"Who, then?"

"Simon," I said, and they all turned to me.

"What?" Aunt Holly asked. When no one challenged me, her eyes widened. "He said Simon pushed him?"

"Yes," the doctor said, almost smiling. "You're Caroline, then. Simon is quite fond of you and—"

"What are you talking about?" Aunt Holly asked. She looked at me and then at the doctor. "What do you mean, yes? How could he push himself?"

"We discussed his multiple-personality syndrome the last time we all met, Mrs. Sutherland. I told you Simon couldn't tolerate himself because he thought his grandfather didn't and wouldn't ever. The Simon he moved in and out of wasn't succeeding as well as he wanted, and I think it might have come to a crisis."

He paused, looking like he had explained everything and was waiting to be complimented.

"What crisis? Damn it, I'm not a dentist. I don't pull teeth. Tell me everything."

"Holly," Uncle Martin said softly.

"Well?"

"In his mind, he might have eliminated the other Simon. We'll have to see if indeed it remains dormant. In the meantime, we'll let him rest—"

"Remains dormant? Let him rest here and wait to see if he bounces back and forth? That's so bizarre. He could do himself harm again. He should be returned to the clinic," Aunt Holly said, raising her voice and folding her arms. "Mrs. Fisher isn't trained in this sort of thing."

"Oh," Mrs. Fisher said, "I've had experience with—"

"Get him back to twenty-four-hour care. Call an ambulance or something!" Aunt Holly practically screamed.

For a moment, no one spoke or breathed.

"Now, there is no necessity to do that," Uncle Martin said. "Just calm down, Holly. Overreacting and drawing more attention to the situation isn't good for Simon and just exacerbates the situation and makes matters worse for everyone."

"Did your father say that or the doctor? I want him back in the clinic under twenty-four-hour watch, just as is done for every suicidal patient."

"Now, Mrs. Sutherland, Simon's situation isn't the same as that of an ordinary suicidal patient . . ." Dr. Sachs began.

"Ordinary? How can you use that word in the same sentence with the word 'suicidal'?"

"Well, for one thing, no two patients are exactly the same, especially with psychological illnesses. There are other complications pertaining only to Simon. You know I've been treating your son for some time now, and I've made certain roads of progress. This still remains the best environment for him to recover," the doctor said. "He's comfortable here. He's motivated to remain and affords me doorways through which to reach deeper into his psyche."

"You mean threatening to take him away from Sutherland gets him to be more cooperative?"

"In a way, yes. The house has become his world, his inner world, too. There is something comforting and therefore healing about it, and—"

"Even letting him continue going down to the basement?" I said. Everyone turned to me again. "I don't think so. As Uncle Martin just said, I think that exacerbates his problems."

The authority with which I spoke and my adult tone left them all speechless for a moment. If I had to, I was going to tell them more, but Mrs. Fisher quickly came to their aid.

"With your own problems still quite fresh, like open wounds, Caroline, I think it's best you let the doctor decide what to do and not do," she said. She raised her eyebrows in a silent warning.

Aunt Holly was visibly annoyed with her. She stepped in front of her to block her from the doctor.

"Is my niece right?" she asked. "The basement is his favorite place here. He as much as drove a stake in that truth from the day he began going down there. Martin and I have had a number of discussions about it. I've been saying it's unhealthy."

"It's just old things, antiques, things my family hoarded. Harmless junk," Uncle Martin said. "In my opinion," he added.

"But not Grandfather's. Otherwise, it wouldn't still be there," I said. I felt I had to defend Simon, even if it meant being insubordinate to Uncle Martin. He looked as infuriated as I'd ever seen him.

"My niece is right," Aunt Holly said. "You wouldn't say that if your father was standing here, Martin."

Uncle Martin blanched.

"We'll see about it," Dr. Sachs said. "Fencing off the basement and even some other places against his exploration might be wise eventually."

"We'll see?" Aunt Holly said. "I mean, what's the point of keeping him sedated in a room? If this whole house is restricted . . ."

She looked at me and then at the others. I could see she was about to explode.

"*No one* is making any sense!" she screamed.

The silence following the echo of her voice was deafening. The grand house was holding its breath.

Uncle Martin went to embrace her, but she pulled away as if his hands were on fire.

"Well?" Aunt Holly insisted. "I asked you a question, Doctor."

"Perhaps in time, if there is no avenue toward progress with the status quo . . ."

"In time? Do you realize how long he has been like this? Don't tell me about time."

She took a step back, looking from one to the other and nodding her head.

"This is my father-in-law's doing, isn't it? Keep everything about an unpleasant Sutherland situation smothered. The servants walk around here like deaf and blind people. Martin, get your head out of the damn sand! Your son nearly killed himself! Again and more dramatically.

Have you forgotten Mrs. Lawson's tumble down those stairs and all the horror that followed?"

"Of course not, but we have one of the most prestigious therapists in the state, if not the country, and—"

"AND NOTHING'S CHANGED!"

I thought her scream shook the very foundations of the mansion. Some of the ancestors in the paintings seemed to widen their eyes.

For a moment, all of us held our breath. Aunt Holly looked like she would start pounding her fists on Uncle Martin's chest. Dr. Sachs took a step back.

"What is this?" Grandfather bellowed from his office door. "A family consultation in the entryway before all the employees! Is this what we've come to?"

Even Aunt Holly looked unable to reply. Grandfather had his walking stick up and poised as if he was going to point it at one of us and make him or her disappear.

"Martin!" he added, now pounding his stick into the floor. "What's going on here?"

"Holly just returned with Caroline from The Oaks, Father, and we were talking about what the next steps are with Simon."

"Take the discussion to the grand room," Grandfather said, sounding calmer. "All of you, except Caroline."

"Me?" I whispered.

"Caroline, in my office. Now."

He tapped the doorframe with his stick, and I hurried toward it. The others were heading to the grand room. Only Mrs. Fisher looked back. I could have sworn she was smiling.

"Sit," Grandfather said. He walked around his desk, but he didn't sit. "I'm quite disappointed in you. I thought we had an understanding about Simon. I trusted you. Did you know he was getting this bad?"

"Yes," I admitted. "He was quite upset yesterday."

"About what?"

"He found some papers, letters, in the basement. He took me down there and told me about it. I didn't know how to tell you. I've been thinking about it, about how it was going to disturb you, disturb everyone."

He nodded. "I assumed as much, but if you worry about how people will react to what you say, you'll never say it. So, from what you're implying, whatever it is, it's directly about me?"

"Yes."

"Did you tell your aunt Holly?"

"No."

"And it's something you think is so terrible that you couldn't get yourself to talk to me about it, even though you knew I was depending on you to come to me with anything that would be harmful to Simon?"

"Yes."

"Well, there are and will be lots of terrible things said and written about me. You know what it's like having people spread rumors about you, don't you?"

"Yes."

"Look at what's happened to you at your young age. Can you even imagine how much crap has been piled outside my door?" he asked in a louder voice. "Do you think I'd still be here if I had been frightened or cowed by it?"

I was amazed at myself. I wasn't crying or pleading. Maybe it was the effect Mrs. Rich had on me.

"No," I said in a voice just above a whisper.

"Okay, I'll help you tell me," he said in a calmer tone. "Get up, go down to the basement, and get the papers you're referring to. Bring them to me."

"What?"

"Now!"

I winced and stood.

This was it, I thought. He'd know what I knew about him, and he'd surely decide he would rather I be sent away. I turned and hurried out of the office, down the hallway, to the basement door. I didn't know how I was doing it without shaking and crying, but I put on the light and went down the steps. Focused only on that box, I wound around other crates and bags and pulled out the box Simon had found. Without opening it, I rushed back to the stairs and out to the corridor. I didn't close the door or put out the lights.

Maybe this was for the best; maybe I'd be happier being more like an orphan than a member of this family.

He had his back to me when I returned to his office. He turned and indicated that I should put the box on his desk. I did so and stepped back.

"You can sit again," he said.

I did. He reached forward and opened the box. He looked at me and then took out one envelope and then another. He unfolded the papers inside each, looked at them, and took out another envelope. When there were no more, he turned one of the papers toward me.

It was blank.

He showed me another and then another. None of them had anything written on them. He pushed the carton aside and sat.

"I don't understand," I said.

"Didn't you see this?"

"No, I didn't read or look at anything. I was so frightened."

"Okay," he said in a softer tone. "Tell me what Simon said was written on them, what they were. Go on," he urged.

"Letters from Mrs. Lawson," I said quickly. He looked away for a moment and then back at me.

"Which said what?"

"That . . ." Did I have the courage? I looked right at him. I could feel his anticipation. Was Mrs. Fisher right? Was this my self-condemnation?

"That? Go on."

"That she was Uncle Martin's mother. And you let her step into Grandmother Judith's role."

"And you believed that?"

"Yes. He was so upset. I ran away from him. He was screaming that he had killed his grandmother."

Grandfather nodded. "What do you think now?"

He slapped the blank pages.

"Well?"

"That Simon is very sick."

"He is. And you kept all that from me. We could have put an end to this yesterday without all the dramatics we have now."

"Mrs. Fisher advised me not to tell you. She had been following Simon. I assumed she knew what he had told me and she thought you would just kill the messenger."

"That's how she put it?"

"Yes."

I looked for surprise and anger in his face, but there wasn't either.

"Then she was only trying to protect you," he said. "I'll have a talk with her."

"She frightens me."

"What or who doesn't these days? I'm hoping you'll build a spine at The Oaks under Mrs. Rich's guidance. More important now, do you think you'll tell me any secret that comes up in the future, about anyone in this family?"

"I don't know," I said.

He smiled one of the best smiles he had ever given me.

This was the time to bring up my mother's urn.

"Will you tell me secrets, secrets about my mother?"

"This isn't a negotiation, Caroline. Besides, honesty is a double-edged sword. On one hand, it can win you a real friend, but on the other, it can lose you valuable business, valuable opportunities, and, especially, it can make you vulnerable, weaker."

"Telling me the truth will make you weaker?"

He stared at me with that wry smile again. "I see more of me in you than I do your mother, Caroline. That's what makes me optimistic about you."

"Sounds . . ."

"What?"

"Arrogant," I dared to say.

"Arrogance is a close cousin to self-confidence. Don't be surprised if you inherited some of that."

He pushed all the papers aside.

"Forget all this for now."

He clasped his hands and sat forward.

"What did you think of the school and Mrs. Rich? It's impossible to think of one without the other," he quickly added.

"My father would like it and her," I said.

"And you?"

"I don't know."

"Honest again. Hard to get used to. Okay. In a few days, you'll attend and make up your mind. We'll discuss it again. At least you'll meet more people your age and—"

"Hudson David invited me to a pizza party at his house tonight with three of his best friends. He was our guide."

He sat back. "Well, that was fast. The seawater practically just dried on you."

I felt my confidence deflate and lowered my head.

"Do you want to go?" he asked, surprisingly.

I thought about Hudson and how handsome and adult he was. None of the kids my age I had met in Hawaii were like him. Maybe I needed to know someone like him. I wished I had enjoyed an early start when it came to Dina and her friends. Maybe I would have acted wiser and listened more to Boston.

"Yes, I'd like to go."

I stared at him, preparing arguments for when he said no. But he surprised me again.

"Good. I think it's best to get you away from what's happening right here now, get your mind on something else, on someone else besides Simon. I made a mistake putting so much on your shoulders, turning you into an audience for Simon's issues. It's time you had a chance to concentrate on yourself."

"Really?"

"Go on to your room, rest, and get ready. I'll have Emerson take you and pick you up at nine."

"Yes, that's what Hudson said, six to nine."

He rose. "Go on. I have to go to the grand room and get them to make the right decisions."

I got up quickly.

"Will Simon be okay?" I asked at the door.

"I'll tell you what you told me: I don't know. But I won't let the question go on much longer. I promise you that."

What did that mean? What was he threatening to do?

"Go on," he said. "Think about yourself for a while."

Why hadn't he ever told that to my mother? I wondered. Or had he, and she had never told me?

I left and hurried to the stairway. I didn't look back, because I was afraid Hudson and the excitement of a party would all pop and disappear.

And I'd be back in the nightmares that resided in every shadow in Sutherland.

If that happened, maybe, just maybe, I'd end up like Simon, trying to escape who I was.

CHAPTER THIRTEEN

Later that afternoon, I went through the dresses I had been given in Hawaii. A few were Dina's hand-me-downs that her mother, Parker, had insisted she give me. One thing about Dina was that she never shied away from being the center of attention, especially with her clothes. Every dress looked like I was trying to focus a spotlight on myself. I settled on the sunset-blue bungee-strap dress and found the shoes to match. Boston had told me I looked very pretty in it, which was why my stepsister thought it was ugly and said she was glad it was one of her throwaways. Jealousy led to a form of blindness, I thought.

When I heard a knock on my door, I was expecting Aunt Holly and news about Simon, but it was Mrs. Fisher, her arms folded and her face a pool of smugness. She probably thought I believed I was getting her in trouble with Grandfather, which I apparently hadn't, actually to my disappointment. I almost closed the door on her, but I wanted to avoid anything that would change Grandfather's mind about my going to the pizza party at Hudson's house. Maybe she had found out and had advised him against it.

"What?" I asked, my tone on the borderline of nasty.

"Your grandfather told me about your discussion. You should have listened to me when I told you it was unnecessary. You put yourself through pointless tension. And him, too. He was in total agreement with how I was handling it."

"I felt it was important. Whatever. It's over with, and talking to him about it wasn't anywhere near as bad as you told me it would be."

I almost smiled, not a happy smile but a smile of satisfaction, more like a grin of glee.

"But I think you knew that ahead of time," I said.

"Knew ahead of time? What does that mean?" she asked, looking as if I had accused her of murder.

"My father told me that people make problems look worse so when they solve them, they get more credit."

"Did he? That's a very good insight. Looks like your father did more for you than you claim."

"I never said he didn't do important things for me."

"In any case, that's ridiculous. I am not looking for any credit to win favor with your grandfather. I've already won enough of that. I'm only concerned about your welfare and your grandfather's peace of mind so he can continue to do his great work and you can continue to develop into a proper young lady."

"Okay. Thank you. So what do you want now?"

"Oh, my goodness. Feeling uppity? Not becoming for a young lady. The reason I'm here, Lady Caroline, is it was left for me to tell you what's been decided about Simon. I imagine you've been waiting to hear."

She paused, looking like she would simply turn around and leave me hanging and feeling bad about thinking only of myself.

"What about him?"

She looked to the side as if she was considering not saying another word. She could tell everyone I was uninterested and thinking only of myself and a party.

"Please tell me," I said, practically begging.

I could see the satisfaction in her face.

"A decision was made to keep him here for the time being. A nurse will visit daily, and the doctor will see him almost every other day now. Your grandfather approved it all."

"Did he? Where is my aunt Holly? Did she approve of this now, too?"

"She and your uncle are still in a bit of a row over it. They were a bit too argy-bargy for your grandfather, who sent them off to work out their problems at their own home. I told you not to depend on her."

I wasn't going to tell her she was right, but I had to push back on the tears that would tell her for me.

"I don't want to depend on anyone."

"Admirable. A dream everyone has, but I told you before, and I'll tell you now: You can depend on me. I hope someday to be able to depend on you. Now, what are you up to, dressing like that?"

"I'm going to a party to meet some of my new schoolmates," I said sharply, trying to end the conversation. "Grandfather has approved of that as well."

"Well, this is good. I'm happy to see that you're mixing with normal children your age. Dwelling on Simon can't be healthy for you. Okay," she said, stepping back and looking me over as if I had dressed for her approval. "You look lovely. Are you in need of anything else before you go?"

I just stared at her. Why did my grandfather like her so much? Why did he trust her, especially after what I had told him following the incident with Simon in the basement? Grandfather either carved out all resistance in people or knew something that was like a sword over their heads. Maybe she had lied about her daughter; maybe whatever had happened was her fault, and he knew it.

"Nothing," I said, and started to close the door.

She put her foot in the way.

"'No, thank you' is the proper response. I can see I have a lot to do."

"Not with me," I said with as much defiance as I could muster, and closed the door.

I stood there, waiting to hear the sound of her footsteps as she walked away, but I didn't hear any. I realized she was still standing there, staring at my closed door. Would she be there when I opened it to leave? The thought sent chills down my spine. Who would do this? I didn't move. Easily, a full minute went by until I finally heard her walking off. I released my breath. My lungs had nearly exploded with the fear.

I sat on my bed for a moment. Was I once again rushing into things too quickly? How was I supposed to have fun at a party? Who there would be worrying about what they would find when they went home? I was so disappointed in Aunt Holly for not coming up to see me and perhaps giving me some motherly advice. Of course, I understood that she was beside herself about Simon. I wasn't her daughter. Instead, I had to imagine my mother being in my room, excited to help me prepare for a party and get to know other students in my new school.

There would be so much delight in her eyes. I easily envisioned her telling me I was growing up fast and already looked like a young lady. I could hear her saying that the boys would be fighting over me. I remembered her telling me what it was like when she first went to parties and how much fun it was for her to dress, even though I now wondered if that ever happened. Did Grandmother Judith pamper her and spend time with her, talking about hair and makeup? I knew that was always important to Grandmother Judith.

Mommy became so beautiful, model beautiful. Did Grandfather ever look at her with pride, or was there always that chasm between them? Surely, there was a time when she looked for love in her father just as I always did. How sad and lonely it must have been when she was my age. I could understand even more now why she often ranted about it, something that often annoyed my father.

But I didn't want to think about those times, especially right now. I didn't want to be introduced to new young people with all that hovering, taking the enthusiasm out of my voice and the light from my smiles. I threw off my depression and sadness like an old jacket and, after checking myself one more time, walked out of my room.

The hollow echo of my steps watered down my excitement almost immediately. I was dressed and ready, but I had no one but Mrs. Fisher to tell me I looked good. I needed someone else, someone I could trust, if for no other reason than to build my self-confidence. How right Mrs. Rich was about its importance.

It suddenly occurred to me that I was about to go to the home of this boy I had just met and meet other strangers who surely knew more about me than I did about them. How careful did I have to be? What questions should I answer, and what ones should I avoid answering? Even Grandfather hadn't advised me about what to say and what not to say. Was that a result of confidence in me or total lack of interest?

Hudson had said his best friends were going to be there. By now, he certainly had described giving me a tour of The Oaks. Surely, they had been or were talking about me. How did he describe me? Did he think I was attractive or simply a curiosity, someone loaded with forbidden stories and experiences, their entertainment? It wasn't going to be like meeting new people in The Oaks itself, where there were boundaries; here there would be no one to protect me from their questions. I could be walking into a swarm of Dina bees. My stepsister might seem harmless compared to these four.

My excitement quickly changed to nervousness, even fear. I could do or say things that would ruin this new chance Grandfather had arranged. Stories about me would be passed around, and that could get back to Grandfather, who might think I had put a stain on the Sutherland image. What then? Back to home tutors, confined in Sutherland? Everything I did or might do was always put under a microscope, especially since my father had sent me back.

Emerson opened the front door and watched me walk across the entryway. As I approached, I saw that his face was pale. He wasn't looking at me as much as he was gaping. What had I done? Put lipstick on my cheeks? Had Mrs. Fisher been deliberately lying? Did I look ridiculous in this dress?

"Emerson?"

I stopped.

"Forgive me, missy," he said, "but as you walked from the stairway, I thought you were your mother at your age or thereabouts."

He smiled.

"You're looking quite posh."

"Posh?"

"Pretty as a young lady going to the king's court," he said.

"Oh. Thank you."

"Let's go take you to some lucky young fellas," he said, opening the door wider.

I started toward it and stopped when I heard something behind me.

Grandfather was standing in his office doorway. He looked at me for a long moment. I had the distinct sense that he was about to say something important. He was holding my attention for a reason, surely. Had he changed his mind? I didn't know why, but I felt more alone and frightened than ever. Had he decided against my going? Did he want to be sure I said nothing to anyone about Simon? Had he rethought everything and concluded that he should be angry at me? Had Mrs. Fisher turned him against me?

And then, to my surprise, he simply stepped back and closed the door.

Emerson must have sensed all that I was feeling. He looked worried, too, and then quickly washed away that look of concern and smiled.

"I remember the first girl I fell in love with," he said, as if Grandfather hadn't ever appeared and we were simply continuing a conversation.

He reached for my hand to walk me through the atrium. I looked back again, anticipating hearing Grandfather calling me back. Emerson continued.

"She was twelve, and I was fourteen. I thought, if she doesn't love me, I'll jump off the cliffs of Dover."

"What?"

"My first love," he said, smiling.

"Oh. Did she love you, too?"

"For a good ten minutes," he said, opening the limousine door. "But I fell in love with another lass twenty minutes later."

He laughed and closed the door. Mommy was so right about how good Emerson could make people feel even at the worst times. "And he could do it as if there was no one else at Sutherland but us," she had said.

"You were that fickle," I said when he got into the car, and he roared again with laughter.

"Aye, I can hear your mum saying the same thing. It'll happen to you, lass, maybe more times than you can imagine."

Maybe it already had. Just thinking about the possibility of falling in love reminded me of the look on Boston's face when we had parted in Hawaii. But were all men like Emerson? Was I one of Boston's ten-minute loves? At this moment, was he in love with someone else?

Wasn't it Nattie who said angrily that men could leave the stain of what looked like love behind, leaving it up to you to wash and wash until it was gone? Were she and my mother thinking of my father?

As you got older, I thought, the things you thought were simple in life became more and more complicated, so much so that you wished you could have been five forever. It was especially true for girls like me who didn't have a mother to help them unravel the knots.

The rear of the limousine suddenly looked so big to me. I started to sit in the middle and then moved to the left corner, where I usually sat, watching the scenery stream by as if we were hovering inches above the highway.

"They're all going to think I'm so spoiled, Emerson," I said as we drove off. "Arriving in a limousine."

He laughed. "Your grandfather would say they were all just lifting their skirts to show their jealousy," he said. "Oops. Don't tell Mrs. Fisher I told you that."

"Are you afraid of her, Emerson?" I asked, curious.

"No, but that doesn't mean you should stir up the bees," he said. "Avoid fights and arguments, even when you're confident you'll win. Most of that is just a waste of good time."

"Are you quoting my grandfather again?"

He laughed again. "More times than I realize, I'm sure."

"You really like him, don't you?"

"Admire and respect," he said. He looked at me in the rearview mirror.

That isn't the same, I thought. Maybe he could hear my thoughts. Looking at the glint in his eyes, I thought so.

I sat back and concentrated on avoiding all the mistakes I had made with Dina and her friends in Hawaii. *Don't accept any drink from any of them* was the number one warning. *Don't get distracted. Let them talk about themselves more than I talk about myself. Measure twice and cut once when it comes to answering any question.*

Most of all, don't show any desperation to make friends. Needy people wore their vulnerabilities on their sleeves. I didn't need my grandfather to spell that out for me, although he practically did when we had discussed what had happened in Hawaii. A little indifference went a great way toward winning respect. The trick was to be that way without looking and sounding arrogant.

Although I was sure it was most likely that egotism wasn't a stranger to the students attending The Oaks. The moment you stepped into it, the school made you feel special. Instead of wiping mud off your shoes on the welcome mat, you wiped off humility.

"This is an upscale neighborhood," Emerson explained after we had taken a turn onto a side road. "Probably no houses under two million or so, and many that price with a fraction of the Sutherland property."

"Well, then, how much is Sutherland worth?" I asked.

"Oh, I wouldn't even venture a guess about that. Let's just say more than more." He laughed.

I wondered how much I could trust Emerson. Did he know about the urn? Would he run to my grandfather with anything I told him? He was so loyal to him, why wouldn't he? It suddenly occurred to me that my going to The Oaks was not only logical but easy to understand. I was already in a world with no one to trust. Aunt Holly was immersed in her own conflicts and troubles now and was limited in the ways she could help me. Simon was suffering so deeply that he was disappearing before my eyes. Mrs. Fisher was truly another pair of ears and eyes for my grandfather, practically transmitting through the mansion walls, telegraphing, every thought I had and any move I made. Why not step out and into a school with Rich-lings? I was living in the world of Sutherland-lings.

I gazed out the window at the beautiful houses, all custom-built, with their stone, rich woods, and slate walkways and drives. I looked past them at the mountains and imagined the places beyond, places where words were not frozen for inspection and smiles were not flashing on faces of deception.

Probably never before did I feel so deeply my mother's longing for her escape. Surely, in the early days of her marriage, when we were what seemed to be an independent family, she thought she might have found it in Daddy because he was so self-confident and firm. Slowly, she discovered he was what my grandfather wanted him to be. In the true sense of it, my mother found the freedom she sought by being with Nattie. For a while, they had it; I had it.

How can I get that back?

"Here we are, Caroline," Emerson said. "I'm not going to be far away, so just hit number three on your phone if you want to be picked up earlier."

"Okay. Thank you, Emerson."

Of course, I was hoping I'd have fun and not want to go home earlier.

He got out to open my door. Hudson David's family home was a sprawling ranch-style house with a beautiful pool and cabana on the left. The lawns and hedges, although quite a bit smaller than those at Sutherland, were as impressive. From where I stood, I could see that the house obviously included acres of land that ran up to a wooded area.

Seconds after I stepped out of the limousine, the front door opened, and Hudson, dressed in a startlingly blue short-sleeved shirt and jeans, stood there gazing out.

I thought it was odd that he wasn't giving me a welcoming smile but instead looked Simon serious. The vibes I felt seemed to smother the excitement that had built up in me as we had approached the house.

Even Emerson paused for a moment and then closed the door.

"Number three," he said, and walked around to get into the driver's seat.

I watched him pull away, and so did Hudson. Only then did he turn to me and give me some glimmer of a grin. He stepped back a little as I walked toward the door.

"Hi," he said with as much enthusiasm as a release of breath. I wasn't sure I should even respond. He held the door open wider.

I looked past him and into the very modern gray-and-white-furnished living room where three other teenagers sat. An attractive, slim brunette woman who was surely Hudson's mother, with his blue eyes, sat with his best friends: Mark Cantor, Paula Reid, and Russel Collins. He didn't introduce them, so I didn't know whether the boy with thick-lensed glasses and curly blond hair was Mark or Russel. Paula was slim, with small facial features. She had rust-colored hair in a pageboy style. They were all looking at me as if they expected me to speak first. But there was something more to their expressions. It occurred to me they looked more surprised than anything. Why?

I could hear the excited voices from a large television on the opposite wall.

"What's happening?" I asked, irked by their silence.

"There is a very bad fire on Maui," Hudson said.

"Lahaina," his mother added. "You didn't know?"

"Is Sutherland on this planet?" Paula asked.

They all nodded and looked at me. I glanced again at the television and backed up.

"Hey," Hudson said when I opened the front door. But I didn't turn back. I pressed three on my mobile and stepped outside.

Adding more to my shock was seeing Emerson right where he had left me. He was looking at his mobile. He looked up at me and then hurried to open the car door.

"What's happening?" I asked, my eyes filling with tears.

"Let's get home. Your grandfather, as usual, is the one with the most information."

"It's a big fire?"

"Yes," he said, and spun out of the driveway.

I fell back against the seat. My heart was thumping, and I held my breath until I had to gasp and hold it again. I did that all the way back to Sutherland. When I closed my eyes, all I could see were the faces of the five of them turned to me. I realized their expressions weren't just filled with surprise. They were almost angry I had come.

When they understood that I didn't know anything about a fire, they were simply astounded. Did they think I didn't care or I was living in my own world, oblivious to everyone else? It was then that I realized why Grandfather had come out of his office to look at me at the entrance. He was going to call me back but decided not to. Did he want me to be embarrassed or simply distracted until it was impossible not to know about the fire? It was almost as if he thought he could will it out of existence, just as he tried to do to many things with regard to my mother. That was the real reason he disliked her: she reminded him constantly that he was only a man with a lot of money, just like his father, and there was nothing he really could do to change that.

Maybe, because I had inherited so much from her, he was more afraid of me.

CHAPTER FOURTEEN

The only fear that mattered at the moment was my fear of what awaited me when we arrived at Sutherland.

Emerson's silence during the trip back only frightened me more. Every house we passed, everything we drove by, seemed to flow as if the world had turned into something liquid, lawns and windows, benches and chairs, everything being washed along, riding a wave. I felt like I was drowning, unable to shout for help, unable to cry. I couldn't get the expressions on the faces of Hudson's mother, Hudson, and his friends out of my mind. They were like a light you turned off but that stayed on in your eyes.

As soon as we stopped in front of the mansion, Emerson practically leaped out of the car to open my door. I stepped out slowly, moving like someone who wanted to hold back time.

"Go directly to your grandfather's office," Emerson said, and started back to the driver's seat.

He never spoke to me like that. Less than an hour ago, he was comparing me to my mother and bringing me tears of happiness.

I walked quickly, my head down, my heart thumping. The mansion was so quiet when I opened the front door that I could hear the door hinges squeak and echo down the corridor. My footsteps reverberated as well. When I approached my grandfather's office, I took a deep breath, as deep as the breath I took when Boston was teaching me how to dive in Hawaii.

Grandfather was sitting but turned completely to look out of his side window facing the golf course and the mountains. He didn't turn around when I entered. I walked softly to the chair in front of his desk and sat. I was beginning to think he hadn't heard me enter, but I was afraid to speak.

"Your stepbrother, Boston, is at the Naval Special Warfare School in Illinois," he began, still not looking at me. "At your father's request, I helped him get into the program."

Suddenly, his voice softened.

"Every choice we make and that is made for us in this life has unforeseen consequences and results that impact most everything we do or can do in the future."

He paused, obviously wanting that to sink deep into my mind. How confusing he was, moving in a split second from an angry, dictatorial man seemingly always at war to a normal grandfather wanting to pass along wisdom and experience. However, until he apologized for how he had treated my mother, and me with that confinement for aversion therapy, I could never see him as my grandfather.

"If necessary, I'll have him come here."

He turned completely around to face me.

"I have people on the ground in Maui gathering information.

What I do know is neither your father nor his wife was at work. I know nothing about your stepsister, Dina.

"As you are aware, I thought your father was being somewhat hasty sending you back. It's in his nature to make a firm, quick decision and stand by it. Ironically, he might have saved your life."

He sighed, gazed at the ceiling for a moment, and then turned back to me.

"I was hoping that after you had your schooling and settled into being a young adult, I would have you return to see if you could all get along. I don't know if that possibility lies out there anymore.

"Now, what I don't want is you sitting in front of a television and watching the news or using your phone for that. Mrs. Fisher is having something prepared for you to eat, and then you can go to your room, read or something. When I find out more, I'll have you brought to my office. Whatever," he said, and started to turn toward the side window again.

"You knew this was happening when I left for Hudson David's house, didn't you?"

He looked at me without answering.

"You did. I just know you did."

"I was expecting you and your new teenage friends to do what most of you do, party and not pay attention to the rest of the world. You should be grateful that I was trying to spare you worry and fear. Most people are not lucky enough to avoid that."

"Most people live in the real world," I said. I didn't know where I had come up with that. It was as if my mother's thoughts really were being passed through me.

His eyes widened. "What?"

"Why would you have Boston come here?"

"Why? It's at times like this that someone would need family. And support."

"Why wasn't that true for my mother?"

"Your mother never needed my support or wanted it. This isn't the time to be discussing your mother. Go get something to eat," he ordered, and waved his hand at the door. "Go on."

I didn't move. For some reason, I felt that Grandfather wasn't as strong as he usually was. His eyes skipped nervously about the room; he looked like he was on the verge of getting up and leaving his office before I did. What my mother would surely call "the Sutherland" in me urged me to go forward, to pounce.

"You know that I know about the urn that was in your inner office until you had it put in that room."

"It was wise of you not to talk to me about it. Sometimes silence is wisdom. The unsaid is like leaving sleeping dogs lie."

"Why?"

"This is all much too complicated to discuss, especially now."

"When, then?"

"When I say!" he replied so loudly that I was sure everyone in the mansion heard it. "Now, go to the kitchen!"

I wanted to continue to defy him, but I was shaking and stood up quickly. He turned away again. I walked out and then hesitated after I closed the door. Where was everyone? Why was it still so quiet that I could hear my own breathing?

Whatever strength had moved into me moments ago moved out. Tears froze over my eyes. I walked toward the kitchen, not looking to my left or right. When I got there, I saw a peanut butter and jelly sandwich on a plate and a glass of milk beside it. At first, I thought no one else was there; then Mrs. Fisher stepped out of the corner on my right, just like I imagined some of the shadows in this mansion doing. She nodded at my sandwich.

"Eat."

"I'm not hungry."

"This is when you need to eat the most. Force yourself. Eat!" she said with such force that it made the veins in her neck bolder.

Why were she and my grandfather yelling at me? Why had Emerson been so curt and silent? It was as if they didn't want me to think. Maybe they were right. If you didn't think, you couldn't imagine terrible things. They had to wait outside your door, and maybe, just maybe, they'd go away and you'd hear good things without ever picturing the bad.

I sat and began to eat. Mrs. Fisher stood behind me, only inches away. I thought she was whispering. Was she saying a prayer? I was afraid to turn around to look. I ate faster and drank some milk. The only thought I had was to get it over with. Almost the second I finished, she scooped up the plate and the glass.

"You should go to your room," she said. "You should go quietly to your room. I have some chores to do, and then I'll come up if you like. Having company when you worry is always good. I remember having some neighbors over when my daughter ran off. They chatted and chatted until they were hoarse. I think I had to clean out my ears. They were so full of their words. Isn't that funny?"

She smiled, and then she looked somber and even a little angry.

"Go on," she said. "I have things to do for Simon as well."

"Where's Mrs. Wilson? Where's Clara Jean? Where are the others?"

"Everyone is in his or her room or together in a room. Never you mind about them. You go to your room. I promised your grandfather I'd see to it. Go."

I got up and walked out quickly. When I reached the stairway, I paused to listen. I couldn't hear anyone talking. There wasn't a creak in the pipes, the water running, anything. The house was holding its breath. The silence rushed me up the stairs and into my room. When I closed the door behind me, I let my tears flow. Seeing myself now in the mirror, I felt silly being so dressed up. But I didn't change. I lay down and stared at the wall, waiting. Fear did drain you, I thought, maybe more than anger. Even though they often did seem to go together.

I closed my eyes.

It was the darkness that woke me. I realized there wasn't a light on in my room. When I looked at my door, I saw the slim slivers of the hallway chandeliers' glow. I sat up and listened. It was still so quiet in the mansion. I rose and went to the door, opening it slowly.

There wasn't any noise downstairs, none of the murmurs of voices I could often hear winding around corners, leaking out of rooms. It was almost as if everyone had fled the mansion and I was the only one left here. I realized it had been hours since I had been brought back from Hudson's home. Surely, Grandfather knew something; someone must know something. I started to the stairway and paused. I should see about Simon, I thought, and I went to his room.

The door was open, and he was sitting and facing it. Mrs. Fisher was beside him, feeding him like someone would feed a baby. He ate and stared, but it was obvious he wasn't seeing me. His blank expression didn't change. I started to cry again, what I thought was sobbing softly, but Mrs. Fisher turned and looked at me. I was sure she would yell or say something about my leaving my room, but she just returned to what she was doing as if I wasn't there.

I started back to my room when I heard footsteps below. I went quickly to the railing and looked down just as Aunt Holly and Uncle Martin entered Grandfather's office. I didn't move until a rippling sensation on the back of my neck told me someone was near. Mrs. Fisher was there, standing as still as the statues in Sutherland.

"Your grandfather told you to wait in your room."

She looked at her watch, which looked more like a man's watch than a woman's, with its big face, encased in silver, with a thick black band. She didn't wear it that often. I had the feeling it had been her husband's. Funny how a detail like that could capture your attention. I was most likely clinging to any distraction.

"There's at least another hour yet until tea."

"Tea?"

She smiled. "That's what we call your idea of supper. Whenever I'm in a tizzy here, I think more like an Englishwoman."

"My uncle and aunt have returned. There must be news. I'm not going back to my room," I said, and started for the stairway.

"You young people are always in a rush to get older."

"Get older?" I said from the top of the stairway. "How is this a rush to get older?"

"That's what bad news does. It makes you older. Look what it did to me," she said, and turned to head back to Simon's room.

Maybe she's right, I thought as I started down the stairway. It seemed so long ago when I thought of myself as a little girl holding my mother's hand and twirling as we danced, the two of us resembling figures in a snow globe awash in tiny bubbles. I imagined Daddy holding us up and watching in wonder. Maybe deep down he was asking himself, *How can I get into the globe, too?*

Grandfather's office door looked taller and wider. It felt thicker and heavier when I opened it. Aunt Holly and Uncle Martin turned. They were sitting in front of Grandfather's desk. He had his hands clasped and then opened them and sat back.

"I told you to wait in your room," he said.

"Willard," Aunt Holly said. "He's her father. She spent enough time with his wife and children to make what happens to any of them important to her."

She turned to me.

"I know her. Caroline is a loving person, but more important, she's a young adult and should be treated as such."

She looked at Grandfather.

"Okay, okay," he said. "I had faith in your father. He is someone on whom you can depend, especially in a crisis. He and his wife, Parker, are okay. They're actually helping other people. I have monetary aid on the way to assist them, and one of my companies is involved with food distribution worldwide." .

I didn't like the way he paused.

"It's your stepsister we can't account for right now. As it turns out, she wasn't at home. The search will continue. I've informed . . ." He looked down at some papers. "Boston. Both your father and I have advised him to stay at his training facility. His commanders agree. It's a test of focus. Men and women, it seems, can't be SEALs if they can be distracted from their purpose. I'd advise you to develop that skill if you want to be successful at anything you do."

"What does it mean that Dina is still missing?" I asked, as if everything else he had said was unimportant.

"It's a chaotic situation right now," Aunt Holly said. "Everyone is working hard and trying. Your father and your stepmother are helping with the search, too."

I was sure I was crying even though I couldn't feel my tears. "Are all her friends missing, too?"

"We don't know them," Uncle Martin said, grimacing. "Right now, our full attention is on what your father needs."

"You can write the names down that you remember, and maybe your grandfather . . ." Aunt Holly began.

"Holly," Grandfather said. Then he sighed. "I'm sure if we find the whereabouts of your stepsister, we'll know about her friends. Now, go get yourself ready for our usual family dinner. When your father gets the opportunity, he will call you."

"He will?"

"If there is one person who does what he says he'll do," Grandfather said, looking at Uncle Martin first and then at me, "it's your father. Go on."

I'm sure that gave Uncle Martin the feeling that Grandfather would have preferred my father to be his son.

"I'm coming up in a few minutes," Aunt Holly said. "We're finishing up a discussion about Simon. Right?"

"Right, right," Grandfather said.

At the moment, I had so many different feelings that it was like a tornado was spinning in my heart. Almost dazed, I walked out of the office. The mansion was coming back to life. I could hear the servants, a vacuum going, and doors opening and closing.

Of course, Grandfather was right about Daddy. I think that was why deep down I wasn't afraid for him, even though everyone at Hudson's house and Emerson had a look of dread. He spent his working hours making sure strangers were safe and protected. When I was old enough to understand his work, I had imagined that his arm could be extended high into the sky and his hand could embrace an airplane and bring it safely back to earth.

Maybe I shouldn't be so angry at Grandfather for planning and arranging his marrying Mommy. Yes, Mommy was right that Grandfather Sutherland wanted to feel like he had a godlike power to control everything and everyone, but he could have chosen a weaker man. He had wanted her to have someone who could protect her, too. Why was Grandfather so reluctant to admit it, to admit he cared deeply for her?

I thought I knew. Being sure had to wait for now, but it was something I desperately needed, not only to live at Sutherland but to live anywhere. Just like Simon tried to do with his exploration of the basement and memories, I would drive every secret out of this house.

As I walked up the stairs, I was more and more confident that I knew what kept Grandfather from revealing his love.

Grandfather thought love was something that made you weaker. If you cared about someone that much, you were vulnerable to so many things. You would worry, and that might put clouds around your judgment. You would be distracted by jealousy, and you would be unable to stop visions of tragedy from invading your thoughts and dreams.

You'd have to mourn her death, and the mourning could tear you in two.

So you wouldn't bury her in the family cemetery.

You'd put her ashes in an urn and keep death from claiming her.

But Mommy's spirit was claiming him. That was why he had put the urn in the dark room.

And me?

She was claiming him through me.

I should be more afraid, but I wasn't, I thought, because he could see it in my eyes.

I could love him.

And he could love me.

It struck me, however, that the only one who would be upset about it would be Simon.

Maybe that was why he was looking at me with a blank face and why he brought me to the basement this last time.

Where would he bring me next?

CHAPTER FIFTEEN

Daddy called me almost as soon as I entered my bedroom after dinner. I suspected that Grandfather had told him it was a good time to call. He sounded different. There was no gruffness, no sternness, in his voice. He spoke more like the Daddy I had when I was little and we played in the snow or went to the park. Oddly, maybe, that made me think about Simon and the diagnosis his doctor had made. Perhaps everyone was more than one person, I thought, even me.

"Parker and I are fine," he began. "Your stepsister, as she has done a few times before, snuck out of the house, so I don't know where she went. She hasn't tried to call either of us. That could be because she's afraid to or . . ."

"Or what, Daddy?"

"She can't."

He paused, perhaps to be sure what he meant had sunk in. My throat tightened, and I held my breath.

"I used to believe in that movie line that annoyed your mother," he continued. "'Don't apologize; it's a sign of weakness.' She said it was your grandfather's anthem. Well, it isn't weakness when it's justified.

"I have mixed feelings about having sent you back. On one hand, you're safer. Dina probably would have talked you into going out with her. On the other hand, I should have given you another chance.

"Anyway, your grandfather tells me you're starting the private school your aunt and uncle attended. Good luck with that. Make the best of opportunities given. It will take a while for us to reorganize here, so don't be surprised if you don't hear from me for a while."

"But . . ."

"I'll speak to your grandfather about Dina when I know."

It was on the tip of my tongue to say thank you, but why would I say thank you to my father for calling me and telling me about himself, his wife, and his stepchildren? Had we become such strangers?

After she had begun her relationship with Nattie, Mommy told me that you could become closer to friends than you could to family. It was less complicated. I really didn't understand what she meant at the time, but oddly, it was those confusing comments that I remembered so well. *You need to be able to recall them when you're older*, I told myself, *because then you'll be wise enough to realize what she meant.*

"Okay," I said. "I hope she's all right."

"Yes, I know you do."

He was silent again, but this time it was as if our words hung in the air and we were waiting for them to be heard.

"All right," he finally said. "Be a good girl."

He hung up before I could say goodbye. I held on to my mobile for a long moment. Grandfather ridiculed how dependent on their mobile phones teenagers today were. But for me, it had suddenly become a candle in the darkness. I put it down and got ready for bed. When I lay down, I stared up at the ceiling and thought about Dina.

All the anger I had directed at her slipped away. Instead, I focused on the excitement I had felt upon first meeting her and thinking I would have a real sister. I was even happier meeting her friends and being a member of a special group. Maybe it was part of the myth of Hawaii, but it did seem to me that there were so many more fun things to do there, and all year round, too.

I also had to confess that I had been attracted to Dina's rebelliousness. She was unafraid of Daddy, probably because he wasn't her real father. Dina's mother didn't disagree with Daddy when he levied punishments on Dina, but the punishments were things she easily wiped away, disregarded, even though she moaned and groaned about the unfairness.

As odd as it might seem, I was jealous of her relationship with her brother, Boston. They teased each other; he was sincerely critical of her. He had warned me about her, but he still loved her, and I know she loved him, too. Sometimes I had caught her expressing her pride in him. She would quickly throw in something critical like, "But he's too much of a goody-goody. You'd think he was as old as your father; two peas in the same pod."

Now, as I recalled those final days in Hawaii, I was more tolerant of her jealousy, especially when it came to Boston's interest in and attention to me. Maybe if our positions had been reversed, I would have felt the same way, if I suddenly had to share my brother with another girl my age.

Although she might not have been the one to put the drug in my drink during our beach party, she had most likely approved of it. As I lay here now, however, I was sure she hadn't wanted such a near-fatal result. I remembered when I left having the fleeting thought that she would call me someday and in her way, a way almost unrecognizable, apologize and even reveal a hope that I would return. I was, after all, possibly the sister she had never had, too.

I was tired of crying, tired of the sick feeling in my stomach. I was eager to fall asleep but terrified that I would be awakened during the night to be told bad news, horrible news. Minutes later, a soft knock on my door sent a chill up my spine.

"Yes?" I called in a voice so tiny that it felt like someone else had said it or, without my realizing it, I had become five years old again.

Aunt Holly stepped in.

"I couldn't leave without stopping in to see how you were," she said.

She looked so feeble, faltering in the doorway as if her legs might give way. All the tension plus what was happening with Simon would knock anyone off their feet.

I sat up quickly. Instinctively, I knew this was not the time to be a young, dependent girl. Maturity was not something that automatically arrived at a certain age.

"I'm okay, Aunt Holly. Daddy called to tell me he and Parker were okay, but he still doesn't know about Dina. She had snuck out of their house to be with friends."

"It's tough when you're both angry at and worried about your child. I'm sure he's doing the best possible search."

She smiled hopefully, and then some rage rolled through her.

"Is Simon okay?" I asked instinctively.

She stepped in farther so she could close the door more behind her.

Her eyes sizzled, and she spoke in an angry whisper. "That Mrs. Fisher. I could wring her neck. Before the nurse arrived, she told Simon about the fire, your father, and his family. It made him very agitated. The nurse called his doctor, and he prescribed a sedative. He's asleep. I hope he forgets what she told him. I bawled her out, of course. ·

"Idiot. She says it's important to keep Simon in the here and now. She claimed that the doctor told her that. I'm going to find out if that is true."

"I'll look in on him, too," I said. "Maybe I can get him to go out to the pool with me. When I start school, I'll probably need his help with math. He'd like that."

"That's sweet. You have so much on your mind, and you still think about someone else. Your mother would be proud of you. I know she would, that she is."

"Thank you, Aunt Holly."

"Okay," she said, coming over to kiss me good night. "Let's hope the morning brings continued good news. Get a good rest. Lots to do in the coming days. They'll be delivering your textbooks, and I'll take you shopping for the school necessities they listed. It'll be exciting. You'll see," she said.

She smiled again before she slipped out, closing the door so softly that I thought it was still open.

Aunt Holly's words eased me into a gentle sleep. I didn't have any nightmares when there was so much reason for them. Instead, her words about Mommy, especially telling me how proud she was of me right now, gave me peace. I suddenly thought that people never died the way we all thought they did. They went to a better place and waited for those they loved to join them. They didn't wish that would happen quickly, but they were comforted by that thought.

"Good night, Mommy," I whispered. The breeze tapped gently on my windows, and I curled up in my blanket, feeling as safe as I would if her arms were around me.

In the morning, everything at the mansion appeared to go on just the way it always had. I heard no one talk about Hawaii, and I wasn't about to bring it up. Grandfather, Uncle Martin, and Mr. Butler held meetings with other businesspeople in Grandfather's office. There was a constant patter of businessmen and lawyers. Aunt Holly arrived to have lunch with Simon. Whatever she had told Grandfather resulted in the nurse being told to be there longer, and another nurse was hired to fill in after her.

Mrs. Fisher was more involved with her work as head housekeeper and didn't even speak to me. Maybe Grandfather had bawled her out after all. Whenever I saw her, she looked like she was sulking.

But as the day went on, I had the growing feeling that people, the employees, everyone, really, was simply ignoring me. I was a reminder that there was still some family tension and a dreaded shadow over the mansion. I didn't blame any of them. I even avoided looking at myself in the mirror, fearful that I would start to cry and put more strain and nervousness on everyone. I did go up to see about Simon, but his door was closed. When I saw Aunt Holly, she told me his doctor was with him.

"Well, how is he today?" I asked. "Did the doctor say anything about his being agitated? Is he still that way?"

"I think so, but you know doctors. They say to give it time, as if time was a pill."

The moment Uncle Martin stepped out of Grandfather's office, she went to speak to him. They stood in the hallway, conversing softly. They looked like they were comforting each other. When you were swimming in sadness, I thought, you put away your anger and clung to other people like life rafts.

I went out to the pool, not to swim but simply to lie on one of the lounges. It was warm, but I could see the wind twisting clouds. Mommy used to say the clouds were God's words. You had to read their shapes to get the message. When Daddy heard her tell me that, he said, "Up there you get only one message: Be careful."

I had started to drift with the clouds into childhood memories when I heard someone call my name.

Hudson David was walking toward me, carrying a white cloth bag that clearly read THE OAKS in bold ruby letters.

"Hey," he said. "Your aunt told me you were out here. First, I'd like to apologize for myself and everyone else last night. We should have understood that you hadn't been told anything so you wouldn't worry. I heard your father and his wife are okay."

"But we don't know about my stepsister."

"Yeah." He looked away. Did he know something I didn't?

"My father promised to call when he found her."

"Sure."

He looked away again, avoiding my eyes, which were searching for truth in his face.

"I've been here at Sutherland, but every time I've come, it's looked bigger and bigger. My father plays golf on the course occasionally. Oh. So Mrs. Rich called me. She knows about everything going on, of course. She said I should bring you these copies of the textbooks you'll be using at The Oaks. She says to tell you it's good to get a little head start.

"I've done that every year. I practically teach the courses to my classmates. By the way, I'm neck and neck with Paula for class valedictorian. She has one of those photographic memories. I try to psych her out all the time by telling her she's out of focus."

He put the bag beside me.

"Thank you."

"There's a copy of the play *Harvey* in there, too."

I gazed into the bag, saw the books, and pulled out the one that said *Introduction to Business.*

"I've taken that business course you're going to have. I want to get involved in that world. Next summer, I'm going to intern at one of your grandfather's companies."

"Oh." I put the book back in the bag. "I don't know much about his companies, except that he's got quite a few."

"Sure, companies that own companies. He has an army of business attorneys."

"Including your father?"

"Yes, for special projects. My father has two partners. They employ about twenty people."

"Why don't you intern with him?"

"I don't want to be just a business attorney. I want to employ them. Maybe someday I'll hire my father."

I could see that wasn't just a joke; he believed it. Was this an example of the self-confidence Mrs. Rich wanted for all her students at The Oaks, or just an abundance of arrogance? How did you know when you had stepped over the line? I wondered if I would ever get to be like him. Was arrogance infectious? Between Sutherland and The Oaks, how could I avoid it?

"Besides, your grandfather's a pretty famous guy. I've seen him on one of the business channels talking about investments. It'll be more impressive on my résumé."

He laughed again, a laugh full of sureness. He liked talking about himself. If everyone at The Oaks was like that, I would surely stand out as different.

"Anyway," he said, looking away again. "Maybe I'll come back and go swimming with you tomorrow. I can show you some neat dives."

"When I was in Hawaii, my stepbrother taught me how to dive."

"I can give you some pointers, too. I was even thinking of trying out for the Olympics. Many people said I should."

He paused, the smile fleeing his face when he looked back at the house.

"Your aunt is coming out."

I rose. She paused. The way she stood caused me to utter a small gasp.

"Come to your grandfather's office," she called.

"I'll bring your bag in," Hudson said.

I looked at him. He looked suddenly pale. I started back to the house, my feet feeling like they weren't touching the ground. When I looked up just before I entered, the clouds were floating into each other.

Aunt Holly waited for me inside. Without speaking, she escorted me to Grandfather's office. She thrust her hand out to open the door. What surprised me was that she didn't follow me in. She just closed the door behind me. My grandfather was standing with his hands clasped behind his back. He was looking out the same window, his shoulders a little more slumped than usual.

"What I had trouble getting used to when I was a young boy was that terrible things could happen to people in other places, even in other parts of this country, and life goes on as if nothing happened. People would go to work, go out to eat, go to the movies, go to parties, whatever. It seemed like indifference, selfishness. That bothered me until I came to realize that's how we manage to go on," he said.

I wanted to ask if that was why he didn't mourn my mother more, but I could see he was talking to me differently from the way he usually did. First, he was telling me about himself, thoughts and feelings he might not have told anyone else, especially Uncle Martin or Aunt Holly. Maybe not even Grandmother Judith.

And second, I wanted him to get to what he knew, what Daddy had told him.

He turned to me. "When I was your age, I had a friend who drowned while on his family's vacation in Cape Cod. He was showing off for a girl he had just met and got caught in an undertow. The ground literally slips out from under you. It was tricky, because the bottom of the ocean changed at a certain point that he wouldn't have known, not having ever been there. He had gone off to a different area, so his parents didn't see him go too far out.

"I think tragedies like that involving young people are harder for young people to accept. You think—we all think—we're immortal when we're younger."

I sucked in my breath. He was preparing me for some news about Dina. It was pretty clear to me that he didn't want me crying. I swallowed back any urge to do so. It made my throat hurt, but I had to find the courage to press forward. He was waiting on me before he said anything more.

"Something happened to her?"

"Your father told you that when he found out about Dina, he

would call so you would know. Your aunt Holly is right. It's important that you're treated like an adult and not a child.

"I shouldn't have let you go to the party. I should have told you what had happened. I kept things from you because I've always kept unpleasant things away from Sutherland. As much as I could. I detest pity. It makes you weaker, and there are vultures out there just waiting to take advantage."

"Even of something like this?"

"We live in two worlds: the imaginary one where good and evil do battle and the real one where winning or losing is the standard. Emotions, feeling sorry for yourself or someone in your family circle, leaves you vulnerable, distracted. I certainly don't want that for myself, and I didn't want that for you.

"However, your aunt and, in fact, your father made me think again about all that. Even someone my age can still change his mind."

He started to smile, but I didn't laugh, so he quickly lost any softness in his face.

"His stepdaughter, Dina . . ." he started.

"Yes?"

"Bottom line is, she was found. She is in critical condition. I had a helicopter take her to Honolulu, where there are better medical facilities. Even if she survives, she won't be the same. However, I am having one of my surgeons flown there. He's very experienced with this sort of thing, has a national reputation, international for that matter.

"I have also gotten the Navy SEALs to give her brother, Boston, a special leave. I've had him flown there as well."

I could feel the surprise and confusion inside me. It was like my right hand wrestling with my left. How could I lose, how could I win? For most of the time I had been here, I had harbored only rage and disappointment. My grandfather had been like some ogre terrorizing anyone who worked for him, even his own son and especially his daughter. Look at what he had put me through. He was easy to fear and hate. I had searched constantly for and clung to any words that would enable me first to tolerate him and then, maybe, to forgive him and even someday to love him like a grandfather.

He had wanted me to spy on Simon, but maybe that meant he trusted me. He had decided to send me to his expensive school, but maybe that had been to protect me. I clung to the hope that maybe someday he would explain everything and wash away the darkness of Sutherland. But every time I wanted to forgive him or have hope, I thought I was betraying my mother.

He was a powerful man; he liked being that, and as my mother had told me, he wanted to outdo and swallow up his father. And now he was helping people in great need. Was he doing that out of the goodness of his heart, or was he, as my mother might say, trying to prove that he could defeat anything?

What difference would it make if, in the end, Dina and Boston were helped? I'm sure Mommy would say there was a difference, but right now I was thinking more like a Sutherland. I could almost imitate his voice: "What's the bottom line?"

"I'm glad you did all that and so quickly," I said. "Can I send a message to Dina?"

"I'll tell you if and when it makes sense to do so."

"Would you tell Boston I'm thinking of him?"

"I'll pass it on through your father."

"Thank you."

"Now I want you to do something for me."

What could I possibly do for him? Continue to spy on Simon?

"What?"

"Put all this aside for now. I don't mean you should belittle or be unsympathetic toward other people less fortunate, but it doesn't do anyone any good if you depress yourself. You want to be ready and strong when you need to be. So for now, I want you to start acting like a normal teenage girl, make friends, and prepare for The Oaks. I don't want to see you moping about the house. I don't want tearful eyes.

"As far as Simon, you can contribute to his recuperation in any way the doctor approves. He has one thing right, at least. You can reach Simon in ways he can't, even with all his voodoo techniques."

"Why didn't you think that of Dr. Kirkwell and her techniques?" I asked, my heart pounding with every word.

He just stared for a moment. Was all the good feeling between us going to be lost?

"That was different. That was recuperation; that was prophylactic, preventative."

He put his hand up before I could argue.

"Maybe someday you'll think of Sutherland as bigger than any one person, even yourself."

It did seem selfish to argue about it right now.

"Okay. Go do whatever until dinner."

"One more thing," he said when I started to turn to the door. "I spoke with Mrs. Rich. She was impressed with you. Cherish the respect of people who can affect your life positively. Don't disappoint me."

When would he ever say something to me that didn't have a warning within it or at the end?

I paused at the door and turned back to him.

"What?"

"I want to change things in my room."

"What?"

"I want it to look more like a girl's room than an anonymous motel. So I'm not ashamed to bring girlfriends here."

I thought he was going to go into a rage, but his eyes brightened, some joy surfacing.

"Careful," he said. "You might become a Sutherland sooner than you think."

CHAPTER SIXTEEN

Hudson and Aunt Holly were talking so softly in the hallway that I couldn't hear anything they said. Usually, voices echoed in this grand hallway. They were at the foot of the stairway, my least favorite place in this mansion. For a few moments, I just stood there staring at them. When they realized it, they both turned to me expectantly. This was going to be the first test of my grandfather's demand to keep my sadness and fears below the surface. I felt myself tighten and stand straighter just the way my grandfather would as I approached them.

"My stepsister was found. She's in critical condition. Grandfather is doing all he can to help. He had a helicopter fly her to better medical facilities in Honolulu, and he got the Navy to permit her brother, Boston, to fly there and be with my father and stepmother."

I said it all almost in one breath, my voice not breaking.

"Where was her brother?" Hudson asked.

"Training to be a Navy SEAL."

"Oh. Impressive."

That is far from the point, I wanted to say, but that might lead me to be emotional.

"Grandfather also has sent his own doctor there to do what he can for her. He's world-famous."

I knew Aunt Holly probably was aware of it all and might have even told Hudson everything already.

"That's great," Hudson said. "When your grandfather gets involved in something, he goes full steam ahead. If anyone can make a difference between life and death, he can."

"My grandfather has money and power. He can get important people to do what he wants, but now it's up to doctors," I said in a coldly factual tone. I realized I sounded almost hypnotized, but I wasn't going to speak about all this lightly.

Aunt Holly's eyes widened with surprise, and Hudson's smile seemed to evaporate like a bead of water on a hot stove.

"Sure," Hudson said.

For a moment, there was a heavy silence, no one knowing just how to continue. Then Hudson smiled again.

"Your aunt thought it might be a good idea for me to bring Mark, Paula, and Russel over tomorrow and have kind of a picnic at the pool. As long as your grandfather agrees," he added quickly.

"He will," I said. "I'll make sure he knows, and then I'll call you."

Aunt Holly actually smiled with surprise at my confidence.

"Great," Hudson said. "We'll all be here about one, and we'll bring pizza from Antonio's. I think your grandfather has actually eaten there."

"Maybe we can get Simon to join us," I said to Aunt Holly. "If the doctor says it's okay, I'll ask Simon. Even if he just sits and watches us."

"That'd be great," Hudson said. "I haven't seen him for about two years."

"We'll see," Aunt Holly said. "Baby steps."

"Oh. I left your Oaks bag of books in the library," Hudson said.

"Thank you."

The grandfather clock announced the time. Each bong echoed and hung over us. As if there was something holy about it, no one spoke until it stopped.

"Uh-oh. Got to get going," Hudson said. "I have some chores at home. My father says I have to earn my keep."

"Doing what?" I asked. What was big or important enough to earn his keep?

"Washing his car," he said. "Which I borrow from time to time. Probably borrow it tomorrow. Can't come here in anything less than a Porsche Panamera." He started away and turned back to add, "Platinum Edition."

"I don't know what that is," I said when he'd left.

"Don't worry. They'll introduce you to the world of the one-percenters. My guess is you'll bring them down to earth," Aunt Holly said.

"One-percenters? I'd better start reading my business text," I said.

She laughed and put her arm around me. "You'll have to tell me more about this conversation you just had with your grandfather," she said. "Unless you want to keep it personal."

I looked at his office again. "I think *he* does," I said.

"Of course," she said, but I could see that she looked even more curious.

We both turned when we heard a door close and saw Mrs. Fisher come out from the direction of the grand room. She gave us a look, which was more like an angry glare, and then she turned and walked in the opposite direction, slapping her shoes on the tile as if she was telegraphing a warning.

"Be careful of what you tell that woman, Caroline. There's something—"

"Not right with her?"

"Yes."

"Maybe that's why she belongs here," I muttered.

Aunt Holly laughed, really laughed. "You're developing your mother's sense of humor. I wish I was that witty. C'mon," she said. "Let's go see about Simon."

She looked at her watch.

"He has one of those doctors who work on a clock first and then the patient."

"That's witty, Aunt Holly."

"Yes. It is, isn't it? Maybe it's catching."

We both laughed and started for the stairway.

She was right about the doctor. As soon as we reached the top of the stairway, he stepped out of Simon's room.

"Well, I've taken him off the sedatives," he told Aunt Holly as soon as he reached us. "Mrs. Clarke will monitor him closely. She's one of my best psychiatric nurses. Works part-time at the clinic as well."

"Which I still think is where he should be again," Aunt Holly said, her voice sharp enough to slice his ear. "He was released too soon."

He was about to start his argument, but Aunt Holly put her hand up. She looked like she was swallowing something bitter and then spoke quickly.

"Maybe we can make some good use of your keeping him here. My niece is having some of her new friends over tomorrow for a picnic and swimming. She'll get my father-in-law's okay. If so, we wondered if Mrs. Clarke or Mrs. Wally could bring Simon out. Perhaps when he is among other young people . . ."

"That's a good idea," he said with relief. "Let's see how that goes. I'll let Mrs. Wally know. If there is any change in the plans . . ."

Aunt Holly looked at me. "I don't anticipate any," she said. "My niece is confident she can get my father-in-law's permission."

"Oh. Well, it's good someone can soften Mr. Sutherland."

He started to walk down the stairs and stopped, turning back to look at me.

"Maybe when you talk to your grandfather, you could see if you can get him to give Simon the impression he doesn't hold him responsible for what happened. By 'impression,' I mean actually saying it. I've suggested it, but if I push any harder on it, I'm sure he'll fire me. He's not crazy about me or any psychiatrist being on this case to start with."

"I've pushed on that, too," Aunt Holly said. "My father-in-law has certain personal principles, expectations."

"Yes, well, sometimes we have to compromise with ourselves to make progress with others," the doctor said.

"My father-in-law believes psychiatry is just a way to provide endless excuses for misbehavior. It's not my belief; it's his."

"Yes. Pity," he said. He started to turn away.

"How much do you charge, and how much do the nurses cost?" I asked.

"What?" He looked at Aunt Holly.

"Just give her the answer," she said firmly. "It's not a state secret."

"No, of course not. Who's more transparent than a psychiatrist?" He smiled nervously. "Well . . . I'm five hundred an hour with an additional charge for house calls. My nurses get one hundred fifty thousand a year for private care."

He stared at me a moment.

"I don't see how that matters at the moment," he said.

"Grandfather might," I quickly replied.

He looked at Aunt Holly, who smiled.

And then he hurried down the stairs.

"As they say, I think you got his number," Aunt Holly quipped.

Maybe witticisms were a way to survive at Sutherland. Before his first breakdown after Mrs. Lawson's death, Simon was the master of it in this house.

We went to his room. Mrs. Clarke, a stout woman with graying black hair cut sharply at the base of her neck, was reading a romance novel with a woman in a low-cut dress on the cover. For a moment, I had a flashback to some of the pictures Dr. Kirkwell had forced me to look at.

Simon was sitting all the way back in his recliner chair, his eyes closed. The instant I said, "Hi, Simon," his eyes opened and he slowly sat up, his eyes fixed so hard and steady on me I was afraid to breathe.

Which Simon was going to speak? I wondered. Maybe neither. I could almost see him thinking, deciding. Should he be angry or nice?

"Did you enroll in The Oaks?" he asked. "I'm sorry I didn't join the tour."

Aunt Holly nudged me, her lips softening with hope.

"I did enroll. It's not the prettiest place in the world, but it might be the cleanest school. The principal, Mrs. Rich, isn't exactly the warmest person, but I think I might enjoy attending. If you'll help me with my homework, that is. Looks like I have to take geometry. I can show you the textbooks. They were brought to me today."

"Good. Are they still using the same one you had?" he asked Aunt Holly.

"I don't know. I doubt it, Simon. That was a while ago."

"Math doesn't change. History changes. It gets rewritten," he said.

"That's very clever, Simon," Aunt Holly said, smiling at me. "Very witty."

He shrugged. "I probably read it somewhere."

Aunt Holly glanced at me. We were both nervous about being optimistic, but this Simon was definitely not the dark side. Maybe he was gone, left at the bottom of the stairway.

He was thinking so hard that I could practically hear the words bouncing like rubber balls down the stairway.

"Maybe I'll audit one of your classes and report to Grandfather," Simon said. "I know he's invested a lot in it. He'd like that, don't you think, Mom?"

"Your grandfather appreciates anyone looking out for his interests," Aunt Holly said.

"Yeah, right. Both Caroline and I can do that."

Simon's tone and look encouraged me to go forward with my suggestion.

"Some of the Oaks students are coming over here to swim and have a picnic tomorrow. I'm sure Grandfather will approve."

He looked up sharply. "What makes you so sure?"

"He's the one who wants me to attend The Oaks."

"Right," he said. He looked at me sharply. "How do you know whom to invite?"

"Oh. Mrs. Rich introduced me to the senior class president, who gave me a tour, and he wanted me to meet his three best friends. They're bringing pizza," I said. "Do you think you might come to the pool? About one?" I asked.

He was silent. I looked at Aunt Holly. Had I gone too far?

"He gave you a tour?"

"Yes. It's his responsibility as senior class president."

He was silent.

"I don't really know him or his friends. Your opinions will be important to me," I quickly added.

I thought I saw a change in his eyes and held my breath.

"I'll check my calendar," he said, then closed his eyes, started to lean back, paused and smiled, and leaned fully back again.

Mrs. Clarke looked at us with warnings flashing. Maybe she could sense when he was going to change into the darker side of himself and she was telling us not to push him. I glanced at Aunt Holly. She nodded.

"See you later, Simon," she said, and took my hand.

He didn't reply. We walked out quickly and paused near the stairway.

"Did I do the right thing?" I asked.

"The doctor thought it was all right. Simon did look a lot better than he has these past weeks," Aunt Holly said. "Of course, we'll have to wait to see if he remembers. Maybe his doctor knows what he's doing. I'm just so hungry for hope."

"Me too, but I just realized Simon didn't ask me anything about my father and his family," I said.

"That's what I mean. Perhaps he doesn't remember being told."

"Doesn't remember? That? And Mrs. Fisher telling him? She drives her words into you like nails."

"Doesn't remember because Mrs. Fisher told the other part of him. Maybe that's the only side who'd listen to her."

I didn't laugh, even though I knew she was being sarcastically funny.

It sounded too much like the truth to me.

"I wish my grandfather didn't trust her so much. Maybe if I tell him . . ."

"Be careful, Caroline. Things have a way of coming back at you at Sutherland. Baby steps."

"Okay," I said.

"Time you took a little break from all this anyway. Maybe just take a little rest before dinner."

"I've got to confirm the picnic with Grandfather first and then call Hudson."

"Right." She thought a moment. "Don't tell him about the possibility of Simon joining you all. If that doesn't happen . . . You've been here long enough to know how he is if something he is told to please him doesn't happen."

"I know. It's safer to tiptoe through Sutherland."

She laughed. "You sure you weren't born here?"

"No," I said.

We started down the stairs and paused outside Grandfather's office.

"Seriously. Afterward, get some rest and get your mind off all this for a while. Maybe start looking at the textbooks. Martin and I are going out for dinner tonight to a small, quiet place, actually a cozy little restaurant we used to go to when we were first married. We need to have what's called a heart-to-heart discussion. I'd take you with us, but . . ."

"I'll be fine," I said.

"You call me if anything changes." She looked at Grandfather's office door. "Maybe I should wait here."

"No, no, I'll call you."

We hugged, and she started away, then stopped and looked back at me.

"There's something you know that you're not telling me," she said.

"Baby steps," I said, and she quickly smothered a loud laugh. I watched her go out and then knocked on Grandfather's door.

CHAPTER SEVENTEEN

When I asked about inviting the Oaks students to Sutherland for swimming and a picnic, Grandfather nodded.

"It was Hudson David's idea. I don't really know anyone yet, but Hudson says he's going to intern for you and his father has done work for you. He's bringing his three best friends."

"Nice boy. Ambitious," he said almost sadly. I imagined he was thinking about Simon. "I'm sure his parents are aware of who his friends are.

"However, socializing is a sort of second schooling for you. From what I know, you weren't very socially active in Colonie and, as we know, you were not very successful in Hawaii. But I never made a mistake that didn't prove to be of some value. You'll probably be able to teach these Oaks students some important things. But subtly," he quickly added. "It doesn't do us any good to make it personal. What happened between you and your father remains locked in a Sutherland safe. Understood?"

"Yes."

"I imagine there'll be questions about Simon. How will you answer them?"

"He's under a doctor's care. I don't know enough about it."

He smiled.

"I really don't. Someone once told me it was better to tell part of the truth than an outright lie."

"Your father?"

I looked away.

"No matter. It's not who gives you wisdom as much as whether it is wisdom. Now, I want you to think of Sutherland as your home. I don't care who these kids are, how respectable their families might be, they are still growing up. When you go to someone's home, you respect that person's home. Make sure they respect yours."

I couldn't recall a time, even when my mother and father came here for dinners and parties, that he had given me the feeling that Sutherland was also my home. It had always been a family castle, a museum with its old portraits and statuary as well as the formality, the rigid way it was maintained. Not least of all, my history here made a homey warmth nearly impossible.

Thinking about his history with it, the bad relationship he'd had with his father, and, according to Mommy, his almost vicious need to remodel and expand it as a way of rejecting and burying his father, caused me to wonder how he could feel it was a home himself. It was always a work in progress, more of a monument to him. But now he was clearly saying I should be sharing it as a Sutherland.

Could I do that? Could I simply blink my eyes and forget everything else? I think he read that in my eyes.

"I've decided to ask your aunt Holly to take you shopping for new bedroom furnishings, to buy anything that is somewhat discreet, of course, that will give you a sense of belonging and pride. I don't want any outlandish sad pictures on the walls. This will be a good test of your character, your innate sense of taste. I'll see to it that it all gets done before you begin school."

He was taking my breath away. *Why wasn't he ever like this with my mother? When will he explain it? I'm afraid to bring that up now and spoil what I have. But what about Simon? I can't just pretend he's not here.*

Should I push my luck? I wondered. It felt dangerous, but I summoned the courage.

"Simon's doctor believes that if you told Simon you didn't hold him responsible for Mrs. Lawson, he might make giant leaps in recuperation. And the doctor and the private nurses are expensive."

"It's not my burden of guilt; it's his. He has to take responsibility and deal with it. That's what Sutherlands do. The psychiatrist is looking for an easy way out. I outlined what I wanted to see happen.

"You see this little notebook," he said, raising a black-and-white one off his desk.

"Yes."

"I keep track of what everyone in this family costs me. It will be deducted from their inheritance."

"Well, who inherits the money deducted?" I asked.

"Whoever gets fifty-one percent," he said, and put the notebook down.

Who could that be? I wondered. There was only Uncle Martin, Simon, and me. Would he leave that to my father, the son he wished he had? My father wasn't really a businessman. And I didn't even have my own checking account. I had a great deal to learn about spending and making money. Was there some other family secret, one not buried in the basement, that involved someone else who could inherit fifty-one percent?

"But I like that you're thinking in terms of profit and loss," he said. "In the end, that's what life is all about."

I didn't think so, but I wasn't going to make him angry.

"Okay," I said. "I'll tell Hudson David that you approve of him and his friends coming over tomorrow."

I could see he didn't like my not agreeing. He sat back, turned his chair, and started to make a phone call. I walked out quickly. Decorate my bedroom? I felt like I had just won a major victory, but would that be included in his notebook of family costs? Although Hudson had said his father was giving him chores to earn his keep with, I was sure he didn't mean something like this. How could you live believing that a profit-and-loss statement was the whole purpose of life? Was that what my grandfather would have on his tombstone? Maybe I would never understand him, I thought. Maybe it was stupid to even try.

I went to the library, picked up the bag of textbooks, and headed for my room to make the phone call to Hudson.

He picked up almost before his phone rang. It gave me the feeling that he was still outside our front gate, waiting for the call.

"Great," he said. "I already told everyone to plan on it. You're like your grandfather. When you say something, you mean it."

"Don't you?"

He laughed. "Most of the time," he said. "I've got to get back to the car. My father inspects it with a microscope when I tell him I'm done. See you tomorrow. I'm anxious to see you dive."

Just hearing the word sent me reeling back to Hawaii after I hung up. My memories were getting jumbled. So much had happened over the past few hours. Aunt Holly was right. I felt drained and not so much dazed but more like I had curled up inside myself. I should try to shut down for a while. Nevertheless, when I sat on my bed, my mind lit up with images of Dina.

She got hysterical over a pimple. How was she going to face never being the same? What did that mean anyway? It was so convenient and comforting to just think it was all up to doctors, to tell myself that there was no sense dwelling on her. That was basically what Grandfather was saying to me.

Would I become like him when I was older and put my emotions in little boxes? Did I want to? Despite what he had told me about losing a close friend, I couldn't imagine him, even younger, shedding a tear. The moment one appeared, he probably slapped himself in the face.

For a few seconds, that made me laugh, and then I lay back. I didn't sleep as much as simply dozed, my eyes half-open. About an hour later, my mobile rang. I had forgotten I had left it on a shelf in my closet. I imagined it was Hudson calling me back to brag about how clean his father had told him the car was. Not really in the mood to talk to him again, I almost ignored it, but the number calling me was from Hawaii. I knew who it was, and for a moment, like before, I debated not answering. I was that frightened.

"Hello," I said on what was surely the last ring.

"Caroline, it's Boston," he said. "Morgan told me it was all right to call you, but I would have anyway," he added. The sound of his voice, the underlying warmth, and the memory of his smile relaxed me instantly.

"Are you in Hawaii?"

"Yes, Honolulu. Your grandfather had me picked up in a private jet. I haven't been here long, but I was with them when the doctor spoke to Morgan and my mother. Dina's been stabilized. The doctor is hopeful, but it's going to be a long, long recuperation. Once she's out of the ICU, she'll go to rehabilitation. There are some surgeries involved that won't be life-threatening. But you know Dina. Once she is fully conscious, she'll be the one who's threatening." He laughed nervously.

"Can you talk to her?"

"Not yet."

"But when you do, would you tell her . . ."

"Of course. All of us are grateful to your grandfather. Without this emergency care . . . I'm looking forward to thanking him personally."

"He's not easy to thank," I said.

Boston laughed. "What's that mean?"

"He doesn't like people knowing some of the good things he does. My aunt says his middle name is really Anonymous."

Boston laughed again. It was so good to hear that, to hear him.

"Nevertheless . . ."

"How long are you going to be there?"

"Maybe a day or so. I have to report to my commanding officer, but I wanted to call you first."

"That was very nice of you, Boston."

"I have to confess, I wanted to hear your voice. I should have used FaceTime so I could see you, too, but I thought for now, for this call, I should just . . . call."

"I was thinking of you a little while ago."

"Were you?"

"My diving lessons."

He laughed. "I hope you remember more about me."

"Oh, yes. Someone was talking about diving, and . . ."

"I'm just kidding. It's all been a whirlwind for everyone."

"Yes. How is my father?"

"What did your mother call him? Captain Bryer?"

"She did, but he didn't like it."

"Don't tell him I said so, but it fits him. He's always in control. A lot of people are depending on him here, especially my mother."

"I used to," I said sadly.

"Lots of things change, and lots change back," he said.

"How is your training?"

"Hard," he said. "But, as Morgan says, the harder it is, the more satisfaction you have when you do it successfully."

"You really admire my father, don't you?"

"Yes, but like an older brother more than a father. So how are you doing back in Sutherland?"

"I'm starting a private school in a little more than a week. It's a little scary, small classes and lots of rules. I think the principal was a Navy SEAL. Her name is Mrs. Rich, and she's very firm, maybe tougher than your commanding officer."

"Really? That's funny. You'll have to keep me up on it all with phone texts. I'm sure you'll do well."

"I hope so. I don't want to disappoint everyone."

"You won't. You've never disappointed me. Morgan will keep everyone informed," he quickly added, as if he had embarrassed himself and also felt guilty for talking about anything other than Dina.

"Okay."

"I have to get moving, call my commanding officer. See you," he said, his voice drifting off as if the winds in the Pacific had turned away all sound.

"See you," I said, even after I knew he had hung up.

I held the phone the way I would try to hold on to his hand for as long as he would hold on to mine. I put it down when I heard the sound of footsteps again, going away from my door. I rose quickly and opened it, just as Mrs. Fisher disappeared on the right, going to her room. The shadows seemed to close in behind her.

It wasn't until that moment that I thought she had to be the lone-liest person I ever met. Should I pity her, fear her, or just ignore her? What I knew in my heart was I could never really like her.

I closed the door and explored my textbooks. I don't know if it was Grandfather's influence or not, but I spent the most time reading the introduction to my business class book. Toward the end, I started to read the play *Harvey*, imagining Hudson as the lead character. I was so into it that I forgot about dinner until Mrs. Fisher appeared to tell me my grandfather was waiting on me. The possibility of my having dinner with only Grandfather both excited and frightened me at the same time.

As it turned out, Franklin Butler and two other business associates were there. After Grandfather introduced me, I was completely ignored until he announced I was attending The Oaks. Both men had grandchildren attending there. It was as if they were now comfortable talking to me, asking me questions about my favorite subjects and sports.

I'm really in a different world, I thought. *It's a wonder we don't speak different languages.* I don't think I had ever concentrated so hard on how I spoke, constantly watching Grandfather's eyes to see if I was doing well. He looked satisfied. Mrs. Fisher followed me out to tell me how perfectly I had done at dinner.

"You made your grandfather very proud of you," she said.

I went to sleep thinking that had become the most important thing to me, almost as important as it was to Simon.

And for the life of me, I couldn't understand how that had happened with so many reasons for it not to.

CHAPTER EIGHTEEN

The next day, Aunt Holly was more excited about redoing my bedroom than I was.

"I know exactly where to go, the stores that have updated furnishings," she said when she came over just before the picnic. "Your mother and I dreamed of this often. We drew up plans, new color arrangements, and sometimes we would leave them lying around the estate, hoping your grandfather would see them and relent. If he saw them or someone brought them to him, he never did, of course, so whatever magic you have, don't lose it."

"I don't know what I have or why he's approving."

She shrugged. "He's even been a little nicer to Martin. We talked about it last night at dinner. Maybe age is softening him up."

"He's not much older than he was when Mrs. Lawson first brought me here."

"Yes, but you are, and maybe he realizes it and that gives him new insights about himself. Anyway, Simon remembered what you're doing today. He's actually considering what he'll wear."

"I didn't mention it to Grandfather."

"Don't. Nothing is until it is, especially here at Sutherland," she said. "Let's take another look at your room. I'll see if I can recall some of our ideas. We'll shop tomorrow. The sooner the better, before your grandfather realizes what he's approved and changes his mind."

My room, the picnic, Simon coming out. It seemed today was starting brighter than most. After Aunt Holly and I went over some details and took some measurements, I changed into my bathing suit, and she went out to do some shopping for Simon.

"I told his doctor and nurses that I would be the one to get him his necessities. I know it doesn't sound important and one of your grandfather's employees can do it," she said, "but I've got to feel like I'm doing *something* his mother would do."

I watched her leave and thought about her pain. It made me realize that I didn't think about Dina's mother as much as I should. I hoped my father was. He was like Grandfather when it came to comforting other people, too worried about drifting into pity. Did they at least cry at night when no one was around? How often had my grandfather gazed at the urn and regretted it? Maybe it wasn't that my mother was haunting him as much as it was that he was haunting himself. Someday I would have the courage to tell him, but I had to wonder, would it make any difference?

On the way out of my room, I thought about stopping by to see if Simon would come now and wait for the Oaks students with me, but his door was closed, and I heard what was surely the muffled voice of his nurse. It sounded like she was lecturing him about his personal cleanliness. It was better not to interrupt anything, I thought, and went down to the entryway, where I would greet Hudson and his friends.

Mrs. Fisher was there, speaking very softly to one of the maids, who had her head bowed, looking like a child who was being reprimanded. She dismissed her with a hand gesture and then turned to me.

"Oh, Caroline. I can greet your guests for you and bring them out to the pool."

"I think I'd rather do it myself, Mrs. Fisher. A little friendlier, don't you think? Less formal."

"Lovely sentiment. We Brits are a little more sensitive to protocol, aware of boundaries: less room for misunderstandings."

"Friendships with boundaries."

"Precisely," she said.

I wondered if she was saying this because of my experience in Hawaii or if she was simply cynical about any relationship. What sort of childhood could she have had? She had never mentioned a brother or a sister. She had said nothing about her parents. She had talked only about her husband. I suspected her parents weren't wealthy; she had made such a big thing about her husband rescuing her from meager earnings. But she had to have gone to school, met others her age. What were those memories like for her?

"Did you ever have a best friend, Mrs. Fisher?"

"What?"

"Someone who was closer to you than anyone else?"

She smiled. "Not until now, dear."

"Really. Who is that?" I was sure she was going to say my grandfather.

"Why, you, dear. Who else? I'll see to it that your guests have everything they need—drinks, towels. Enjoy the day," she said, and walked away.

Sometimes, even in the daytime, I felt she went down a hallway or around a turn like another Sutherland ghost.

When I turned back to the entrance, I heard their laughter before they rang the doorbell. Perhaps Emerson had let them into the atrium.

Hudson stood there in a pair of dark blue shorts, a plain white T-shirt, and dark brown sandals. He wore a black cap with the words THE OAKS on the front. His friends stood around him. Paula was almost as tall as he was and dressed in a bright blue-and-white bathing suit cover-up, her hair pinned up.

"I never got a chance to introduce you properly," Hudson said. "This goofy-looking guy on my right is Russel Collins, and always a step behind the rest of us is Mark Cantor."

They were similarly dressed, although neither had on an Oaks cap.

"Hi," I said.

"Yo," Mark said.

"Ditto," Russel added.

"I think you can figure out this is Paula Reid," Hudson said, smiling.

She extended her hand. She wore no nail polish or rings, not even a bracelet.

"Sorry about how we all behaved the other night," she said.

"I understand. Thank you," I said, taking her hand. "So, there's even an Oaks cap?" I asked Hudson.

"Oh, there's lots of stuff for bragging. Some are prizes, and some are gifts. Russel has an Oaks wallet."

"I have an Oaks hairbrush set," Mark said.

"Nothing can help his curly hair," Hudson quipped. "Our pizzas are being delivered in about twenty or so minutes."

"Come in. I'll show you to the pool."

I stepped back, and they all entered, Hudson's friends looking up and around, more like gawking, like people who had obviously never been here.

"It's a castle," Mark said.

"Without a moat," Russel declared.

"Or a dragon," Paula said.

"Oh, there's a dragon," Hudson said, looking at me. "Right?"

"No, it's just a big home," I replied, instantly wiping off their smiles. "This way," I said, turning. "It's the fastest and least dangerous route to the pool."

They all laughed, and I went forward, all of them following, Hudson's friends definitely gaping at the statues and pictures. I wondered what they were really thinking. Did they envy me or pity me? I was too young at the time to recall my first impression of Sutherland, and as I grew older and we visited, it always seemed a little different each time. It was as if the mansion was slowly revealing itself back then. More and more of what had lingered in the shadows stepped forward. I knew that nothing terribly new or different had been added. It was just too big to be gulped. It had to be visually sipped. The same was true of its vast and beautiful grounds.

Everyone exclaimed about it when we stepped out and started for the pool.

"I bet the whole of The Oaks could fit in here," Mark said.

"I'm surprised your grandfather doesn't start a corn farm or something," Russel added.

"There are beautiful gardens," I pointed out, "and there is a vegetable garden the cook and some others maintain on the south side."

"The south side," Paula said. "I don't even know if our home has sides. I could get lost coming home at night here."

They all laughed. Was their response to Sutherland made easier if they made fun of it? I looked to Hudson. If anyone should be raving about Sutherland, it should be he, I thought. Didn't he idolize my grandfather?

"Great pool," Russel said, charging forward.

"And a diving board," Mark said. "Going to give us a demonstration?" he asked Hudson.

"We'll let Caroline show us first," he said.

"Oh, I only dive off the side of the pool."

"Then there's something very new to teach you," he said.

I looked back. Was Simon told they were here? Was he on his way?

The four charged forward toward the pool. They threw their things at mats, Paula tossing her cover-up in a ball. She looked like a tall, lanky boy with those long legs. Mark, Russel, and she dove into the pool. Hudson went to the diving board. As he stepped out, they all cheered, and he looked toward me, put his arms up, and then rushed forward to do what was, to me, close to a perfect double somersault.

They clapped and splashed each other. I had barely taken another step, but none of them, not even Hudson, seemed to notice. It was almost as if I were some sort of caretaker who had opened the gates for them to enjoy Sutherland. I walked forward, took a seat on a lounge, and watched them laugh and fool around. Hudson did another dive, not so well, and hurried to correct it.

"Let's see what you've learned," he called after the dive.

The others stopped talking and teasing each other and looked my way as if they had just realized I was here.

"I told you it's not much," I said.

I rose, walked over to the side of the pool, envisioned Boston instructing me, and did my dive. I know it was good, because I hardly splashed.

Hudson clapped. The others followed without much enthusiasm and returned to their conversation and silly splashing games.

Could it be, I wondered, that I had grown so much older than they were because of all that had happened to and around me? I remembered an expression I had once heard. You could be a ten-year-old going on twenty because of hard events in your life, or you could be twenty going on eleven because you were a pampered, spoiled child. Was that who a one-percenter really was, a pampered, spoiled child?

"Hey, here's our pizza!" Russel shouted.

"Just in time. I'm starving," Mark said.

I turned to see Mrs. Fisher leading Clara Jean and another maid toward the pool patio tables, the maids carrying the boxes. Hudson and his friends got out of the pool and watched with smiles across their faces as Mrs. Fisher arranged the plates, napkins, and silverware, had an array of sodas presented, and even adjusted the seats.

"Cloth napkins," I heard Paula say.

"Only the best for the best," Mark declared.

I looked back at the house. Where was Simon? Then I saw him, standing at a window in the library, gazing out at us. I waved at him, beckoning him. When the others saw where I was looking and looked too, he stepped back and disappeared within.

"C'mon, let's eat," Russel said.

"I didn't bring a tie," Mark quipped.

They all dried themselves off and finally looked back at me still in the pool.

"Aren't you hungry?" Hudson asked. "Or did you have a late breakfast? Swimming always makes me hungry."

"No, I'm hungry," I said, and got out to follow them.

"Afterward, I'll teach you the board diving," he said.

Mrs. Fisher looked at me with a smile of approval and then stepped away with Clara Jean and the other maid. Hudson and his friends began eating and talking about the upcoming Oaks opening party.

"What sort of party is this?" I asked as soon as there was a pause in their conversation.

"The social committee, of which Paula is chairwoman," Hudson said, nodding to her, "clears the cafeteria and puts up the annual decorations, which were approved by Mrs. Rich five years ago."

"Six," Paula said. "Accuracy."

"Six," Hudson said begrudgingly. "It's our form of what public schools call a prom. You don't have to have a date, but many do. I'm going to ask you to be my date, before either of these bozos does," he said.

"There's nothing like a prom queen, but Hudson is the master of ceremonies, being the class president," Paula quickly added, maybe anticipating what I would think being Hudson's date meant.

"It's a dress-up," Hudson said.

"When is it?"

"Two days before opening. Saturday after next," he replied. "All the faculty will be there chaperoning. It's a great way to get to know them. And there are many students who've been away all summer. People have second homes in Europe or England. So it's kind of a reunion. Fun, you'll see. Everyone will have pictures to show."

Not me, I thought.

Hudson could see me worrying.

"Mrs. Rich will be there," he said.

"Practically checking our breath," Mark said.

They were complaining, but all I could think was *Good*. Would I ever fit in? Anywhere? It made me think again of Simon. I looked toward the house. He was at the window again. I saw Aunt Holly step up beside him, and he backed away. Maybe she would bring him out. I'd love to see the old Simon, I thought, witty and sarcastic. In his way, he'd surely bring them back to earth. It hurt me that right now he was the most vulnerable.

"Are the maids going to clean this up?" Paula suddenly asked.

"Yes," I said. "The housekeeper, Mrs. Fisher, will have it looking like no one was ever here."

"See? That's why I can't have a party," she said. "My mother won't let me use the maids to clean up, and I don't do a good enough job for her."

"For anyone," Russel said.

She hit him with a paper plate, and he pretended it really hurt. He threw a piece of pizza at her, and she threw it back. Hudson stopped them from wasting more food. They continued to make me feel so much older but also a bit sad. I was thrown back to Grandfather's telling me about Dina, what he had said first.

". . . terrible things could happen to people in other places, even in other parts of this country, and life goes on as if nothing happened."

He justified it by saying, "That's how we manage to go on."

But this didn't seem important enough to go on. Was it my fault? Was I too serious? Would I never have fun, fully?

When they were finished eating, they got up quickly and returned to the pool. Hudson insisted I do more diving with him, and then shortly afterward Paula announced that it was time for them to leave. The boys groaned, but it was as if she was in charge.

"I told you my parents were taking the family out tonight," she wailed.

They groaned again but began to get their things together. I looked toward the house. Aunt Holly was standing out on the patio, looking our way. Simon was nowhere to be seen. The moment we started to leave the pool, Mrs. Fisher and two maids started toward us.

"She must have been sitting by a window, watching," Hudson quipped.

The others laughed.

"Probably," I said.

"Wow," Russel said. "You're kind of the lady of the house, huh?"

"I don't tell her what to do, if that's what you mean," I said.

"You don't have to," Paula said. "Good servants anticipate what to do."

"Does everyone who attends The Oaks have maids?" I asked.

"No, there're a few who snuck in," Mark said, and laughed.

"Your grandfather never claims it, but everyone knows he gives scholarships here and there," Hudson said. "That's a sign of confidence, when you don't have to brag."

"Then most of those students with pictures at the party lack self-confidence," I said. "Mrs. Rich will be unhappy."

"Whoa!" Russel cried. "You walked into that one, Hudson."

"Yeah, I did," he said, looking at me. There wasn't a twinkle in his eye. There was something closer to fear.

I walked them all to the front entrance. Of course, Hudson had to point out his father's car and how clean it was.

"I'll be picking you up for the opening party in that," he said as the others got in.

"You forgot to ask me," I said. "You said I was your date."

"Oh, I just thought . . ."

"I'll let you know," I said. "I hope you all had a great time."

I left him standing there, looking after me, and suddenly thought my grandfather would be very proud of that.

Later I'd realize that I was jumping to conclusions, conclusions that were not there yet.

But would be.

CHAPTER NINETEEN

Aunt Holly was waiting for me in the hallway. She raised her arms, her face full of disappointment, her eyes tearing.

"I couldn't get him to come out," she wailed. "I know that would have been a great move forward for us, for him," she said. "I tried and tried. I could feel how much he wanted to, but he wouldn't do it. He told me he would explain why not to you. The good thing is, it really bothered him that he had disappointed you."

"I'm sorry, Aunt Holly. I kept looking his way and even beckoned. He would appear and disappear."

"I know. Did you have a good time anyway?" she asked.

"I don't know. That sounds funny. I wanted it to be a good time. Grandfather won't like to hear it, but I had nicer friends in Colonie public school. I think finding a shy person at The Oaks will be harder than finding a pin in a stack of hay. My father called it 'dry grass.'"

She laughed. "Well, don't blame them for being self-absorbed. Once they get to really know you, they'll be different. It's always hard to be the new kid on the block."

"They don't live on a block. They live on a mountain," I said.

She laughed again and hugged me. "Linsey is here. That's for sure," she said.

"Yes, we both know that. In more ways than one."

She winced, lost her smile, and took a breath. "Let's fight one battle at a time. I'll pick you up about nine thirty. The stores we're going to open at ten. Okay?"

"Yes, thank you, Aunt Holly. I really do appreciate it, and I am very excited."

It was just then that the effects of the swimming, diving, and being in the sun hit me. I couldn't help a yawn. I was really tired. Aunt Holly could see it in the way my eyes closed and the lids fought to be opened.

"Go take a shower and relax, Caroline. I'll ask Clara Jean to make you something simple for dinner and have it brought up. You've had some pretty big emotional days. They catch up to you when you least expect it."

"Okay," I said. I couldn't resist even if I wanted to. "Thank you in advance for tomorrow."

"It'll be my pleasure."

She gave me a kiss, and I headed for the stairway. Thinking about what I had said, I realized it was funny in a way that I didn't prefer Dina's friends to the Oaks students. Dina's friends were wilder in an obvious way because of the drugs and drinking but somehow friendlier. I suspected that all of that prohibited activity was more subtle with my new friends.

Nevertheless, somehow I was thinking it was my fault for not being like any of them. I wasn't really like my friends in public school either. Everyone's life was looser, not filled with so many fears, perhaps.

Buried in the basement was Prissy, the girl who had suffered from progeria. She had never had a chance to be a child, much less a normal teenager or young adult. That was a genetic disorder. Scientists and doctors could see it and identify it. In a strange way, my genetics, my life, was causing me to suffer from a different form of progeria. I thought my mother, my father for his own reasons, and my grandfather had suffered the same fate.

For a very short time, my mother had escaped it. Maybe that was truly what my grandfather resented the most. Deep down, he was envious. All he had done to her was punish her for refusing to become what he and his father were. Now he was realizing it through me.

But it was more than just that. I could feel it. His wall of resistance was crumbling. Even if he wouldn't admit it now, I believed there was a way to be a Sutherland and free and happy. However, it was far from inevitable or even around the corner to reach that. There were still secrets to destroy. Right now, Grandfather was battling and suffering from what he considered his worst weakness, love.

And I had no idea how I could change that for him. It was better to think like Aunt Holly did: one battle at a time. Just getting up the stairs was challenging enough at the moment. I took a deep breath at the top, looked toward Simon's room, and headed for my own. I didn't even have the energy to wash my face and get out of the dry bathing suit. I just flopped onto my bed facedown, almost like a dive in the pool. In minutes, I was sure, I was asleep.

I had no idea how long I slept, nor did I know how long he was stroking my hair and gently kissing my shoulder. It was finally his breath on my neck that snapped my eyes open. Realizing Simon was beside me, I turned onto my back quickly and pushed a few inches away.

My second shock was the realization that he was completely naked. He didn't move, and for a moment I couldn't find my voice.

"What are you doing?" I cried. "You know you can't do this. Where are your clothes? We've talked about this. Get dressed, please. Simon!" I cried when he wouldn't stop his smiling.

"Simon!"

"Being cousins doesn't matter," he said. "I told you about all those cousins who married."

"It's not only that, Simon. I don't love you this way. It has to be different. You know that; you can't have forgotten it all."

The smile flew off his face. His eyes filled with that steely anger, his lips tightening with every muscle in his body. What was he going to do? If he started screaming and he was found here like this . . . Grandfather would somehow blame me. Mrs. Fisher would certainly help that along.

"You're not going to love that boy from the school, are you? He's not a good boy to love," he said through his clenched teeth.

"I just met them, Simon. I'm a long way from falling in love with someone from the school. Please, get dressed. How did you get out like that? Where's your nurse?"

He sat up.

"How long have you been here?" I said.

He pulled on his underwear and turned back to me, smiling. "A long time. I watched you dreaming, smiling and then looking sad and then smiling. I even whispered in your ear, but you didn't wake up."

"That's not nice, Simon. That's really spying on someone."

He shrugged. "Everyone spies on me," he said. "They even take notes on everything I say or do. If I belch, they'll tell the doctor. I might as well be in a store window."

"I'm sorry about all that, but where is your nurse?" I asked, sitting up and folding my arms. "She's supposed to be with you, and then another nurse at night."

"This one reads too much. I slipped a few of those sedatives they gave me into her drink. She never saw it. I watched her eyes closing. She put down the book and lay back, and not long after, she actually snored."

He started to lie down again, bracing his chin on his hand to stare at me.

"That's terrible, Simon. Maybe you'll get her fired."

He just stared, smiling.

"Why didn't you come out to the pool? You saw me beckoning."

"I didn't want to know those kids. I could see I wouldn't like them, and I thought if I came out, you would make me be polite."

"Of course you should be polite. You can't like everyone you meet, but you don't have to be nasty."

He looked away, glaring angrily at the wall.

"You used to help other kids with their tests and questions. You didn't have to like them, but you could be friendly."

"I don't care to remember any of that."

"What *do* you want to remember?"

He was silent.

"Simon, do you remember what you showed me in the basement? Those papers, those letters—what you said were letters?"

He started to say something, paused, and then turned to put on his pants. After he put on his shirt, he turned back to me.

"I haven't been down there in some time, Caroline. You have to forget those old memories. And don't trust those kids from The Oaks," he said, and started out.

"Simon?"

"I'll see you later," he said, and left.

For a moment, I thought I had dreamed it. Still tired, I leaned back. Maybe I should be happy he didn't recall the basement revelations. Maybe he was actually getting better. I fell asleep again and woke when Clara Jean brought me some dinner.

"Mrs. Fisher said for you not to worry about the dishes," she said. "If she doesn't send me for them, she'll get them."

"Thank you. Clara Jean . . ." I said when she reached for the door.

I had known Clara Jean even before I was brought here. She was one of the people who worked for Grandfather the longest. I knew she had begun working here after the man she was engaged to had been killed in Iraq. Mommy used to say that Clara Jean was so distraught, she had joined a nunnery called Sutherland.

"What does everyone think of Mrs. Fisher?" I asked her now.

She held the door slightly open, thought, and turned back. "We don't think of her, Caroline. Just like we didn't think of Mrs. Lawson. Everyone makes faces, but no one says anything to anyone. These walls have ears," she said, then touched the wall and walked out, closing the door softly.

I wondered if Grandfather knew how the people who worked for him thought of his housekeepers. More important, did he care? If they did their jobs, it didn't matter if they were happy or sad or even afraid.

I looked at the food, decided I was hungry, and ate my dinner. I read some more of *Harvey*, again imagining Hudson in the main role. He could probably do it well, I thought. He could probably do everything well, but I wasn't sure that made me like him more. Hours later, Clara Jean returned for the dishes. I was surprised Mrs. Fisher hadn't come. It was almost like she was suddenly avoiding me. This time, I was sure. I wasn't upset about it, just suspicious.

All these thoughts were washed away in seconds the next morning when Aunt Holly arrived to take me shopping for my room. I was having breakfast on the patio, earlier than usual. I hadn't seen Mrs. Fisher until she came out of the house and started toward me. She was wearing a darker blue dress with the hem down to her ankles. The smile on her face was odd; it was like someone had plastered it on. Her arms swung only slightly as she walked in my direction.

"Your aunt is waiting for you in your grandfather's office," she said.

"Is she?"

"They're discussing your budget. You didn't think you had carte blanche, did you? Your grandfather knows every nickel that's gone into Sutherland."

"Yes, my mother told me that once, and I hid a nickel in the mansion. Guess what? It's still there."

"Doesn't mean your grandfather doesn't know it is," she said with that soupy smile. "Your aunt expects you in ten minutes," she added, and returned to the house.

I finished what I wanted to eat quickly and hurried inside. Both my grandfather and my aunt were standing outside his office door.

"Ready?" Aunt Holly said with obvious excitement.

"Sure."

"That boy from The Oaks called this morning," Grandfather said.

"Boy? Hudson?"

"Yes. He wanted my permission to take you to the opening party. I said it was fine with me if he brought you home right after. Fine with you?"

"Yes, sir."

He nodded.

"In that case, we'll look for a special dress, too," Aunt Holly said.

"In good taste, I hope," Grandfather said.

"Oh, that's our first concern for everything," she said, smiling.

Grandfather smirked. "Well, I have a closing this morning, so . . . so you're on your own," he added, and went into his office.

"When aren't we, right?" Aunt Holly said. She threaded her arm through mine. "Let's have a great day," she said.

She was so much happier than usual. I decided it was the wrong time to talk about Simon's visit, what he had done and said. *Have fun*, I thought. *Whenever you have a chance to here at Sutherland, grab it.*

We left in her car and talked about color schemes and beds with matching tables, a new computer desk, but with some elegance and style. Aunt Holly had obviously done quite a bit of scouting. When we arrived at the stores, she knew just where to go to look at the bedroom furniture. She had the matching sheets and comforter, pillows, and side tables set aside as well. For everything we looked at, she had another option if I didn't like the first, but I loved just about everything she first showed me. I had never had a shopping experience like it. Her excitement buoyed my own. It was like she was buying it all for herself.

"I couldn't do it for Simon," she complained. "I was lucky I could do it for myself, with your uncle walking in your grandfather's footsteps, evaluating every choice I made as if the Sutherland empire could rise or fall on the choice of a lamp."

"I love the choices we made for the bedroom set and everything that goes with it," I said.

After placing that order, we went right to bureaus and a warm, light blue rug. The salesman showed us matching curtains. On the way out, we chose some accessories. When I saw the final bill, I was shocked at the number Grandfather had approved.

"He actually approved a bit more, but we've been nice to him," Aunt Holly said, laughing.

Afterward, we went to look for a party dress. Some of them she admitted were quite standouts. For this first time, I was more comfortable with something nice but not so loud. Truthfully, I wanted to disappear in the crowd and not be the subject of everyone's attention. I realized that was going to be hard, dating the president of the class, who appeared to be the most popular boy at the school. Even Mrs. Rich obviously favored him.

We ended up choosing a jewel-waisted, pleated black high-low dress. I was surprised myself that my size had gone up. She insisted on buying me a new bra and a set of panties.

"One more thing," she said. "It sort of matches your topaz ring."

She took off her white-gold blue-sapphire bracelet.

"Wear this with it. You can stand out that much. I'm sure the other girls will be outdoing you, if not wearing just as much. I'd like you to wear it. Makes me feel young again to know it's with you and at a party."

"Oh, thank you, Aunt Holly."

I put it on. Then I hugged her, and we left for lunch, during which she talked about some of her early dates with Uncle Martin when they were both what she described as "young and restless. And hopeful."

"We wanted so much for our own lives. As you should for yours," she said.

"I can't help but be afraid," I said.

"That's natural. Girls who are so in charge that they don't fear going out with someone for the first time are unusual. The worst that happens at this age is you part friends."

"Are you and Uncle Martin still friends, too?"

"Up and down, but right now we're being more honest with each other, and it's helping. We have Simon to think about more than we think about ourselves."

"I'm sorry."

I was about to tell her about Simon's latest visit when she asked for the check, and I thought again. Nothing Simon did seemed permanent right now. Who knew what he would say tomorrow or even who he would be? Why add worry? It managed to find its way into Sutherland no matter what we did. I wondered, was it ever a really happy place, glorious and as beautiful as strangers first thought of it?

As we headed back to Sutherland, Aunt Holly, maybe sensing my mood, talked about happier times there, like her wedding celebration, the births of her children, even my mother's wedding. I wondered, did you exaggerate happiness because you were so afraid of unhappiness, or was it all accurate? For a while, at least, brighter lights could have shone.

The moment we entered Sutherland, Mrs. Fisher came rushing

toward us. *Oh, no*, I thought, *something bad about Simon, something I could be blamed for.* She paused when she was closer and just walked up to us.

"Your grandfather has had a visitor," she said, "and he has remained to talk to you," she told me. "I've given him something cool to drink and set him down on the patio, facing the garden."

"Set him down? What is he, a dish?" Aunt Holly said.

Mrs. Fisher glared at her and then changed her expression. "I imagine I'm to expect deliveries."

"Yes, during the remainder of the week. I have a decorator who will arrange what we've bought. You merely have to politely show him the way."

"Is there any other way to show him?" she asked, smiling.

She started to turn away.

"Who is it? Is it my father?" I practically shouted at her.

"You have better manners than that, Caroline," she said, and kept walking away.

"Maybe it's better that it's a surprise," Aunt Holly said, shaking her head as she watched Mrs. Fisher continue down the hallway. "I'll go report to your grandfather as to how much of his money we've spent."

As she walked toward Grandfather's office, I started to the exit to the patio that revealed my mother's favorite garden. Maybe, if it was Daddy, he had come to take me back to wherever he had found a new home in Maui.

As I entered the patio, he stood up and turned to me.

It was Boston in his SEAL training uniform. By the smile on his face, I knew it wasn't bad news, but it was news.

CHAPTER TWENTY

"**B**oston! What are you doing here?" I asked as he moved quickly to embrace me.

He looked so different, so mature, filled out, not that I hadn't thought he was mature for his age when we had first met. But right now, it was as if I hadn't seen him for years. His rust-colored hair was even shorter than it had been, and although I knew it was just the impression he gave, he looked taller. He couldn't have had firmer posture than when he was living with my father, but somehow he did. His hazel eyes were gleaming as he stepped back.

"I never expected you to come from Hawaii and not go right back to your training," I said, not hiding the joy in my voice.

"Someone high up wanted a personal message delivered to your grandfather. He does have a lot of influence with senators—even the president, I imagine. Word got out about all he had done for us and my wish to thank him. I was given a sealed envelope and simply put on a different flight with a military flight connecting and actually waiting for me to take me back to training camp."

"How was Dina when you left?"

"Clearly getting better. She was complaining nonstop."

"I'm so sorry for her," I said.

"Believe me, when you see how other people suffered, she's lucky. One thing I've already learned in SEAL training is there is a resilience in us if we search hard enough to find it. Your father and my mother are setting the examples. I'm proud of them both. Your grandfather . . ."

"He's a confusing man, maybe deliberately," I said.

We sat, and I noted that he had held on to my hand until we did.

"Maybe. You were right about him. He looked uncomfortable being thanked profusely. He changed the subject quickly. How's he treating you?"

"I think we're finally getting to know each other," I said.

"Men as successful as he is are books with more pages," Boston said with that warm, twinkling smile. "My money's on you reading them clearly."

He looked at his watch.

"I was afraid I'd have to leave without seeing you," he said. "I'm in a world where being late is being dead on arrival."

We both laughed.

"I started reading about Navy SEALs. So many don't make it through the training, right?"

"We're given those statistics right away so no one has any illusions. SEALs are only about one percent of all active-duty members of the Navy. About twenty or twenty-five percent make it through the training.

"Every time the mere thought of giving up occurs, I see your father's face of disappointment and push on, and when I'm really desperate to get out of the darkness and the pain, I see you."

"Me?"

"Didn't realize until you had left how great the impression you made on me was. Despite all your history, the problems, you brought a kind of sweet brightness that wasn't there before. I kept thinking, 'She's suffered in so many ways and yet she still has that innocent, hopeful, hungry-for-happiness look.' I think that's what I envisioned."

I felt my heartbeat quicken at the way he was looking at me when he spoke. For a moment, I was speechless, but before I could say anything, we heard the scream.

It was Aunt Holly.

We both stood up as groundskeepers were rushing toward the house. On the west side, we could see smoke rising. I heard Aunt Holly scream again: "Simon!"

"That's my aunt Holly. My cousin . . ." I said, as if that explained everything.

We hurried into the house. Down the hallway, we could see the smoke coming through the basement door. Grandfather came out of his office quickly and stumbled, falling onto his side. Boston went to him and helped him back up. Uncle Martin joined Aunt Holly, who had her arms up, looking like she was reaching for something to pull her out of a hole.

"Your cousin?" Boston asked, returning to my side.

"Yes, Simon. He must have gone down to the basement secretly. He has a nurse with him, but he knows how to get away. He must have done something to cause a fire and be still down there."

The smoke was thickening. Everyone was shouting for us all to get out of the house. Mrs. Fisher was going from room to room, ordering others to hurry out. Uncle Martin was at Grandfather's side, steadying him. Suddenly, Boston rushed forward to the basement door. I screamed after him, but in seconds, he was in and charging down the stairs.

"OUT! OUT!" Grandfather screamed at me.

Aunt Holly took my hand and practically pulled me toward the main entrance. Emerson was there, guiding everyone else. He then assisted Grandfather.

"Boston!" I yelled at him. "He went down to the basement!"

Grandfather looked in that direction, shook his head, and went out. Aunt Holly and I followed. We could hear the sirens of the fire trucks. Groundskeepers had hoses on. The billowing smoke blackened. Emerson kept moving us all farther from the house. Aunt Holly kept her arm around me. I saw Mrs. Fisher emerge and join Grandfather and Uncle Martin.

Just as the fire trucks arrived, Boston came out of the house with Simon over his shoulder. Aunt Holly rushed to him as he lowered Simon to the ground. He was obviously unconscious.

"Smoke inhalation," I heard Boston say.

Paramedics leaped off the fire truck and ran to them. We all stood back to watch them work to revive Simon. An ambulance arrived while they were working on him. Aunt Holly and Uncle Martin stood back to watch, holding hands.

I turned to Boston. "Was he on the stairway, trying to get out?"

"No. He was lying right beside one of the fires he started," he said. "I saw the pack of matches. The smoke from the other fires must have overwhelmed him. I think they'll contain it. Just a few small fires, but one or two had some oil or something with grease in it."

"Family heirlooms, old papers, clothes," I rattled off. "Simon liked to explore it."

"Yes, your grandfather told me about some of it."

"Why?"

"We were talking about when you lived with your mother and father. He was thinking of getting your father back some of his things I guess he had left behind. They're in the basement. He likes your father."

"I know," I said. It sounded like I was unhappy about it.

When Simon regained consciousness, there was some cheering. He looked totally confused, frightened. Aunt Holly and Uncle Martin joined the paramedics as Simon was placed on a stretcher. Grandfather and Emerson, who had been with the groundskeepers and firemen, came over to us.

"They've got it contained," Emerson said, looking toward the paramedics carrying Simon to the ambulance. "It's great that you got to him in time," he told Boston.

"We'll have to work on the house inside to rid it of the odor," Grandfather said, looking mostly at me. "When I tell you that you can go in, go up to your room and open the windows."

Mrs. Fisher was standing right behind him.

"Oh, I'll go in and get it aired out, Mr. Sutherland. No worries," she said.

He nodded. We all watched them place Simon in the ambulance.

"I guess your aunt was right. He should have been brought back to the clinic," Grandfather said, mostly, I thought, to himself.

He turned sharply when we heard people driving up to see the fire from outside the main gate. A small crowd was forming. Someone beeped his horn. People stepped out of their cars with their cell phones pointing at all the activity, the fire trucks, and the ambulance.

"Emerson, do what you can to make this less of a carnival."

"Yes, sir," Emerson said.

Grandfather turned to Boston and put his hand on his shoulder. "I'll make sure your commanding officer knows what you did here, Boston, and don't worry about being late for your flight."

"Thank you, Mr. Sutherland," Boston said.

They shook hands.

Grandfather looked at me and then walked toward the firemen again.

"I can't believe you did that, Boston, charged down a smoke-filled stairway, not knowing how bad it was."

"If you think too much about it, you won't do it," he said, and looked at his watch. "I'd better get going. With your grandfather's help or not, they might make me do a little more than everyone else just to prove I'm not some well-connected recruit. The SEALs don't want anyone getting special treatment. We're all part of the one fist.

"I'll try to get back to see you in six months or so, but I want you to enjoy your new school and friends. Your social life is an important part of your schooling."

I was hoping he would kiss me before he turned away to leave. Maybe he would have, but Aunt Holly and Uncle Martin grabbed him to thank him. Clara Jean joined them. Others started to come toward him. I saw how embarrassed he was at all the attention.

He glanced at me a few times, smiled, shook Uncle Martin's hand, hugged Aunt Holly, and started for the car that Grandfather had arranged to take him to his flight.

The ambulance pulled away first, its siren blaring as it headed toward the gate. Aunt Holly and Uncle Martin got into the limousine, and Emerson drove them off to follow it. For a few moments, I stood there, confused, tears mixing with a feeling of amazement. This wasn't the first time I had thought about the fact that our lives could change in moments.

I watched Grandfather shouting orders at groundskeepers and conferring with some firemen. Although he had first stumbled and lost control of himself, he now looked like he was once again in charge of everything and everyone.

Unaware that Mrs. Fisher had returned and was right behind me, I nearly screamed when she spoke inches from my ear.

"You don't want to have new furniture and such brought into this house until it's free of the smoke stench," she said.

I turned to look at her.

"Don't worry. I'll make sure your aunt postpones it all."

"I wasn't thinking of that," I said.

"Of course not, dear. That's why I'm here: to think of what others do not."

She whipped out a smile and walked back to the front entrance. I now understood what people meant when they said he or she or this or that made their blood boil.

Rather than stand there waiting for the green light to go inside, I walked around the other side of the mansion toward the pool and sat on a lounge. The world around me seemed to be spinning. I lay back and closed my eyes. I saw two images. The first was Grandfather's face when he had fallen. I had never seen so deep a fear in him. Sutherland could have been lost. His life would have gone up in smoke, too.

He was thinking of that, I felt sure, rather than of Simon, although I did see a look of relief when Boston rescued him.

And then I saw Boston smiling at me and on the verge of saying something he didn't think he would say. I was hoping those words would return before he had left. They didn't. They lingered in the air, or maybe in my imagination. I remembered Mommy telling me that if you wanted something enough, you'd believe it had happened.

The only danger was, you might be the only one believing it.

Later, when everyone was leaving, the fire trucks driving off, I wondered if any of them had seen Prissy's grave while they were down there. Of course, I knew it wouldn't matter. No one would say anything. And once again I thought about how you might find yourself to be the only one believing in what you saw anyway.

What was lonelier than that?

When we were given the all clear to return to the house, I learned that Simon was in the hospital but would be transferred back to the clinic. Aunt Holly called my mobile and rattled off the details. She then ended by telling me that Mrs. Fisher had spoken to her about the new furniture and other things for my room.

"I hate to say it, but she's right."

"That's the worst thing about her, Aunt Holly."

"What?"

"That she's always right."

She laughed with relief. I couldn't see her, but I was sure it was a laugh with tears streaming down her cheeks.

Grandfather ordered a buffet to be served for dinner and invited the groundskeepers as well as the maids, along with Emerson, of course, and Franklin Butler. Aunt Holly and Uncle Martin remained at the hospital until they could feel confident of Simon's recuperation from the smoke inhalation.

When my mobile rang, I was hoping it was Boston, but it was Hudson.

"Tell me all about it," he said. "Were you in any danger?"

When haven't I been? I thought.

"No."

"And your cousin did it?"

"Grandfather doesn't like us talking about it," I said. I couldn't say anything stronger to shut him down.

"Sure. Well, I'll visit you in a few days. My parents plotted a trip I didn't know about."

"Okay," I said. "Have fun."

"I doubt I will. They always go to these ritzy, stuffy, elegant hotels, but I have to be a grateful son."

"Have to be?"

"Checking all the boxes," he said.

I wanted to scream how lucky he was to have parents, to feel he was part of a family and not living in a house where there was a Cemetery of Memories. But I said nothing. I listened to him talk about the

Oaks party and all the responsibilities he had as senior class president, making them sound like great burdens.

"You could always resign," I said.

He laughed. "Mrs. Rich would kill me."

"I don't doubt it."

He laughed again. For someone competing for class valedictorian, he seemed unable to pick up my sarcasm.

I told him my grandfather was beckoning to me.

"Sure. Go. I'll call you from the elegant, snotty hotel and tell you how I'm suffering."

"Thank you," I said.

Before he could respond, I hung up and went to sit at the table where my grandfather was, looking like someone celebrating the most important rescue, that of Sutherland.

His eyes went to me. There was a twinkle of appreciation in them.

Why? I wondered. What had I done?

And then it came to me. Boston hadn't come here mainly to thank Grandfather for all he did and was doing for Dina.

He had come here to see me.

What did that mean? Would it mean anything?

Suddenly, my wanting to get older returned. And all the hesitation and resistance, along with the worry, went up with the smoke that had been caught in the wind and thinned out to nothing.

"Tomorrow" was a hopeful word.

I hoped I was right.

CHAPTER TWENTY-ONE

All my new furniture arrived the day before the Oaks party. I was so excited watching it being installed that I didn't realize Grandfather had come up to see my new room decor. He was standing just to my right. This was the first time since I had been here that he had come up. I waited for him to say something, but all he did was nod a few times before he turned and headed back to the stairway. Aunt Holly was in my room, directing the movers. She hadn't seen him. When I told her, she said, "A nod is about as close to a stamp of approval as you will get from him. Your mother said she could count on the fingers of one hand how many times he had come to her room when she was a teenager.

"Maybe he's just old-fashioned that way. Fathers from his generation especially are uncomfortable, even though it's his own daughter's room. Their masculinity is very fragile. Seeing a pair of their daughter's panties or a bra will make them tremble.

"Perhaps it's not only his generation," she continued after thinking a moment. "Most fathers I know are shocked to learn that their daughters have had their first periods. I suppose we can't blame them for wanting to hold on to their little girls longer.

"My mother told me my father paced about most of the night after I had experienced my first period and when I went out on my first date after that. Fathers don't worry like that about their sons on first dates. Except, of course, when it comes to getting their car dented." She laughed.

"Did Simon ever have a first date?" I asked.

"Sort of. It was more like an arranged date, and when he came home that night, he reviewed it like a date critic. Kind of telling your uncle and me not to try it again."

She paused, looking sad for a moment, and then smiled.

"And here you are, going on your first official date tomorrow night. It's exciting, right?"

"Yes," I said.

She tilted her head. "You sound more frightened than excited. You have nothing to worry about, Caroline. You're a bright, attractive young lady.

"And we both know what will be tolerated and what will not be at The Oaks," she added. "So no one should embarrass you. Hudson knows that better than any other student."

"I know," I said.

"Let's finish with your room."

"What will happen with Simon, Aunt Holly?"

"That's another 'wait and see,' honey. No sense in your worrying about it. I'll keep you updated on the progress."

"Okay," I said.

I knew I had to lock away a number of things and do what dreadful Mrs. Fisher had said about concentrating on the here and now.

Later, I did put on my party dress and work on how I wanted to do my hair. My mind returned to my memories of Mommy preparing for a party or for a dinner. I even recalled how she and Nattie would do their makeup and hair together. Remembering those moments made the silence in my room that much louder.

Hudson came for me in his father's car the following day. Aunt Holly had called to tell me she was still at the clinic, getting feedback from Simon's doctor's there. Uncle Martin and Grandfather were at the city office, reviewing some business venture that involved the city building department. When I came down to be picked up, Mrs. Fisher was waiting at the bottom of the stairs.

"Your grandfather asked me to check you out and send you off," she said.

She stood back with her arms folded and looked at me. Then she stepped forward and reached out to push at my hair. I jerked away.

"You just have a rebellious strand," she said.

"I'm fine."

"You young people today," she said, shaking her head. "So stubborn, a little arrogant, too. Don't think everyone older than you is a threat to your independence. You should rather appreciate our sharing of hard-earned wisdom."

A loose strand of hair is wisdom? I thought. Simon would have a field day with her. Strangely, maybe, I missed his biting sarcasm. In a way, it had become our secret language.

Mrs. Fisher kept talking, following me to the main entrance.

"I wish I had listened more to my parents. And less to my husband," she said.

I didn't turn around.

"I'm simply trying to give you valuable cautions. Young men are experimenting all the time. I tried to get my daughter to realize that, but . . ."

Thankfully, the door buzzer sounded. I practically lunged forward, opened it, and saw Hudson standing there with a rose. He was wearing a dark blue sports jacket with a lighter blue tie. He did look handsome.

As I walked toward him, Mrs. Fisher called out, "Be careful with your driving, young man."

"You look great," he said, both of us ignoring her.

"Thank you. So do you."

He handed me the rose. "Senior class presidents' dates always carry a rose into the Oaks opening party."

I took it, but after what he said, it didn't feel the same as I was sure it would have if he had just thought to give it to me and not made it a traditional thing.

Of course, he had his father's car. He opened the door for me.

"It smells new," I said after he got in.

"Actually, it's only ten weeks old."

He looked into the rearview mirror and then started out.

"I thought I would smell the fire still, but I didn't."

"Grandfather has already had that part of the house repaired."

"Probably an hour later," he said, smiling.

"Not quite."

All the way to The Oaks, he talked about how many new students there were besides the incoming class and how many tours he had done. Listening to him go on and on about himself was actually good, I thought. It kept him from asking me too many personal questions. It was like that old joke Nattie would use: "I'll stop talking. Let's talk about you. What do you think of me?"

Remembering it, I just broke into a laugh.

"Huh?" he said. "What's so funny?"

"Nothing."

He gave me an odd look, turned into the school parking lot, and then parked the car without saying anything until he had.

"Okay," he said. "Don't worry. I know you're nervous, but everyone will be coming up to us. I'll do introductions."

He took a paper out of his pocket and unfolded it.

"You should talk about the following things: going to school in Colonie, Sutherland, the property, and you can say your parents had divorced. There are a number of students here who come from families with divorced parents, all but one living with their mothers. Of course, talk about your favorite subjects, music, movies, whatever."

"Who gave you that list?" I asked.

"Mrs. Rich. I have the agenda, the things Mrs. Rich wants said before the party starts. Every senior class president does that. She believes it makes more of an impression if one of the students describes a new rule or a change to a rule, whatever."

"So you have an agenda?"

"Yeah, you know, when I start the party with my introductory speech. I hope I beat Paula and make the valedictorian speech. It will be like bookends . . . start of the school year and then the end."

We got out, but he stopped as we started toward the building.

"You forgot your rose," he said.

"I did."

He looked annoyed for a moment and then hurried back to the car to get it. I watched other students being brought by parents and some driving here themselves. Somehow, even though all the students were dressed for it, after hearing him go on about it, it didn't look as much like a party as it did a meeting. There wasn't any music on when we entered what had been converted from a cafeteria to a party scene. There were decorations, balloons, and tables with party favors on them, but I didn't feel the festive atmosphere I had been anticipating. Other students who had arrived before us were milling about, talking, many excited to see friends. At least they had that, I thought.

Hudson took my hand and directed me to the right where Mrs. Rich was holding court. Four men and two women surrounded her. As we approached, they all stopped talking to look at us.

"Good evening, Mrs. Rich," Hudson said.

She sat back in her chair. She wore a navy beaded mesh dress but no more makeup than and no change of her hair from when I had first met her.

"Well, you both look very appropriate," she said.

She then introduced her husband, a stout man who looked quite a bit older with his balding head and deep-lined face. His smile was very tight and short.

"How is your grandfather?" he asked me, checking with Mrs. Rich instantly as if he had to be sure that was appropriate.

"He's fine, thank you," I said.

Mrs. Rich then introduced the faculty members, placing obvious emphasis on Mr. Kaplan, a tall, lean man with bushy dark brown eyebrows. He nodded at me.

"You'd better get ready to start the festivities," Mrs. Rich told Hudson.

"Yes, ma'am," he said, and turned me toward a small stage that looked like it could be instantly put together and taken apart.

"We have the front table," he said. He pulled out my chair, took the rose from me, and placed it on the table. Mark, Russel, and Paula quickly joined our table with their dates. Everyone was introduced.

Suddenly Mrs. Rich announced, "Everyone be seated."

I watched the students hurry to their tables. Hudson rose, winked at me, and stepped onto the makeshift stage. I heard what sounded like someone tapping a spoon on a microphone, and the place grew silent.

Hudson took out a paper from his inside jacket pocket, unfolded it, and began by welcoming everyone, especially the new students. He nodded at me. He then read the updated rules, describing in detail what articles of clothing were now not permitted. He emphasized that cell phones, mobiles, whatever anyone wanted to call them, were not to be on in classrooms or hallways. Certain bathrooms were designated phone-accessible. Someone groaned, and Hudson paused. From what

I could see, no one, not even the teachers, breathed. Whoever it was, I thought, must have the quickest heartbeat in the room. After a few more seconds, Hudson continued.

He described how the opening party would go, when the buffet would be out, and when everyone should prepare to go home. He thanked Mrs. Rich and the faculty and then, like some gatekeeper, raised his hand, and the music started again. Everyone applauded, and he stepped off the stage and reached for my hand.

"First dance," he said, "always starts when the senior class president starts."

It was a slow dance, and for a good thirty or forty seconds, no one joined us. Then his friends and their dates rose, and others, mostly the older students, began to dance.

"So how'd I do?" he asked.

"Very nicely."

"Think I could become a politician?"

I pulled back so he could look right in my eyes. "I think you already are," I said.

He looked surprised, and then he laughed.

We danced only twice more because Hudson spent so much time talking to other students and introducing me. I knew the names and faces wouldn't connect for days. Other boys asked me to dance, and Hudson told them it was fine.

"Maybe I should decide that," I said.

The girls who heard me clapped, Paula the loudest. Hudson just shrugged.

I did decide to dance with a few other boys. One was a fast dance, and while I was doing it, my mind turned back to the memories of my mother and me dancing, especially to "Sweet Caroline." It didn't make me sad. I was sure I moved even better to the rhythms, which encouraged other boys to ask.

Finally, Hudson noticed and cut in.

"Looks like you'll fit into this place just fine," he said, sounding angry.

I stopped dancing. "I need a rest," I said.

"No wonder."

We returned to the table, where Paula and I had a nice enough conversation about things we liked to cause me to believe that whatever test I was taking, I had passed.

When it came time to leave, Hudson made sure that we said good night to Mrs. Rich. She had apparently been watching me most of the night.

"I'm glad you had a good time, Caroline. I hope it bodes well for the upcoming school year."

She simply nodded at Hudson. I saw his face sink a little. He was anticipating compliments.

"I hope I didn't disappoint you, Mrs. Rich," he said, fishing for them.

"You lived up to expectations," she said.

Her husband turned from his conversation with Mr. Kaplan to say good night to us.

I could tell from the way Hudson walked out to the parking lot that he wasn't as happy as he had anticipated he would be. For the first time since I had met him, I felt sorry for him. I knew if I said anything remotely like that, he would practically break out in tears.

"I hope you had a good time," he said as we drove out.

"Mrs. Rich told me I did. Isn't that the same thing?"

He looked at me as if I was some alien from outer space and then smiled to himself.

"You're a Sutherland," he said. "No doubt about that."

I was far from ready to claim that and still had good reason to wonder if I ever would.

What happened next would put that question in bold capital letters.

CHAPTER TWENTY-TWO

Hudson leaned over to kiss me when we reached Sutherland. I turned my head slightly, and his kiss, meant to be on the lips, grazed my cheek. He sat back. He didn't look that disappointed, nor did he look like he was going to make another attempt at a real good-night kiss.

"I'm going to go meet Russel and Mark," he said. "We always do an after-party review before we head home. It would be too late for you, and I don't want your grandfather coming after me."

I handed him the rose.

"You're supposed to keep that," he said. "Press it into a book or something."

"It's okay. I've already pressed it into my memory," I said, and left it on the top of the dashboard as I got out of his father's car. "You can tell Russel and Mark that I enjoyed some of the party."

I closed the door before he could speak and headed for the atrium and the main entrance. I wasn't tired, but my disappointment in so much of the evening put me a little in a daze. When I stepped into the atrium, I didn't close the door behind me all the way. But I didn't notice until I heard Emerson talking.

I turned around, took a few steps back, and peered through the partially opened atrium door, just in time to see him take out a small fold of dollars and hand them to Hudson.

"Thanks," Hudson said. "That was an easy night's work for this."

"Lovely. You can leave," Emerson said, stepping back. "Immediately."

"Whatever," Hudson said, rolled up his window, and drove out.

Emerson stood there watching him go. When he turned around, he saw me standing there staring at him.

"I thought you had gone in," he said, his voice heavy with guilt.

"You paid him to take me to the Oaks opening party?"

"Not me, as such. I'm sure he would have been happy to have you as his date, but you know your grandfather. He likes to guarantee that a deal will be resolved the way he wants it to. He's used to that. He was only trying to ensure that you would have a successful evening at the school.

"He's not going to be happy with me, happy that you saw this, Caroline. I mean, it is my fault. I should have been sure you were definitely inside first, and . . ."

"Don't worry about that, Emerson. I won't say anything to Grandfather, but I'm confident that Hudson will reveal what you did, at least to his so-called best friends, despite all the promises of being discreet at The Oaks. His ego will overcome any rules or expectations for students. As far as Hudson goes, if anything, you convinced me to put my attention and energy elsewhere at The Oaks.

"Good night, Emerson."

"He's a fool indeed for making a big mistake with his priorities. He took silver instead of waiting for gold."

"Somehow I think my grandfather will know that without us telling him. He's always testing people."

"Aye, that he does. Did you otherwise have a good time?"

"Now that I think about it, whenever he and I were apart."

Emerson laughed. "Okay, Lady Caroline. Sleep well."

I stepped back and closed the door. I wasn't surprised to see Mrs. Fisher seated in the entryway chair, waiting for me. She rose quickly. I wondered if she had eavesdropped and heard my conversation with Emerson. If she had, she was sly enough to keep it hidden.

"How was your evening?"

"More than I expected. Tiring," I said, walking quickly past her.

Although she said nothing more, she followed me to the stairway. I didn't look back. Before I reached the top, she called out.

"Nevertheless, I hope it gives you sweet dreams."

I didn't respond; I pretended I hadn't heard her and walked quickly to my room. I couldn't help thinking about her, however. Somehow my grandfather, who was so renowned and powerful, so successful, and insightful enough to instantly recognize the strengths and weaknesses of his competitors, had been blinded by this woman. It wasn't enough to say he was comfortable with her because of her loyalty and past service. Grandfather could instantly recognize false compliments and deception. He had all sorts of antennas and sirens at his disposal. There was something I was missing, something that was perhaps beyond my insight or abilities to see and understand.

When I got to my room, I was so exhausted from the tension at the party, the dancing, and then the discovery I had made just outside the front of Sutherland, I simply fell face forward on my bed and folded my arms under my head. I knew I shouldn't just close my eyes, but I did. Hours later, just before dawn, I awoke and realized I still had on my dress.

Groggily, I rose, took off my clothes, brushed my teeth, and went back to bed. Late in the morning, I heard a knock on my door, groaned, and sat up as Aunt Holly entered.

"Hey," she said. "Are you all right? Mrs. Fisher told me you were still sleeping."

I ground the sleep out of my eyes and straightened up to look and sound more awake.

"I'm okay," I said.

She studied me a moment and then sat at the foot of the bed. "Tell me about your evening, your date. Was he unpleasant to you, anything like that?"

"No, he was a proper gentleman. If anything, he was enjoying the extra attention he received from Mrs. Rich for bringing me as his date."

"Oh. Well, that doesn't sound as terrible as I feared."

"No. There's more," I said. "But you can't tell Grandfather that I know. I promised Emerson."

"What goes on between you and me will always be our secret," she said.

I was happy about that, but it did seem like new secrets were born here daily.

I told her what I had seen and heard soon after Hudson had brought me home.

"I'm not surprised at your grandfather. You know all he did behind the scenes when it came to your mother and father."

"Yes, I thought of that."

"If we want to be generous, we can say that he wanted things to be good for your mother and wants that for you."

"Or?"

"He is simply a control freak."

We both laughed.

"I suppose he could be both," she said. She rose. "What are you going to tell him when he asks you about your night?"

I thought a moment. "I'll tell him what my father used to say, sometimes annoying my mother."

"Which was?"

"The jury is still out."

"You know, I think I've heard your grandfather say that."

We both laughed again. She left, and I rose to shower and dress. Clara Jean made me a late breakfast, and I went out to the pool lounge to read some of my Introduction to Business text. Maybe there was something genetic about it, but my interest in that world had grown. Later Grandfather did ask me about the party, and I gave him my father's answer. It brought a tight smile to his face, and we didn't talk about it again.

I wasn't expecting Hudson to call me before school had begun. I wasn't disappointed at all that he didn't. What surprised me was that one of his so-called best friends, Russel Collins, called to ask me on a date. I knew what my stepsister, Dina, would think. I was actually grateful for the social education she had laid on me in one of her many rants about boys. "If a good friend of a boy you've been out with calls you for a date, it's probably because the boy you were out with made up things to make himself look better." She had put it in language quite a bit nastier. Whatever, it rang warning bells in my ears.

"Thank you," I told Russel, "but I have too many things to do for school preparation and other things I have to do at Sutherland."

"Oh. Well, maybe later," he said.

"Maybe," I said without a single note of hope. It made me think even more vividly of the things Hudson surely had exaggerated about me. What I might do, I thought, was drop hints about it at Grandfather's feet.

There I go again, I concluded, *thinking more like a Sutherland*.

When school began and I started to develop closer girlfriends, especially Paula, I learned that most had similar opinions of Hudson and his buddies. I didn't try out for a part in *Harvey*, not because of Hudson getting the lead but because I was simply too into my classes and reading. I invited a few of these girlfriends to Sutherland, with Grandfather's permission, of course. Somehow I managed to keep the sadder events in my life not so much hidden as avoided. And true to Mrs. Rich's prediction, other students didn't pursue me with shocking questions or comments. There were lots of questions about Sutherland, suggesting that an invitation to visit was as significant as an invitation to the White House.

Even though I had been afraid I would hate attending The Oaks, I did manage to navigate among my classmates to find those who didn't have the arrogance most others did. I enjoyed my teachers, and occasionally, when he asked about the school, I told Grandfather things he was pleased to hear.

I received emails and texts from my father describing what they were rebuilding and how Dina was coming along. When we spoke, our conversations, although short, were warmer. I didn't ask him about Boston, and he didn't tell me anything new.

And then, one night after dinner, Boston called me. I was so happy to hear from him that my fingers trembled holding the phone. I knew I babbled when he asked me about The Oaks and the other students. I told him about some dates and parties, but I didn't suggest that anybody had made a significant impression on me. He didn't specifically ask about that, either.

He didn't tell me much about his training. What did excite me was his saying he hoped he would have a sufficiently long leave before he was assigned a base or even deployed somewhere. He didn't go so far as to say he hoped this so that he could visit Sutherland, and I felt too guilty to ask him to do so. Of course, I thought, he should first think about his parents and Dina.

What he did say at the end was that he missed everyone, and then he added, "Especially you."

For a few seconds, I was speechless, and then I said, "I miss you, too."

"I'm glad of that," he said.

"Do you still think of me when you're facing a difficult challenge?"

"Sure do," he said.

"I often think about the short time we spent together. And of course, what you did for Simon!"

"I probably did it more for you."

"You did it for me?"

"To impress you. Even more than impressing your grandfather."

"You'd better never risk your life to impress me again," I said.

He laughed. "Now you're really talking about a challenge."

Once again, I was speechless for a few moments.

"Hey, I've got to go," he said. "Wonderful talking to you."

"You too. Stay safe."

"It's good to have more reasons to," he said. "Bye, Caroline."

"Bye," I said.

Despite the thrill and excitement I had talking to him, I felt a deep sadness and a deeper emptiness when we said goodbye. Maybe it was simply because of all the tragic things I had experienced, but I had the fear that I might never hear from him or see him again. The gloom that came over me seemed to wash away the moments of happiness and hope that new friends and challenges had brought. I felt thrown back so far. I didn't get much chance to think about it, however.

Mrs. Fisher, who had been avoiding me, seemed to swoop in moments after my phone conversation with Boston. It was as if she was tuned in to my every feeling. Surely she had been listening in the doorway.

"It's not proper for you to have so intimate a conversation with your stepbrother," she said. "He's old enough to know better, too. If your grandfather finds out about this, he'll forbid him to ever come here. All of you young people misuse the phones. Secret calls, secret text things. You spend far too much time on it."

"Don't tell me whom I can talk to and whom I can't. You were eavesdropping. That's very sneaky. I'll tell my grandfather that."

She stared at me in an odd, harassed way for a few moments. It was like a shadow had come over her.

And then she smiled. "Well, you use 'who' and 'whom' correctly. Most Americans don't. We say you don't speak English; you speak American."

She cackled, turned, and left. I could feel the blood rising through my neck to my cheeks. No wonder her daughter ran off, I thought. I bet it was mostly her fault and not her husband's at all.

And then I thought, *Maybe she made it all up. Maybe she never had a daughter. Maybe that would be more frightening than anything.*

I considered it and then called Paula.

"Hey," I said. "Could you do me a favor and look someone up on the internet? I don't want to be caught doing it."

"How could you be caught doing that?" she asked.

"Let's just say the walls at Sutherland have ears. Everywhere."

"Oh. Look up who?"

"Whom," I said, laughing to myself. Hudson would love my correcting her. "Her name is Claudia Fisher. She's from London."

"Your housekeeper?"

"Yes."

"She looked kind of scary. What specifically do you want to know about her?"

"If she had a daughter," I said.

"Someone would have had to make love to her with the lights off," she said.

We both laughed.

"What else do you know about her? There could be a hundred with that name and around that age."

"Her husband's name was Arden Fisher."

"Okay. I'll call you when I find anything."

"Thanks. Don't tell anyone, please," I said.

"Of course, but don't you know a secret can be kept between two people if one dies?"

"Seriously."

"Okay. Stay tuned," she said.

I didn't know why, but I suddenly had the need to walk through the mansion, looking at everything like someone who was seeing it for the first time. Everything we had seen in our lives, although it never really changed, seemed to be different when we looked at it again over time. My mother used to say that although most of Sutherland remained as it had been for decades and decades, it sometimes looked smaller to her, "as if the walls had inched closer to each other. Of course, it's probably that your feelings have changed, and your feelings will always determine how you see things."

Strolling through Sutherland, I could hear Mommy's voice so clearly. It drew me to the secret bedroom where I knew her urn remained. Would it be crazy to think she was speaking to me? Would I tell that to Grandfather someday? Was that really what had happened to him and why he'd had Mrs. Fisher place it in there? I doubted that he would ever admit it. But maybe I could tell from looking at him.

Sometimes when Daddy would get angry at Mommy for saying things about her father or her life at Sutherland, she would say, "You can't lock up your thoughts, Morgan. Not even you can do that."

Now, as I walked about the mansion and recalled how I would run through it as a little girl when we did visit, it did look so much different, and not because of the ugly things that had happened in it. It was just . . . different.

When I heard footsteps in the other direction, I started back. I saw Uncle Martin talking to someone in a business suit in the entryway. They shook hands, and the man left. Uncle Martin started back to Grandfather's office and paused when he saw me.

"How are you doing, Caroline? I heard you were having a good start at the school."

"Yes, thank you, Uncle Martin. Did you like it there?"

"For the most part. I've never really remained friends with my classmates. I mean, I see them here and there, but . . . thank goodness for your aunt," he said. He started on and paused again. "Be careful who you choose to spend your life with," he warned.

"My mother wasn't that careful, was she?"

"Whatever regrets she had, you made them go away. I'm sure of that," he said, smiling. Then he looked at Grandfather's door as if he was afraid he was listening and continued on.

I thought about what he had said. All the happiness I had felt when I was young, the happiness I thought we enjoyed as a family . . . was it all because they had me and had to be that way? Was that the way it was for so many married people? How foolish it was for young people my age to think they knew everything they had to know about the people they loved, the people closest to them. Yes, Mommy was right. Things, places, were different to you when you grew older, but so were people you knew.

As if she could hear me thinking, Paula called.

"Hey," I said. "That was quick."

"It's not as hard as people think. So, yes, she has a daughter. Her husband died about five years ago. Her daughter lives in London, too, but in Mayfair, a far more expensive place. Mrs. Fisher still has their old home in Newham. I can print out a lot more detail if you want. Things like where she worked, relatives, how much her net worth is . . ."

"No, that's fine. Thanks."

"Well, does any of that mean anything?"

"It's enough. Thanks again."

"Well, nothing sounds exciting to me."

"I just wanted to know more about her. Thanks."

"Okay. See you tomorrow."

She hung up.

I held my phone near my ear and thought. Did Grandfather know she had lied about her daughter? Would it even matter to him? If it was so easy to know the truth, why did she make up that story?

Instinctively, I knew that someone who lied to herself was worse than someone who lied to others. But how much worse?

Why did Mrs. Fisher really come here?

CHAPTER TWENTY-THREE

The weight of secrets at Sutherland will eventually topple it or overcome us all, I thought. Paula was constantly after me to tell her more. She was a very smart person. In fact, I was confident she would beat out Hudson for valedictorian. After a while, she gave up, and we talked about other things. She clearly saw my relief.

Hudson's other male best friend, Mark Cantor, asked me out twice, and when I refused him the third time, he said, "Maybe you just don't like boys. Figures."

One of Mrs. Rich's Rich-lings must have overheard him. Next thing we all heard was he was pulled into her office with his parents and put on what was called "a very thin probation." Over the next few weeks, I could see how terrified he was of even looking in my direction. Gradually, most of the boys in my class and the senior class were, but that didn't bother me at all. My romantic interests and dreams had gone elsewhere.

Paula was amused by it. "Rejection wasn't even in their vocabulary until now."

Back at Sutherland, things were quiet, except I saw the way Mrs. Fisher would look at me when she thought I wasn't aware of it. There was an underlying anger that she took out on other employees. I found it easier and easier to ignore her, which only made her more upset.

Boston called me again. We had an even more intimate conversation. I was outside at the time, just walking the grounds, so I felt confident Mrs. Fisher heard none of it. By now, he felt self-assured of his Navy SEAL training. In fact, the next conversation I had with Daddy was almost all about Boston and how proud of him he was. Daddy concluded by describing a town house he and Parker had bought in Wailea, Hawaii, which was still on the island of Maui. He then surprised me by almost offhandedly saying, "This is a good place for you to spend some of the summer."

He didn't talk much at all about Dina. In fact, neither Boston nor he did, which put me into very dark and troubled thoughts.

What buoyed me most during these months was Grandfather's interest in my schoolwork, especially my interest in business issues. He surprised me one day by asking me, in a voice that sounded more like his telling me, to attend a meeting he and Franklin Butler were having with a major investor in one of his strip-mall projects. I could see that the investor, an elderly man with the beadiest eyes I'd ever seen, was quite curious about my presence during the conversations about his net worth and other investments. My grandfather simply said, "My granddaughter, another member of the Sutherland family."

Afterward, I apparently surprised both Grandfather and Franklin Butler with my detailed questions about the corporate laws and the use of banking funding. I had already learned about priority lines of credit and collateral. The truth was, when I went up to my room afterward, my mind was spinning with all the details. I couldn't help but have

even more respect for Grandfather, who could handle so many different businesses and corporate concerns almost all by himself.

But like always, whenever I felt something good about him, I felt
guilt. It was like I was slipping away from Mommy, and I hated even
the thought. That night, though, my troubled feelings were whisked
away when my phone rang. I thought it was Daddy again because it
had a Hawaiian area code.

"How's my lucky, creepy, rich stepsister?" Dina asked. "You gloating?"

"Oh, God, no, Dina. I think about you a lot, but it's all worry.
Well, not all. Sometimes I am thankful for things you taught me. In a
nasty way, maybe, but still valuable."

"Oh, and what could I have told you that mattered to the girl who
has everything?"

"Well, as you may or may not know, I'm in a new private school
called The Oaks, a school my grandfather built practically single-
handedly, and most all the students come from one-percenter families."

"Huh?"

"Wealthy people."

"Why am I not surprised. So?"

"I suppose the boys are the same as boys everywhere, except these
think they're more entitled. I went out with the class president to the
school opening party, but as you once said about a boy named Lloyd
something, 'He can't pass a mirror without stopping to look at himself.' It got worse."

"How?"

"He did exactly what you predicted others would do once they
took you out and didn't get what they wanted."

"Oh. You're a victim."

"It's not funny. Or . . . maybe it is. I know if you were at this
school, you'd mow them down like bowling pins. But don't misunder-
stand me. I like the school and the teachers."

"Um," she said, thinking.

"Well, what about you?"

"I'm no longer a candidate for Miss Hawaii. I'm still in therapy."

"I'm sorry, Dina. I really am. What about your friends?" I asked, my voice heavily weighted with trepidation.

"They were all luckier than me. Leave it at that. The real reason I'm calling is because you hypnotized my brother," she said.

"What?"

"I wait weeks for him to call me, and every second sentence has your name in it."

"Oh."

"Yeah, oh." She paused and then said, "So you're coming here this summer?"

"Maybe. I hope so. For a while anyway."

"I walk with a cane," she admitted.

"Are you going to poke me with it?"

She laughed. "Looks like we'll be sisters one way or another," she said.

"I hope so."

"Maybe I'll visit your palace one of these days."

"Would you? That would be so exciting. I could bring you to my classes, we could use the golf carts and explore the property, we could . . ."

"Calm down. I said maybe."

We were both silent for a moment.

"Anyway," she said, "with all this time to think, I agree what was done to you was wrong."

"Thank you."

"Oh, brother. If you're going to say thank you after things I tell you, I'm going to vomit or shut my mouth."

I laughed, and then she did.

"I have to go," she said. "They're ringing a bell or something. My therapist used to run a torture chamber."

"I'll call you sometime. Soon."

"Whatever. If I don't answer, it's because I'm in a pressure cooker or being drowned. Oh, and say hello to Boston for me. I'm sure he'll call you more than he calls me," she said.

She hung up.

I sat there soaking in one of my happiest moments since I had been sent back from Hawaii. What it gave me was a feeling of hope, hope that I would have a sense of family again and that I wouldn't feel so alone for so much of the day.

But I wasn't naive about it. There was still so much to overcome, maybe even too much.

She was right about Boston. He was closing in fast now on completion of his training, and he said his group had become one person with many hands. They practically breathed in the same rhythm. He talked so much about them that I even felt a little jealous.

Weeks went by. There were tests and outings with some of my girlfriends. Grandfather had me attend two more business meetings and ask questions. Aunt Holly seemed more surprised than Uncle Martin. One afternoon, when I returned from school, she told me that Simon was making some progress. He had been able to confront some of the ugliness he had blocked out. She was happier with his new doctors.

The persistent shadows in Sutherland seemed to wilt. Maybe it was just my imagination or the moving spring sky, but there was more light in the hallways. However, the happier I became, the grouchier Mrs. Fisher appeared to be. More of the employees were voicing complaints about her, but Grandfather's confidence in her, as odd as it seemed to me, didn't falter. No one had the courage to confront Grandfather directly with a complaint about her.

And then one day, the day that would mark the biggest change in my life, I returned from school, settled my things in my room, showered, and changed my clothes. Then I sprawled out on my bed to talk to Paula about some of the social events being planned for the school year's end.

I reached for my phone in my bag and couldn't find it. I thought for a moment. I was positive I'd had it when I returned from school. I had moved some other things about in my bag when I was in the limousine and Emerson was driving me home. I looked everywhere in the room, thinking I might have dropped it. I even looked under the bed, but it was nowhere.

Frantic, I hurried downstairs and out to see Emerson, who was detailing the limousine. I knew that meant he had been cleaning the inside as well.

"Did you find my phone?" I asked as soon as he looked up and saw me.

"No, I didn't, Caroline. Are you sure you had it when you got into the car after school?"

"Yes, I saw it in my bag."

"It might have fallen out in your room."

"I just went through it carefully."

He wiped his hands. "Well, perhaps it fell somewhere in the house. Let's go talk to Mrs. Fisher and Clara Jean."

He saw how frantic I was and followed me back into the mansion.

Mrs. Fisher was just coming out of the kitchen area and stopped.

"What's going on?" she asked.

"Caroline's phone is missing. She had it when she returned from school."

"Well, did you look in your room?"

"Yes."

"I haven't seen it, and I was up and down that stairway twice in the past hour."

Emerson turned to me. "I'll go back up and look again with you," he said. "You just walked in and up to your room, correct?"

"Yes."

"These phones," Mrs. Fisher said. "You might as well have them sewn onto your body."

"You don't have one, do you?" I asked. It had just occurred to me that I had never seen her with one.

"I'm not desperate to talk to someone constantly." She looked at Emerson. "Her generation is terrified of silence."

"Well, I'm not fond of it either, mum. I prefer music and conversation."

"Yes, well, we're all different, some more dependent on others. Sorry, I haven't seen your device," she told me, and walked off.

"Let's just re-search your room and the hallway," Emerson said. First we checked any downstairs area onto which the phone could have fallen, and then we walked the stairs carefully and went to my room.

"Sometimes we put things down and just forget where. Our minds are on other things. I'll look at the obvious area. You check every drawer and shelf, and the bathroom, too."

He got on his knees, and I did what he said. We both came up empty.

"Wait," he said, pulling out his mobile. "Why didn't I think of this? See, we miss the obvious. I'll call your number."

"Oh, it was off. Remember the rules at The Oaks? It couldn't be on, and I usually don't turn it on until I'm home."

"Oh. I'll check the limousine again. You might just have to get another. We'll have to call to see if anyone who might have found it is using it."

After we did all that, I decided I had to tell my grandfather.

"He's misplaced things. Don't let him convince you otherwise," Emerson said, winking.

I headed for my grandfather's office. When I entered, I told him the issue and how Emerson and I had searched so hard. Grandfather wasn't as angry about it as I had anticipated.

"We'll give it a day, and I'll have Franklin call, cancel it, and order a new one. I believe I had instructed him to take out the insurance."

"I'm positive I brought it home," I said.

"Then keep looking," he said. He rose. "I have to leave for the city office, after which I'm having dinner with some associates."

He started to gather his things and place them in a briefcase.

"Okay," I said. I left and walked slowly over the ground Emerson and I had covered. We hadn't missed it.

There was such a small gap in time between when I had last seen it and when I couldn't find it. I sat on my bed and thought and thought about it, finally realizing the biggest gap was when I had gone into the bathroom to take a shower, dry my hair, and put on my clothes. I could feel the heat building in my face and my heart skipping beats. There was no doubt in my mind.

She had come into my room, heard and realized that I was in the shower, and then taken my phone. If she had, she would most likely have thrown it into the garbage. I rose, hurried downstairs, and went directly to the kitchen. Both Clara Jean and Mrs. Wilson turned, surprised at my rushing in without saying hello. I looked at the garbage bin and then reached in to move things around.

"What are you doing?" Clara Jean asked.

"I'm looking for my phone."

"Oh, it's definitely not in there. I changed bags."

"How long ago?"

"Two hours, at least."

"Okay," I said, and rushed out again, practically running through the house to check every bin. It wasn't anywhere. Still frantic, I went out to the garbage cans and looked through them. There was no sign of it, and I knew she wouldn't just throw it somewhere on the grounds, not the way these grounds were kept.

When I reentered the house, I saw her coming down the stairs to start her preparations for dinner. She certainly wouldn't be carrying it around on her, I thought. I watched her go down the hallway toward the kitchen and dining room and then I slowly, quietly, went up the stairway.

I had never been to her room, never even been in the hallway that led down to it from mine. I knew she could come back up for some reason, but I was willing to risk it. I moved quickly to her hallway. The lights were always dimmer there to me, but on this early evening, they looked more so. I listened for a moment, and then I went to her room.

There was no way I could even begin to imagine that the moment I opened her door, I would start on the path toward changing my life . . . forever.

CHAPTER TWENTY-FOUR

The room was barely lit by a single battery-operated candle. It flickered in the far left corner of a dark walnut desk with neatly piled paperwork, receipts and bills, some notebooks, and a canister of pens and pencils. Next to the lit candle was the silver-framed picture of a little girl, most likely not much more than five or six at the time of the photograph.

I picked it up and studied her features. There was no question that she had enough resemblance to Mrs. Fisher for me to assume this was her daughter. But unlike pictures of me taken at about this age and photographs of classmates I had seen framed of them at similar ages, there was an eerie absence of any joy in Mrs. Fisher's daughter's eyes. Most photographers ask you to smile, and even parents urge you to do so. If anything, this was a picture that captured a little fear and uncertainty. Why would Mrs. Fisher choose this photograph to display? Maybe she didn't have anything different.

I put it down and looked about the room. Her window curtains were only slightly open, permitting a sliver of illumination from the wall lights outside. If anything, that gave her room a darker gray aura of mystery. The strong breeze outside rubbed some of the vines against the walls around the windows, sounding like a faint scratching.

Along with what was carefully distributed on her desk, everything else in her room was neat and organized. There were no articles of clothing left out, nothing dropped on the floor, and not a lamp or any piece of furniture out of place. The closet was open, and I could see all her dresses, blouses, and skirts in neat sections. The drawers to the dresser were closed. I began opening them top to bottom. Again, socks and undergarments were immaculately folded and arranged. I ran my hand under everything in every drawer and found nothing.

I paused to look around again. It occurred to me that there were no pictures of herself and her husband or any of just her husband on display. I hadn't found any in the bureau drawers, so I began to look at the four side desk drawers. The bottom left drawer had only the Holy Bible in it. The top left drawer had a somewhat crudely hand-painted black and gold jewelry box. When I looked in it, I didn't think any of it looked terribly valuable. It looked like old costume jewelry. I did recognize some of it from her wearing it at dinners.

The bottom right-hand drawer had more papers in it, all to do with the Bank of England. I ran my hand under them and felt nothing. The top right-hand drawer had something covered in a black silk scarf. I unwrapped it and stared down at a picture that had been cut in half. The remaining half was of me. I was not much older than her daughter in the picture beside the battery-operated candle. I picked up the half that had the picture of myself and thought about it, realizing that what had been cut away was the picture of my mother holding my left hand. This had to be one of the pictures placed in a box stored in the Cemetery of Memories. It was eerie and frightening to see that my mother had been snipped off crudely.

The neatness of the room beside the madness I sensed gave me a chill. Those vines on the outside walls seemed to be scratching harder, as if they were trying to warn me to get out. I went to the door and listened but heard nothing except the distant sound of the employees preparing the dinner. Perhaps Aunt Holly was joining me. Grandfather had told me he was eating out. Regardless of how many were to be at dinner, Mrs. Fisher always had it prepared as formally as she would if the governor was attending.

I returned to searching the room. Pessimistic and disappointed so far, I went over to her bed and riffled through the night tables; there I saw her various medicines and a flashlight but nothing else. Just like a detective I had once seen in a movie, I ran my hands under her mattress and under the pillows. There was nothing. Afraid I already had spent too much time in here, I started to leave. How, indeed, was I going to explain this intrusion to my grandfather if Mrs. Fisher appeared, even in the hallway, and saw me walking from the direction of her room?

I looked about to be sure there was no evidence of my search, nothing out of place. I even readjusted the picture of her daughter a little. Mrs. Fisher was so exacting when it came to anything she supervised or personally did at Sutherland that I was sure she'd notice the picture a quarter of an inch more to the left or right.

I might have missed it; I might have missed everything, and everything would have returned to the way it had been. She would have continued to go on unchecked, and somehow, in some way, she would have hurt or changed my future to satisfy her insane vision for me, probably a vision she had created for her own daughter.

But just as I had gone to the door and peered out to be sure it was safe to leave, I heard it. Thankfully, she was as unacquainted with the workings of mobile phones as she had claimed to be. My phone had been turned off following the rules Mrs. Rich had written in stone for The Oaks, but sometimes I, and a few others, would turn off the ring but forget to turn off the vibration. In a noisy school setting, that was usually unheard or ignored anyway, but here, in the eerie, almost morbid silence of this room threaded with what I thought were ribbons of madness, the vibration was as loud as a bass drum.

It came from her closet.

I turned and hurried to it just as my phone vibrated for the last time. I reached in, fumbling through dresses, and finally searched the pocket of a raincoat to find my phone. Paula had just called me.

"Thank you, Paula," I muttered, and backed away from the closet as if Mrs. Fisher was hanging in there, too.

For a few moments, I stood there enveloped in the heat of my rage. I would show this to my grandfather and especially to Aunt Holly. I ransacked my mind, imagining all the excuses or claims Mrs. Fisher would make. Yes, it was there; she had just found it and was going to return it, or it had slipped her mind. She might even say I had misplaced it and was so embarrassed about the hysteria over it I had exhibited, having this one and that one distracted from his or her work, that I had made it up and falsely accused her. And on top of that, that I had violated her privacy.

Aunt Holly wouldn't believe her, but could I depend on Grandfather? Look at how much about her he tolerated as it was, and I couldn't figure out why. This could fall right into that bag of mystery. What would life be like here then? Should I just keep it and how I had found it to myself, maybe just letting her know I knew? Would that be enough to keep her off me? Would that suffice?

I stood there looking down and thinking and then suddenly realized that I was staring down at the floor of her closet, on which was a wrapped black shawl. In a suite as immaculate and as organized as hers was, why would such a thing exist on the floor? Surely, she saw it often. Why didn't she put it away as neatly as she put away everything else?

I knelt down slowly and unwrapped it. Tied in a black ribbon were at least a dozen envelopes. I plucked one out, opened it, and read. It set off an explosion of images, all of Simon's hysterical expressions, his cries, and his scream.

These were Mrs. Lawson's letters. They were not in Simon's mad imagination. It was all true. Did Mrs. Fisher completely concoct the blank pages Grandfather showed me, or did he know she had found these and asked her to substitute the blank pages? After having done that, was she blackmailing him with them?

The famous bottom line for either choice was that it was true: Mrs. Lawson was Uncle Martin's mother. Simon had accidentally, in a rage, caused the death of his own grandmother. I could just take these letters, burn them, and keep it all to myself.

But I was tired of secrets, confronting them and especially hoarding them. And I was angry, angry at the possibility of Mrs. Fisher lording it over my grandfather and in a real sense, every sense, actually, over me as well.

If I had ever doubted or questioned the possibility of what Simon had discovered, that doubt was all dead. I had come here as a helpless young girl, arrived that way more than once, but as I walked out of Mrs. Fisher's room, the letters in my hand, I went down that hallway as a Sutherland, for now and forever. I would never be a helpless young girl again.

I paused to hide two of the letters in my room, and then I went downstairs to the kitchen to tell Clara Jean I wouldn't be coming to dinner.

"Don't tell Mrs. Fisher anything more, please, Clara Jean."

"As you wish, Caroline."

"Where is she, anyway?"

"She took May and Lisa out to the golf clubhouse to clean it all again." She leaned over to whisper, "I think she's trying to drive some of us out of Sutherland."

"She won't be driving anything here much longer," I said.

Her eyes lit up as she gestured a prayer. I left her and walked quickly to Grandfather's office. After I entered, I closed the blinds and put the letters and papers on Grandfather's desk. Then I sat in front of the desk and stared ahead at where he would sit, building my courage with every passing minute.

I knew I'd be sitting here a long time, but ironically, there was no other place in the mansion that felt as safe. With the lights off and none of the illumination leaking under the door, Mrs. Fisher would not enter the office. No one would.

I didn't fall asleep or doze. Instead, I sat there reliving all the important things that had happened in my life before I had been brought to Sutherland for that terrible aversion therapy. The eyes of the young slipped easily from dreams to fantasies, clinging to laughter and smiles. It was as if I had lived with different people, my mother trimming herself, swallowing back what made her unhappy, becoming more like a piece in a puzzle that had to be scraped and cut to fit in. Back then, she was surely a beautiful marionette.

And then there was my father, the perfect man who was easily cast in the role my grandfather had created for him. If my mother lacked what my grandfather called discipline, my father personified it: Captain Bryer.

And then that all changed. I was certainly aware of Mommy's unhappiness with my grandfather. I had heard and seen some of their arguments, and I could recall almost every disagreement my father and she had had when Mommy had one of those incidents with Grandfather. I was never drawn into it. She never told me to hate him or even to dislike him.

Of course, I disapproved of what he had arranged to have done to me and with me, and I disapproved of what he had done with Mommy. I feared him; I was often angry at him. And I always felt

Mommy's tension when she came here, but I couldn't recall a time when Grandfather would look at me with similar rage and frustration when he was upset with her.

Goodness knows, I tried to hate him just to please Mommy, but I knew Daddy would be even more upset if I displayed those thoughts. Until this very moment, I did feel entrapped. I was lost because I didn't know who I was or who I should be.

Tonight I did.

The hours ticked by faster than I imagined they would. I didn't fall asleep. I hardly moved. And then the door opened; Grandfather flipped on the light and saw me.

"What the . . . you actually frightened me for a moment. For a moment, I thought . . ."

"My mother had come back?"

He didn't answer. He put his briefcase down and started for the desk.

"Why were you sitting in the dark? How long have you been here?"

"Shortly after I found all that in Mrs. Fisher's suite, as well as the phone you gave me before I left for Hawaii. I didn't misplace it."

"Really." He looked down at his desk. "Where did you find this?"

"Wrapped in a shawl and poorly hidden at the bottom of her closet," I said.

He picked up one of the envelopes and read for a moment. "I imagine you read everything," he said, putting it down.

"I knew what it was; I didn't have to read it all."

He sat.

"You didn't know she still had it all, did you?"

"I suspected," he said, and then sifted through the papers and envelopes. "There's something missing."

"Two letters," I said.

"Where are they?"

"Somewhere in Sutherland," I said.

He sat back, the amazement softening his face. "What are you . . . what is it you want, Caroline?"

"Let's begin with Mrs. Fisher's departure tomorrow. By noon at the latest."

"Departure?"

"That's the kindest way to put it. She no longer has any hold over you. It would be her word against yours, and I'm sure you know how unstable her life was in England. She has no friends or allies here. You made a mistake bringing her here. You mistook her dependence on you for loyalty. I'm going to believe that you didn't know all the things she's done to me, said to me.

"And to Simon. She was very harmful to him. You should have listened more to Aunt Holly."

"Send her on her way?"

"Exactly, and I might recommend, as I heard you say the other day when you were talking about changing executives at the bottling company, that you promote from inside. I would suggest you make Clara Jean head housekeeper. She's not rigid or as domineering, but the other employees like her very much and would not want her to fail. It will probably improve the atmosphere here and yet keep it all as perfect, if not more so."

"So you're telling me who to hire and fire?"

"'Whom,' as Mrs. Fisher would say."

He started to smile and stopped. "You know what this would do to your uncle Martin, how much damage it would do to us all."

"Yes. I don't want anyone to be hurt, not even you."

This time, he did smile.

"That doesn't mean I don't have some requests, Grandfather."

"Really. You're doing what your mother would never do, you know."

"And what's that?"

"You're letting yourself become more Sutherland. I told you that you were, and that has obviously not slowed you down."

"I've been reading a lot this year, especially the Shakespeare assignments. I think, like in any great family, there is good and bad. When the family is as established as ours, it all just stands out more, I guess. I'm not arrogant enough, as some of those Oaks students you've launched into the world are, to believe I haven't got a lot more to learn about us, about myself, about everything."

"That sounds good, Caroline, but you haven't told me your requests," he said, and leaned forward. "I imagine what's missing here will then appear."

"It will."

"Okay," he said, leaning back. "What are they?"

"Two mainly, Grandfather. The first is that you visit Simon, maybe even hug him and tell him that you want him home."

"Okay. I actually do. It was in the back of my mind. It's probably good that you gave me a little shove."

"Oh, it's more than a shove, Grandfather."

He laughed. "And what," he asked, "is your second request?"

I leaned forward.

"I want you to tell me why you really didn't bury Mommy in the family cemetery, why you kept her ashes hidden here, and why you moved them to that terrible place in Sutherland."

CHAPTER TWENTY-FIVE

"I hated my father," Grandfather began, "and I hated myself for hating him. I don't think that was unusual for Sutherlands. He didn't like his father, and my grandfather wasn't very interested in his children. Sometimes I thought he resented the fact that we'd inherit anything he had achieved. No question, my father had some of that attitude.

"This sense of entitlement, our belief in royal blood, was passed down from generation to generation. I hate to tell you, but our ancestors, the first so-called colonists, were against the Revolutionary War. Spies and colonial traitors, the whole lot of them. You had two ancestors who were hung."

"I did?"

"You won't find a portrait of them here. Eventually, none of that mattered to me. I'm just a businessman. But I did have a sense of Sutherland tradition. Tradition gives your identity some legitimacy.

My grandfather and your great-grandfather used to end their day with a toast of scotch in the grand room, standing in front of our family emblem. I always thought that was a bit much. But I adhered to most of our rules, some down in writing and recorded."

"But what happened with Mommy . . . afterward . . ."

"One of those Sutherland codes affected our family cemetery. We had a cousin, my grandfather's brother's son, who was gay. If you think some people's attitudes are anti- . . . what is it called . . . LGBT today, you would be shocked at what they were then. It was literally against the law.

"I'm not going to fall back on that excuse, Caroline, but there is a codicil in our family cemetery paperwork that forbids any gay member of the family to be buried there. Your grandmother didn't even know that. Very few know it. I never publicized it, but when your mother had her affair, which I knew was heading for a marriage certificate . . . well, your father and I were quite enraged."

"But my father was seeing someone—Parker."

"Yes, and I was quite upset about it, but he claimed your mother drove him to it, and he pointed out that at the time, she was involved with another woman. That was indisputable. I hated being at a disadvantage in any negotiation."

"It was family, not business."

"Yes, well, maybe I never saw the difference until you came along. Anyway, what is what you're doing right now? Negotiating, aren't you?"

"Yes."

He smiled. "That's all right. But getting back to your mother, we were always at each other. She was a very independent thinker, too independent for a proper Sutherland. When she was younger, she actually threatened to change her name legally. I didn't know what to expect from her after a while.

"I readily confess that I manipulated her into a life that I thought would shape her into more of a Sutherland. It backfired. That played a role in what was done with you. It may not be of any solace to you to tell you I regret it. I think it was another way I was getting back at your mother."

"If it wasn't the old rule, why didn't you place her in the family cemetery? Why did you keep the urn here and then put it in that horrible room?"

"Sutherland vengeance, at first. I had her under my control finally, but as time passed, I couldn't stop thinking about her in there. I'll never say this to anyone but you . . . I could still sense her defiance.

"Not being anyone close to perfect, as you know," he said, patting the letters on his desk, "I began to feel more guilt than anger, so I moved the urn out of here, tried to bury it somewhere else in Sutherland. But that's not working either," he said. "Actually, that was Mrs. Fisher's suggestion."

"She used it against me," I said angrily.

"Apparently, she did a lot more than I knew. As I said, Sutherland was running like a Swiss clock again, so I didn't pay attention."

"And she followed Simon to the basement, and she found those letters. Who came up with the idea to replace them with blank pages?"

"She did. At the time . . ."

"You felt it was a solution, a quick solution."

He winced like someone who had been given an electric shock. I knew what that was like from my aversion therapy.

"Yes, yes," he said. "When you don't admit your mistakes to yourself especially, you risk compounding them. I hope you're taking notes."

"More like they're taking me," I said.

He nodded. "Okay."

He opened a drawer and took out a ring of keys.

"The right one is here. You take the urn out of there and maybe put it in your room."

"Why are you really doing this, confessing all this?"

"You don't trust me? Good. Trust is always a disadvantage, at least in my world."

He looked out the window toward the golf course.

"I keep myself occupied day and night with my business interests. It was always convenient to have someone else do everything else, but at some point, relatively recently, I thought of myself at your age, and Simon's. I had other dreams, fantasies. My father mocked them when I voiced any."

"And your mother?"

He turned back to me.

"She was unfortunately treated more like an accessory. My father was unpredictable when it came to relationships. You know about Prissy. I don't think anyone was more surprised than I was, surprised that my father could have deep feelings for someone else. He was even more bitter after that. He took his bitterness out on everyone, maybe mostly me. I don't like sounding like a complainer. That's weak."

"It's honest."

"Whatever. Sometime about then, I got more satisfaction by outdoing him."

"Which you still are trying to do."

He laughed. "I love how your mother comes out in you. I'm getting kind of used to it."

He took a deep breath like someone who had been underwater.

"All right, I think that's enough self-analysis. I'm starting to think like those doctors or whatever they are who are treating Simon."

He looked down at the desk.

"So what about what's missing here?" he asked. "When do you return it?"

"Trust," I said.

I thought he was going to explode, be Grandfather Sutherland again, the ruler of the kingdom, but he didn't.

"Okay. I'm glad to see the Sutherland in you win out when it needs to. We'll attend to your requests. And then you'll complete the deal."

"I'm hoping it's that you want to complete it more than that I'm making you."

"It's all right to hope. Just be sure you've done all you can to make it a reality. I'm tired, and it looks like I've a lot to do tomorrow," he said, standing.

I picked up the keys on his desk and started out.

"Caroline," he said when I reached for the door to leave.

"Yes?"

"Be careful. I'll be watching how you wear your self-confidence."

"I know you will, Grandfather."

I opened the door and turned back to him again.

"In fact, I'll be depending on it."

I would swear I heard laughter inside after I had closed the door.

Later I put the urn beside my bed and said good night to Mommy. I hoped she was proud of me.

In the morning, I heard the commotion shortly after I had showered and dressed. I recognized Emerson's footsteps in the hallway outside my door and peered out. He saw me and winked. He was carrying Mrs. Fisher's suitcases. She was a few feet behind him and saw me looking out.

"You'll be sorry," she said.

"Go talk to your daughter, Mrs. Fisher," I said. "Apologize. She's the only family you have and ever will."

She walked faster, catching up to Emerson at the top of the stairway. I closed my door. A short time later, I had breakfast with Grandfather. He said nothing about Mrs. Fisher except to announce to everyone within hearing range that Clara Jean was taking her place.

Aunt Holly was puzzled as to why it had all happened. She studied me to see if I would have a response, if I knew. I gave her one of my father's quotes: "Don't look a gift horse in the mouth."

She laughed.

Everyone was full of smiles and laughter after that day. A great shadow was washed out of the mansion. The lightness I felt in my footsteps followed me to school. I was more tolerant of the classmates who annoyed me with their boisterous arrogance. It didn't surprise me that they liked me more for it, no matter how I tried to convince them that I wasn't looking for their approval. In fact, everyone thought I was hoping to be nominated for senior class president.

I wasn't, and when my name was introduced, I declined immediately.

"I'm sorry, but I'm going to be too busy. I'm interning with my grandfather as well as attending The Oaks, and I've already applied for early admission to a well-known business school."

No one questioned that, especially not Mrs. Rich or Hudson when he heard. He was quite upset, in fact, because his intern position at one of our companies fell through. He had to work for his father that summer before he went to college. On top of that, Paula beat him out for valedictorian.

After Grandfather visited Simon in the clinic, Simon began to improve and was carefully given permission to return to Sutherland for a week and then two. He was more into reading and talking about his favorite subjects. Whenever he found a good listener, he'd cling to him or her. One person in particular was the daughter of the head of the grounds department. I was amused and very happy about the long walks they took, Simon lecturing on one subject or another, his hands flying about like sparrows.

That summer, I did visit my father, Parker, and Dina in their new home on Maui. I could spend only ten days, because Grandfather had a major consolidation of businesses he was undertaking, and he wanted me in on every important meeting. I think for a while Uncle Martin felt a little threatened by all the attention Grandfather was giving me. Would I slip by him, take his coveted place in the Sutherland line? Grandfather put a quick end to that by appointing him executive vice president of Sutherland Enterprises and giving him far more authority and responsibility.

When I left to return to Sutherland, Dina made plans to visit that August. I was disappointed that Boston wasn't visiting the family when I was there, but his assignments were always top secret. We talked on the phone whenever he had the opportunity, and he would never tell me where he was.

And then in late August, just before I was to start my senior year, Clara Jean informed me we were having an overnight guest. Boston was actually spending two days with us. I should say with me, as we were constantly together most of the day and night. He still couldn't talk about anything he had done, but I sensed the danger and worried aloud for him.

He liked that.

Our second night together was the most passionate. I knew he was very worried about how my father was going to react.

"And you're so young," he said.

"We're both so young," I told him.

Our kisses grew deeper, longer, and I knew when he touched me that this was going to be a new lesson in diving, diving deeply into desire, into love, and into a commitment that Grandfather would call the most dangerous because it relied so much on trust.

We saw each other as much as possible my senior year.

In the spring, Grandfather sent me to the city of Boston to sit in on a meeting held by the executives of a shipping company we had acquired. I asked some questions and took notes. Grandfather and Uncle Martin complimented me on it.

Meanwhile, Dina, who had returned to school, enrolled in a community college. She had no definite plans, but Daddy said I was a big influence on her. I laughed to myself, thinking how once she had been a big influence on me. Maybe it was the ping-pong effect real sisters had on each other. If she had any reluctance, Boston's interest in me gradually dissolved it. I was feeling something I hadn't felt for years: a sense of family.

Just before my high school graduation, Boston arrived for a surprise visit and brought with him some disappointment. He was not going to be able to attend the ceremony and celebrate with me. It didn't take me more than a few moments to realize this was going to be one of the most dangerous assignments he had been given.

When he was ready to leave, he gave me what he said was my graduation gift. It was in a box that could hold a blouse or a jacket, and I imagined it had something to do with the Navy SEALs.

"Don't open it until then, so I can feel like I'm here," he asked.

I didn't.

I left it in my room and didn't touch it until I returned from the ceremony and was about to go down to celebrate with family and friends. In fact, I didn't start to unwrap it until I was in the grand room where Grandfather, Uncle Martin, Aunt Holly, and Simon had stepped out of the party to watch me. Simon had been telling everyone, or I should say lecturing to everyone, about the Navy SEALs.

"He promised to get me a shirt with the Navy SEALs emblem, too," Simon said as I began to tear away the paper.

I opened the box, in which there was another box and then another. Everyone was laughing until I was down to the last, small box. I looked at Grandfather. He nodded, and I opened it to find an engagement ring.

I didn't put it on. For days, I tried everything I could to distract myself. I even sat for one of Simon's new studies about nuclear fission. I don't know if I heard a word.

And then, at about four o'clock, my phone rang with a call from an unknown number. I held my breath and barely uttered, "Hello."

"Does it fit?" he asked.

EPILOGUE

On a cool August day, Emerson drove Uncle Martin, Aunt Holly, Simon, Grandfather, Boston, and me to the family cemetery. We had waited for Boston's leave. Except for Simon commenting on the seasonal changes and what caused them in nature, no one spoke.

There was only one man there. He had it all prepared. The six of us gathered at Mommy's tombstone only a few feet from Grandmother Judith's.

A week earlier, with only himself present, Grandfather had exhumed Prissy's coffin from the Cemetery of Memories and given her a place in the far-right corner, not four feet from Great-grandfather Sutherland's grave. No one commented. It was something Grandfather wanted to do himself. When Simon saw it, he looked very happy about it. Grandfather had put him in charge of everything in the basement, telling him to separate what was important from what was nonsense or meaningless. He relished the assignment.

Everyone waited for me to step forward with the urn to have it placed in the spot in front of Mommy's gravestone. We watched in silence when it was covered.

Then Grandfather turned to me.

"May she rest in peace," he said.

Everyone but me headed back to the limousine. Emerson stood with the door open for them and waited beside Boston. I touched the stone, but I didn't cry.

"You know," I whispered, "how Grandfather hates to lose.

"But somehow, Mommy, I don't think he hates it this time."